Purrder She Wrote

Purrder She Wrote

CATE CONTE

St. Martin's Paperbacks

This is a work of fiction. All of the characters, organizations, and events portrayed in this novel are either products of the author's imagination or are used fictitiously.

PURRDER SHE WROTE

Copyright © 2018 by Liz Mugavero.

For information address St. Martin's Press, 175 Fifth Avenue, New York, NY 10010.

ISBN: 978-1-250-07207-8

Our books may be purchased in bulk for promotional, educational, or business use. Please contact your local bookseller or the Macmillan Corporate and Premium Sales Department at 1-800-221-7945, ext. 5442, or by e-mail at MacmillanSpecialMarkets@macmillan.com.

Printed in the United States of America

St. Martin's Paperbacks edition / August 2018

St. Martin's Paperbacks are published by St. Martin's Press, 175 Fifth Avenue, New York, NY 10010.

10 9 8 7 6 5 4 3 2 1

*In memory of the real Junkyard
Johnny, whose spunky, unique spirit
will live on in these books. Run free
with all your old pals, JJ. xo*

Acknowledgments

Cat cafes are becoming a huge part of the fabric of our society here in the U.S., and it's a delight to watch people and cats reaping so many benefits from this concept. The Meow Parlour in New York City was the city's first cat cafe, and served as a model for other cafes. I want to give them a shout-out for the great work they do and for helping so many felines—and humans.

I'm so grateful to my editor, Hannah Braaten, and the whole St. Martin's crew who brought this series to life. It means even more to me now to have a way to memorialize Junkyard Johnny, my real feline companion who served as the model for JJ in the books. The cover art captured his likeness so convincingly.

Special thanks to my agent, John Talbot, for being such a wonderful partner, as always.

When I began working on this book, it was during a creative crisis. Sometimes you need a little help to get out of your own way and back to the page. A huge thank you to Ken Lauher for helping me get clarity about where I was in the world, put processes in place to help me truly take back my power, and ultimately led me back to my creative self. I am grateful.

My Wicked Cozy Author sisters—Barbara Ross, Sherry Harris, JA Hennrikus/Julianne Holmes, Edith Maxwell/Maddie Day, and Jessie Crockett/Jessica Ellicott—as always, I couldn't do it without you all. Thank you for being the people I can always count on.

And to the readers who are following this series—thank you, from the bottom of my heart. You make it all possible.

Chapter 1

Grand opening day of my new cat café, and I was envisioning long lines of cat lovers and a plethora of adoption applications. Instead, I got a catfight. Between two humans.

This was not how I pictured the Daybreak Island version of rescue work.

I know the rescue business has its moments. I mean, I wasn't a cat rescue virgin or anything, having done years of the work out in San Francisco. But that was different, in-the-trenches stressful. Going to a shelter every day and working with different personalities, even with the kitties' welfare as top priority, had its challenges. But here, back at home on Daybreak Island, it was supposed to be different. Here I'd had visions of people coming from all over the island to visit JJ's House of Purrs, simply looking for some love from a fur baby. They'd sit on the floor and coo over the cats. The cats would purr adoringly—never swat or hiss—and wait for someone to say the magic words: *I want to fill out an application to adopt.* We'd have happy endings every day, and find homes for all the island strays.

I used all my visualization techniques to bring this story to life. I was convinced it couldn't go any other way.

Instead, it was my first day open and I had two women

facing off. One, my volunteer, with her hands clenched into fists and coarse, graying hair frizzing out around her head like a steel halo. The other, an indignant blonde wearing designer flip-flops, poised to grab a can of the latest organic hairspray out of her Louis Vuitton purse and use it like Mace. And my purring, happy cats? Scattered to the nearest hiding places for safety.

Nothing in my world was destined to be easy.

"The only way you'll be getting one of these cats is over my dead body. Maddie, you tell her." Adele Barrows, my volunteer, wasn't budging. She directed her words to me while clenching those fists tighter, training an impressive death stare on her adversary. Her stocky, five-foot-seven frame alone might have been intimidating to the wispy woman still clutching one of my cats, a pretty calico named Georgia. And that was notwithstanding the look of utter rage on Adele's face at the notion that this woman would even consider herself eligible to look at a cat, never mind take one home.

And frankly, I wasn't sure what I was supposed to be telling this other woman, because I had no idea what was going on here. Although she looked vaguely familiar, and I was a little distracted trying to figure out why. It wasn't strange that anyone on this island looked familiar though. I'd grown up here, and even though I'd been gone for a decade, most of the players were still the same.

Grandpa Leo's eyes widened in panic as he watched the scene unfolding before him. "Maddie," he stage-whispered finally. "Do something!"

Despite the situation, I nearly laughed. Grandpa Leo, in addition to being the best grandfather in the world, was also Leopold Maloney, the former police chief of Daybreak Island. Our island was comprised of five towns and in the summer months there were more people than could reasonably fit on its total square footage. He'd seen a lot in his years on the job, and no doubt faced down more dangerous criminals than two ladies arguing over a cat. But I had to admit, for a sixty-year-old woman, Adele could be pretty scary when she got cranked up. And cats definitely got her cranked up.

"Don't worry, Grandpa," I said, patting his arm. "I got this." I strode over to the face-off and planted myself in between the two. "Ladies. What can I help with? I'm Maddie James," I said to the blonde, offering my hand in a lame attempt to defuse the situation. "I'm one of the owners here."

She stared at me, disdain seeping out of every pore. Her tiny button nose flared slightly at the indignity of the situation she'd found herself in. She was pretty, but in a pampered, rich-person way. Flawless makeup, lips that had an exaggerated puff to them, suggesting some sort of collagen treatment. Gold jewelry dangled off her earlobes, around her neck, and from her wrists. She had a tiny gold ball in the side of her nose and a defiant set to her jaw.

Clutching Georgia closer, she glared at me. "I know who you are. And I didn't come in here to be verbally abused. I came in here to do *you* a favor and take one of these cats."

Georgia arched her back, her eyes wide. I could tell she was seconds away from digging her claws into Blondie's perfectly tanned arms to gain purchase for her great escape. Smoothly, I reached over and plucked the cat from her, setting Georgia down on the floor. She bolted for the nearest cubby.

"She gets nervous around tension," I said apologetically. "So, Miss . . ."

"Holly," Blondie supplied with a haughty toss of her hair. "Holly Hawthorne. Don't you *remember* me?"

Holly Hawthorne? I peered at her more closely, fascinated. The last time I'd seen Holly Hawthorne had been in high school. Which was the case for so many people I ran into on the island. But usually there were remnants of the person they'd been ten years ago. In Holly's case, not so much. I remembered her as being pretty nondescript back then, with glasses and long, straight hair, nose in a book most of the time. And quiet. In fact, most people probably didn't notice her half the time. Which was not jibing with the person standing in front of me.

Holly and her twin sister Heather had been two years ahead of me in school. Their family was old-money Daybreak Island and really well-known, involved in charities and fund-raising and all the sorts of things wealthy families around here did. Heather had been the one to play off of her family's status. She'd been the loud, outgoing one, head of the drama club and obsessed with all the things her parents' money could buy. While Holly didn't style her hair to death or wear fancy clothes, or even seem to notice she could have whatever she wanted.

So what the heck happened to her? Had she and Heather swapped personas just for fun? Did twins do that in their thirties?

"Of course! Holly. So great to see you again," I lied. "So you're interested in Georgia—"

"She's not getting her!" Adele piped up, appearing around my right shoulder, her finger jabbing the air in front of Holly's face. "Not after what you did last year. And the year before that. I'm still feeding the offspring from the orange cat you just *had to have* that you *loved more than life itself.*" She mimicked what I assumed had been words uttered by Holly in a previous encounter with exaggerated air quotes, then dissolved into a coughing fit. "You're a disgrace. And you don't deserve a cat," she said, when she'd recovered enough to talk.

Blotches of red crept up Holly's neck to stain her cheeks. "Just who do you think you are?" she demanded. "You can't talk to me that way!"

I could tell Adele was about to throw a punch, so I took her arm and swiftly guided her to the back of the room, away from the curious stares of my other guests. They'd come in to relax and instead were getting front-row seats for a reality show. A crossing guard by day, taxi driver by night, and cat feeder and rescuer pretty much the rest of the time, Adele had one goal—to make feline lives better across the island. Her salaries went almost entirely to caring for cats. I admired her for it. But sometimes she got a little overzealous. This was one of those times.

"Can you please stop?" I said quietly. "I don't need a scene in here."

"But Maddie, she's not fit to have pets!" Adele protested, still too loudly. "Are you telling me that just because she's rich you're gonna give her what she wants?"

Across the room, I could see Holly bare blindingly white teeth at Adele and open her mouth. I held up a hand to stop her.

"I get it," I said to Adele, keeping my voice calm and reasonable. "Let me handle it. Okay?"

Adele stared at me, clearly evaluating whether or not she could trust me to do the right thing. Finally she gave a curt nod. "Fine," she said. "I'll be in the kitchen." She turned and stalked out of the room.

Heaving a quiet sigh of relief, I turned back to the other half of my problem. Holly's arms were crossed over her chest. She glared at me, one foot tapping an annoyed staccato beat on my floor. I breezed back over to her and handed her an application from the stack next to the door.

"Why don't you fill this out and we'll go from there?" I suggested.

"I would like the cat now," Holly said. Her tone strongly suggested I should do as she said. "Don't be difficult, Maddie. You know very well who I am and what I can provide an animal."

Yeah. Lots of love, from the sounds of it. Had this nasty woman really lived underneath that quiet high school gal? I reattached my hopefully pleasant smile to my face and tried to speak as if I wasn't gritting my teeth. "We have a routine we do for all our applicants," I said. "We don't send the cats home right away. We need to do vet checks and home checks, and talk to references."

"I've never heard of such a thing." Holly's phone trilled and interrupted her new tirade. She glanced down and narrowed her eyes, punching at the screen. "Heather. Chill. Out. I said I'll be right out." She disconnected, then looked back at me. "So you're not giving me the cat now."

"I'm happy to consider your application," I said. "But again, we don't send cats home right away." It wasn't a total lie. We looked at each request on a case-by-case basis. Some cats we *did* send home right away. Katrina Denning, Daybreak's animal control officer and my cat supplier, had given me the authority to do what I felt was right, given my prior experiences as an adoption counselor. In this case, I had no intention of adopting to Holly Hawthorne at all, based on this scene alone. I just wanted her out of my café.

"Then forget it," she announced. "Your loss. This place is a joke." And she sailed out the front door in what I'm sure she considered to be a dramatic exit.

Chapter 2

The room was silent for a minute, then the rest of the patrons erupted into laughter.

"What a piece of work," one woman said, coming up to me. "You did the right thing, sweetheart. She doesn't need that precious cat. The Hawthornes have such big egos I'm surprised there's room for anyone else on this island."

"Indeed," an older gentleman said, looking up from where he played with a gray and white tomcat. "They aren't the kindest people in town, not by a long shot." He stroked the cat from his head down to the tip of his tail. The cat arched his back in pleasure.

"I think he likes you," I said, nodding toward the cat. I didn't want to perpetuate the gossip about my irate guest. Whatever drama Holly Hawthorne was involved in, I wanted it as far away from JJ's House of Purrs as possible. Although I was dying to ask around about when she'd turned into her sister. Had Heather turned into the nice one?

"I think he does," the man agreed. "I'm going to have to ask my wife if we can bring him home."

"Can I put in an application on Georgia?" the woman who'd spoken up asked me. "She's so cute. And I want to make sure Holly doesn't go near her again. I'm sure the poor thing is traumatized."

I handed her the application I'd been holding for Holly. She took it and hurried to a table to fill it out.

Adele poked her head back in from the kitchen and glared at me. "Maddie? Is the coast clear?"

I nodded.

"Good. Did you tell her to go pound sand?" she asked eagerly, stepping back into the room as the man holding the gray and white cat reached over and gave her a high five.

I wanted to ask him not to egg on her bad behavior, but something told me the point was probably moot. Besides, I had to admit I didn't actually blame Adele for her vehement disapproval of Holly. I would've handled it differently, but Adele wasn't me. She simply didn't care about anything but the cats. There weren't too many people who would take their role as a defender of animals so seriously. Me, I had to consider my brand. And the fact that if I shouted at visitors, people probably wouldn't want to come in to the café.

"It's fine, Adele. She left without even filling out an application."

Adele narrowed her eyes. "You were going to let her fill out an application?"

"I was trying to defuse the situation. She didn't, so it doesn't even matter. Don't worry."

Adele watched me with those slate-gray eyes long enough that I shifted uncomfortably under her gaze. "You better worry," she said finally. "She'll be back. And she'll bring nothing but trouble with her."

"Who'll bring nothing but trouble?"

I whirled around at the voice that suddenly appeared behind my left shoulder. Katrina Denning stood behind me, nodding in approval as she took in the cats' new digs. Katrina and I went way back. She'd been my childhood babysitter. She wasn't that much older than me—when I'd

been an awful middle schooler she'd been in high school—
so once we got past those weird ages, we'd actually become
friends. Which made her approval even nicer now. And in
addition to supplying cats, she'd promised to supply me
with volunteers to help me run this place. She was the reason Adele was here. She'd recommended her to me months
ago, when I first decided to move back to Daybreak and
commit to the café.

"This place is *awesome*," Katrina declared, reaching
down to stroke the black cat rubbing against her leg. "Any
applications or adoptions yet?"

"One, actually," I said. "The little orange kitten. I knew
he wouldn't last long. Hopefully we can get the references
checked quickly and get him into his new home. The
people seem really great. And that lady's putting in an application on the calico."

I heard a squeaking sound at my feet and turned around.
JJ, my own cat—short for Junkyard Johnny—sidled into
the room, checking out the goings-on through his brilliant
green eyes. He had a catnip toy in his mouth, one that
Adele had hand-made specially for the café. She'd begun
work on them as soon as she'd heard what we were doing.
Created out of bright colors and fun patterns, they were
full of catnip and ranged in size from one a kitten could
play with to larger ones for adult cats. They were the café's signature toy—not only were they for the resident cats
to enjoy, but we were selling them too, to raise money for
the café. And when a kitty was adopted, he or she would
be sent home with one.

JJ, finally having captured my attention, rubbed ur-
gently between my legs. I bent down and stroked his orange fur. I'd picked him up as a stray when he appeared at
my grandmother's grave earlier this summer. He got all the
credit for starting this whole strange journey I was on.
Mostly, I wanted to thank him for it. Then there were days

like today when I wondered what on earth I'd gotten myself into. And it was only the official day one.

JJ dropped his mouse right on my foot. He looked up at me and squeaked, louder this time. I took the toy and threw it. He looked at me disdainfully, as if assuming he would fetch was absurd, but he walked over and retrieved it, then brought it back to me and sat with it hanging out of his mouth. Staring at me. Odd behavior, even for him. Usually he'd be rolling around with it and getting high as a kite.

"That's great," Katrina said, yanking my attention away from him. "I have a list waiting to get in, so the more adoptions the better. It really does look great in here."

I glanced around. To me, it still looked like Grandpa's living room, with some hasty adjustments made so we could open before we lost the momentum of the summer season. We'd presently allocated the living and dining rooms for the café, since they were our largest rooms on the first floor. We'd added lots of cat furniture, as well as comfy chairs, some cushions, and a few café tables. It looked nothing like I wanted it to look yet—I envisioned a professional entryway with a nice desk area where people could check in, modern cat-related art on the walls, and those fancy leopard-print cat perches all around. But on the positive side, it was homey and comfortable and there were plenty of spots for the cats to sleep, hide, and play. And lots of closed doors to the rest of the house so no kitties could wander off.

Luckily, Grandpa's sunny yellow Victorian, which had been in his family for generations, had room for a couple of cat cafés, as well as our whole family if we ever all wanted to live together again. As it was, my business partner Ethan and I *were* living here. The house was four stories plus a basement, and it sat on a prime corner lot down the street from the ferries. It was only a five-minute walk into the center of Daybreak Harbor, which was the largest town out of the five on the island. Which meant it was in a great spot for visitors. The balconies dotting the back of the house offered obstruction-free views of the ocean.

It was still my favorite place in the world, so being able to live here again was special. And sharing it with some of the island's four-legged friends was an added bonus.

"So you've had lots of people?" Katrina asked.

I nodded. "There have been people in here since I opened the doors. And everyone's had positive things to say. Well, mostly everyone." I frowned, remembering Holly's angry parting words.

"Yeah, so you didn't answer my question." Katrina tucked her dark blond hair behind her ears, blowing her too-long bangs out of her face. As usual, she wasn't devoting much time to self-care. Or even a haircut. "Someone's bringing trouble?"

"That spoiled, rotten diva Holly Hawthorne," Adele supplied, eager to fill Katrina in. "She came in and wanted precious Georgia, then threw a hissy fit when Maddie wouldn't give the cat to her."

Katrina rolled her eyes. "That woman is a nightmare. She wants a cat like I want an aneurysm. I mean, she'd have to hire someone to scoop the litter box. Which wouldn't be a problem, but seriously. She just wants the idea of a cat. She should get a stuffed animal."

I hid a smile. Holly certainly had gained a reputation. "I don't remember her being anything like that in high school. Wasn't she kind of nerdy? And I don't mean that in a mean way. I was a nerd."

"You were?" Katrina looked surprised.

"Of course I was. A trendy nerd, but still a nerd." I winked.

"Oh." Katrina nodded. "Well, yeah. She used to be nice back then, actually. Her sister was always crazy. And loud.

Holly went away to college and came back just as crazy. Maybe her family demanded it so she would fit in. Whatever happened, she's just like her sister now. So they can't even stand each other, and they're practically the same person."

"Yeah. I heard Heather yelling at her on the phone while she was in here. Well," I said. "I'm not going to worry about it. She's gone, and from the sounds of it, she's not coming back. And I have a grand opening to celebrate. You guys in?"

Chapter 3

Despite the unpleasantness Holly Hawthorne left in her wake, I managed to push the whole scene out of my mind and focus on the happy people crowding JJ's House of Purrs. Grandpa, of course, who was taking his role as a co-owner seriously. He worked the room, a presence in his red pants and Hawaiian shirt covered with cats in various sunbathing poses. A red baseball cap with a cat in a yoga stretch was perched on top of his thick white hair. He offered food to people like he'd been a waiter all his life, and made sure the cats' bowls were all full.

The rest of my family had come to celebrate. My parents and two sisters brought a giant bouquet of yellow roses and two large bags of food to donate for the cats. My best friend Becky Walsh, the editor and pinch-hitter reporter for the *Daybreak Island Chronicle*, was here to personally do a feature story on the café and its fabulous owners—that would be me and Ethan, as well as Grandpa.

I watched Becky, meandering around with her notebook, jotting down quotes from visitors with whom she'd struck up a conversation and stopping to pet the cats and take photos. She'd already snapped a bunch of pictures of Ethan working hard in the kitchen and me chatting with visitors and potential adopters. And of course, JJ, who'd been the inspiration for the whole venture. He enjoyed his stardom, posing for pictures whenever he sensed a camera in the vicinity. He was nothing if not smart, that cat.

People were milling around, playing with feather toys and lasers with the cats, or snuggling with them on one of the funky cushions I'd scattered around the floor. Others perched at café tables with a cup of Ethan's coffee or a muffin. Humans and felines looked happy.

The cat café concept was fairly new to the States, and virtually unheard of on a small island like ours. Usually reserved for urban areas, the cafés served as a place where people who either couldn't have cats or didn't have time to properly care for them full-time could come and get their cat fix, with a cup of coffee or a pastry on the side, for a minimal entry fee. On the island, the model was a little different. Actually, it was brand-new. I'd seen a couple of needs to fill—those who were here for summer vacations and missed their pets, and those who simply couldn't afford pets. The Holly Hawthornes of the island didn't encompass the entire population. There were people here who could barely make ends meet, the ones who worked eighteen-hour days in the summer in the hopes of surviving through the winter. And thirdly, I could provide some relief to Katrina, whose small quarters at the animal control center were full more often than not, with the result that some of the residents ended up in her own house.

All in all, I was confident our recipe was a good one.

Grandpa and I, with the help of my dad on the weekends, had worked hard the last two months to turn the house into both a livable space for the café cats and separate our living space. In honor of the cats, we'd moved our area, with the exception of the kitchen, to the top two floors of the house. But we had a long way to go. We were putting the kitchen to double use, baking and making coffee for the café, and cooking for ourselves. Ethan, who also co-owned a juice bar with me out in California, was in charge of the food and drink. So far he hadn't complained a whit about our MacGyver approach, but I knew he was remodeling in his mind to make the place work even better. And since he was staying here at the house too, I knew he'd be happier with a dedicated kitchen for "real" café prep.

"Relax," Ethan said, coming up behind me. "I can read your mind. It's looking good in here. Stop worrying."

I grinned. One of our friends in California had dubbed Ethan "the Maddie whisperer." He always knew exactly when I was working myself up into a frenzy. He was also one of the only ones who could talk me off a ledge. "I know, I'm getting ahead of myself. I just wish it was all set up the way I want it. But I can't find a stupid contractor to save my life."

"You say you need a contractor?" Adele appeared behind me with a glass of wine in her hand. Apparently she'd found a way to get over her Holly Hawthorne sulk. "Why don't you call my nephew?"

"Your nephew? Is he a professional?" I asked, perking up.

Adele frowned at me. "'Course he is. You think I'd send you a concert pianist if you need a builder?"

I sighed inwardly. Adele's delivery could be a bit rough, even with me. Ethan hid a smile and backed away. "What's his name? Does he have a card?"

"His name's Gabe. Gabriel Quinn. My sister's boy. He works for himself. Been in business for fifteen years. Here." She rooted in her pockets, pulled a receipt out. Grabbed a pen from the table holding the stack of adoption applications and scribbled a number. "He's a good worker. Builds furniture too. Those fancy Adirondack chairs? He makes most of the ones they sell on the island."

Adirondack chairs? I wasn't so sure that meant he was

overly qualified as someone who could do house remodeling. But I wasn't about to argue with Adele, not with the mood she was in. "Thanks," I said, pocketing the tattered receipt. I noticed it was for East's Liquor Store.

"Actually, I'll call him for you," Adele decided. "As soon as I'm done here."

"Oh, I can do it," I started to say, but she shook her head.

"I said I'd call." Her tone left no room for argument, so I shrugged and let it go. One less thing for my to-do list.

Chapter 4

"Maddie. I'm in love," my mother declared, rushing over to me with another resident black cat snuggled in her arms. My dad trailed behind her, a concerned look on his face. I don't think my dad wanted a cat.

"Moonshine is supersweet," Adele said, reaching out to stroke the cat's head. "Hates dogs, though. Do you have a dog?"

"We're just playing with her," my dad interrupted, before my mom could speak. "Right, Sophie?"

My mother gave him her best evil eye, then followed it up with a pouty face. "But Brian. Our house is so empty these days. Especially with Sam moving out. And no, we don't have a dog," she said to Adele. "I'm going to need something to love. Besides you, of course." She winked at my father. He blushed. They were too cute for their own good. I thought it was sweet.

"Plus you're working so much lately, I need company," my mother declared. "So, it's settled. Maddie, do I need to fill out an application? Do you need references?"

I hid a smile. "I think I can vouch for your character, Mom."

"Excellent," she declared.

"Hang on," my father began, but I cut him off.

"Sam's moving out? She didn't tell me that." I looked around for my youngest sister, but didn't see her anywhere.

My mother nodded. "She's renting a place with three other girls. I suppose it's time. I mean, she's done with college and all. It's just . . . she's our baby." Her eyes filled with tears and she hugged the cat closer. My sister had commuted to community college on the mainland, so she had yet to live away from home.

My dad sighed, but I could see him softening. "Let's go talk about it over here," he suggested, leading my mom toward one of the comfy couches I'd found at the local thrift shop to replace Grandpa and Grandma's ancient furniture.

I left them to it and waded back into the crowd, looking for anyone who needed help, or a coffee refill, or anything. And my heart did a little flip when I saw Lucas Davenport heading my way, a brilliant smile lighting up his face. Lucas owned a pet grooming salon on the island. He'd recently started working with Katrina to help with the strays she picked up around the island, which meant we had a professional connection now since a lot of those cats would be coming my way. Which meant he'd be coming over to the café to do some of the grooming here.

Lucas was also a musician. He sang and played guitar in a local band called the Scurvy Elephants. He was gorgeous too. At least, my type of gorgeous, with messy dark hair, icy blue eyes, and a smile that could melt you into a puddle.

And oh yeah, we were kind of dating. I say "kind of" because we hadn't made it official yet. But we'd been casually seeing each other once or twice a week since I'd been back and things seemed to be going pretty well.

Actually, so far, Lucas was awesome. Although in the back of my mind I feared his musician status would ultimately reveal him to be a worm. I had a habit of dating musicians, and they usually ended up not being worth my time in the end. It seemed like one of those patterns I was hard-pressed to break.

Unless Lucas was all about breaking the pattern, because he was a Good Musician.

"Happy opening," Lucas said when he finally reached me, and produced a bouquet of gorgeous colorful gerbera daisies from behind his back.

"Oh!" I stared at the flowers, horrified to feel tears filling my eyes. I'd told Lucas once, way back on our second sort-of date, that I loved gerbera daisies. For him to remember something like that—well, let's just say I wasn't used to it. "These are beautiful," I said, accepting the bouquet once I was sure I wouldn't cry. "Thank you so much, Lucas." I was acutely aware of everyone staring at me, including my parents. Great.

"Of course. Congratulations." He pulled me toward him for a kiss. I could feel my face burn.

To make it worse, the people around me started to clap. I guess my status as a perpetual single female had made its way around the island, even though I'd barely been home for three months. I hoped this would put all the questions about me and Ethan to rest, because of course everyone thought that since I'd brought Ethan across the country with me, we had to be together. Well, everyone except the people who thought I was going to get back together with my high school boyfriend Craig, now a local police officer.

Leading the clapping was the island's quirkiest character, Leopard Man. That wasn't his real name. I'm not sure anyone knew his real name. He and Grandpa were friends, but I had no idea what Grandpa called him. Leopard Man was another resident who'd been around at least since I was a kid. I'd made friends with him at a very early age, when I'd pulled his tail once on the street. My father had nearly died with embarrassment. Kind of a straitlaced guy, my dad had never been sure how to react around a guy who dressed in leopard garb from head to toe and wore a tail on days he was extra happy. Most people thought Leopard Man was homeless, mentally ill, or both. I had no idea about the homeless part, but I didn't think he was mentally ill. Quirky, sure, and cool in a totally unique way that most people on this island were used to at this point.

Leopard Man winked at me and tipped his leopard fedora. "I can express no kinder sign of love, than this kind kiss," he murmured.

I suppressed a smile. That was the other fun thing about Leopard Man. He spoke mainly Shakespeare. He had a quote for every life situation imaginable. I didn't really know what to say to that, so I didn't say anything. Turning back to Lucas, I tried to not pause awkwardly. "Do you want coffee?" I asked.

"I'd love some."

"Cool. Come in the kitchen with me. I'll get a vase for these."

"Hey Maddie!" Becky rushed over, brandishing her notebook and yanking a pen from behind her ear, managing to tangle it in blond, American Girl Doll-like curls. Cursing, she yanked it out. I cringed, thinking of the hair she'd just pulled from the roots.

She didn't seem to notice. "I didn't think I'd have so much fun writing a good-news story. Usually I like crime. Listen, can we do a series featuring the cats once a week? It might help them get adopted and it will definitely get you some extra publicity. Cool?"

"Really cool," Lucas said before I could even respond. "Maybe you can even put in a plug for the awesome groomer helping out the strays." He winked at her.

"I'll think about it," Becky said. "No promises." She might look like an American Girl Doll, but she was a ruthless journalist.

"I can live with that," Lucas said.

"We're getting coffee," I said to Becky. "Want any?"

"No. Going to get back to the office and write this up. Nice job, Mads."

She turned to walk away just as Gigi Goodwin, Adele's volunteer-in-training, shoved through the crowd until she reached my side. "Maddie," she said in a stage whisper. "There's a cop here looking for you."

Chapter 5

I spun around, craning my neck to see the front door. Sure enough, Officer Craig Tomlin stood there, a bit awkwardly in full uniform, hat in his hands, shifting his weight from one foot to the other. In addition to being one of Daybreak's finest, he'd also been my high school boyfriend. We'd sort of tried reconnecting when I first came back. Mostly Craig's efforts. He'd grown up nicely, for sure, but I had this real issue with going backward in life. And then, of course, there was Lucas.

Still, Craig was a good guy. And I was happy to see him here to help me celebrate my opening. I smiled at Gigi. "It's okay. He's a friend."

Gigi didn't look convinced, but the girl seemed like a bag of nerves anyway, weighing in at barely a hundred pounds, with hair in a perpetual ponytail and eyes that were always huge and concerned. She chewed on her short red nails. I could see where the polish was chipped and wondered if she was ingesting it. I hoped she was using the nontoxic stuff.

"He's not looking too friendly," Becky said. She didn't seem too eager to get back to the office anymore. I could see that flash of *maybe there's a story here* in her eyes.

"Excuse me one second," I said to Lucas. He didn't look thrilled to see Craig, but he nodded. Lucas and Craig had picked up on each other's vibe, and they spent any time in the other's presence circling each other warily. It was annoying on a regular day, and today I had no time to entertain them. I left Lucas and made my way over to Craig.

"Hey! Thanks so much for coming on our opening day." I went to give him a hug, but he stepped slightly back. I frowned. "What's up?"

"Maddie. The place looks great. Congratulations. Is Adele Barrows here?" he asked.

"Adele? Sure. She's right . . ." I turned to point at her, then slowly dropped my hand as it dawned on me. He wasn't here to support my opening. He was here in an official capacity. I narrowed my eyes. "Why do you want Adele?"

He sighed. "I'm sorry to do this on your first day open, but we've had a complaint. A woman said she was verbally abused by one of your employees."

"You're kidding. This is because of Holly?" I shook my head. "First of all, Adele isn't technically my employee. She's a volunteer. And secondly, the two of them were guilty of bad behavior."

My café patrons had started to inch closer to us and pretend not to be listening, or had blatantly stopped what they were doing and stared. Becky headed our way, the scent of a story ripe in the air. Craig took my hand and pulled me to the side of the room so we were a bit out of earshot.

"So you know what I'm talking about?" he asked. "Holly Hawthorne?"

I gritted my teeth. "Yeah. She's a joy, for sure. She came in here thinking she'd just walk out with a cat. When we told her it didn't work that way, she lost her mind."

"Really?" Craig consulted his notes. "Because she said Adele told her she was 'a disgrace' and 'not fit to have pets.'"

"So what if I did?"

We both turned to find Adele behind us, arms crossed, foot tapping defiantly. "You gonna arrest me for telling the truth?"

"Adele. Let's not take it out on Craig—Officer Tomlin. He's just doing his job, okay?"

Adele snorted. "If I'da been the one to call and cry abuse, would you have come running? Or is it just 'cause she's rich?"

Craig looked pained. "Of course I would've come. Listen." He glanced around, then lowered his voice even more. "I have to respond to the call. And I have to ask some questions to do that correctly. Now that I know what happened, I can make my report and say it was a mutual disagreement. Okay? If you see her again, ignore her. And it's done." He looked satisfied with himself for breaking it down into such simple terms.

I looked at Adele. She clearly wanted to argue with him more, but then something inside her seemed to give up. "Sure," she said, and her tone sounded defeated. "It's done." She turned and walked away, her shoulders slumped.

I turned to Craig and sighed. "I can't believe she called you guys. What a drama queen."

"Oh, you don't know the half of it with that family," Craig assured me. "They think they own the island. Anyway, I'll let you get back to your day. The place looks great, Maddie. Truly." He looked like he wanted to give me a hug but wasn't sure if he should while he was there officially. He ended up patting my arm awkwardly, then turned and left.

Becky grabbed my arm as I walked by her. "What was that about?"

"That jerk Holly. She didn't like the way Adele spoke to her so she called the cops. Who does that?"

Becky rolled her eyes. "Most people are just too polite to tell her what they really think. Good for Adele."

"I've never met a woman with a bigger cheerleading squad," I said dryly.

"Oh, sweetie. You have no idea. Let's just say Holly hasn't made any friends since high school." Becky patted my shoulder. "Most people can't stand her. And she's not even on the island full-time. I'll talk to you later."

I headed back to Lucas, who'd been watching the whole scene through narrowed eyes. As had most of the rest of my guests. My mother started over to me, but I shook my head and lifted my chin, grabbing Lucas's hand. "Come on. Let's go get that coffee." The heck with Holly Hawthorne. This was my day, and no one was going to ruin it.

Chapter 6

When we disappeared into the kitchen, I let out the breath I'd been holding. Ethan turned from the oven, where he'd just removed a gorgeous tray of scones. "Perfect timing," he said in that soft voice that never failed to take any stressful situation down a notch.

Ethan was my other guru. I guess in addition to attracting musicians, I also had a talent for attracting people who were good for my often-neglected spiritual side. Too bad they were never relationship possibilities. Ethan and I tried to date once, and realized we were way better as friends and business partners. He was cute enough, with his curly red hair, longish hippie beard, and gentle brown eyes. Basketball-player tall, his typical uniform consisted of baggy pants and tank tops. He usually avoided shoes if at all possible. He rode a skateboard around the island and practiced Kundalini yoga. Zen was his middle name. He and Cass had already hit it off. Next to Becky, he was the person closest to me. And the fact that he'd moved across the country to get into another business endeavor with me reminded me of how lucky I was.

I sniffed the air. "Yum. What kind?"

"Blueberry lemon." He studied me, noting the flowers,

then glanced at Lucas. "What's going on out there? Nice flowers," he added.

I smiled. "Lucas brought them. Can he get coffee?"

"Sure thing. What can I get you? Espresso? Cappuccino? Mocha?"

"I'll just take a regular coffee," Lucas said.

"Mads? Anything?"

Despite how yummy the scones smelled, I'd lost my appetite. "No. I'm annoyed."

"What happened?"

"I just had a visit from one of Daybreak's finest. The spoiled little witch who threw a fit earlier called the cops. Can you believe it?"

"You're kidding. Because you wouldn't give her a cat?"

"It was more about her complaining about Adele's big mouth, but still." I sighed and dug around in one of the cabinets until I found a vase. I fixed the daisies into a colorful splash, then placed it on the counter. "I'm going to take them upstairs later," I told Lucas. "If I leave them in the café the cats will knock them over. Or eat them."

He nodded, as if it made perfect sense. "Sounds good to me."

"So what ended up happening with the cops?" Ethan asked. "Is everything okay?"

"Well, Adele told Craig off. I don't think he took it personally." I paced the kitchen looking for something to do. "I'm sure he has to report back to the Hawthornes. Maybe he'll get instructions to come back and arrest somebody. On second thought, I'll take an espresso."

Ethan looked at me doubtfully. "You sure? Maybe a juice would be better."

"No. I need some caffeine." No doubt Ethan was right about the juice being a better choice, but I was sulking.

He handed Lucas his coffee, then went to his fabulous new machine and began making my espresso.

"You've got a good turnout," Lucas said, trying to shift the conversation back to happier topics. "Any adoption applications?"

"Yes, a few so far. And my mother wants to adopt Moonshine, but I think my dad's trying to talk her out of it," I said.

"I think you're going to have a lot of success. People seem to love it. It's a cool concept in general, but even cooler out here on an island where you wouldn't expect something like this. Proud of you, Maddie." Lucas squeezed my hand.

His words left me kind of speechless. In a good way. "Thanks," I managed. "I hope you're right and people keep loving it."

The door to the kitchen opened and Becky stuck her head in. "Maddie, there's a bunch of people who want applications. I can't find Adele or Gigi and Katrina's jumped in. Can you come out?"

"Sure, sorry." I cast an apologetic look at Lucas, then dropped his hand and hurried out. "You can't find Adele?"

Becky shook her head. "Not since she yelled at the cop. Gigi seems to have vanished too."

"I saw Adele take off out the back door," Mr. Gregory, one of Grandpa's friends, said, looking up from where he sat petting Snowball, an all-white cat. "She took the wineglass with her," he added with a disapproving shake of his head. "That lady's gonna get herself in real trouble one of these days with that drinking habit. Pair it with that temper and boy, oh boy." The word temper came out as *tempah* with his strong Massachusetts accent. "I don't know about the other one, but she looked mighty nervous when young Officer Craig came in."

Took off? And with one of my wineglasses? I gritted my teeth. Seriously, the woman needed to get a grip. I'd have to sit down and have a serious talk with her about all this nonsense. And what was with Gigi being afraid of the cops? My café was supposed to be a drama-free zone, and it was only day one and already anything but. I needed volunteers to help reduce my stress level, not make it skyrocket.

I'd have to worry about it later though. I had customers to attend to, and cats to adopt out.

Chapter 7

By the time we saw the last guest out of the café and finished cleaning up after the day's festivities—which meant
scooping all the litter boxes, sweeping and mopping the
floor because a couple of people, in their excitement to
pet the cats, had spilled their coffee or other beverages—
it was nearly eight thirty. The café had technically closed
at eight, but people had been having such a good time I
didn't want to throw them out. Plus the cats were happy to
have the attention.

But when I flipped the cat-shaped sign to CLOSED and
locked the door behind the last guest, I realized how exhausted I was.

My parents lingered behind. "So," my mother said finally. "It was nice of Craig to come by to wish you well
today." She blinked innocently at me.

I had to laugh. Sophie James was anything but innocent. Anyone who didn't know her might be fooled by her
appearance, with her unruly brown curls, long gypsy skirts,
and sweet smile. Really, she was the smartest woman I
knew, and she was used to getting what she wanted. Usually her wants were for the greater good. When it came to
her kids, she just wanted to know we were okay.

And her eagle eyes had caught on to the fact that Craig's visit wasn't just a social call.

My dad, though, seemed totally preoccupied. He kept disappearing into the other room with his phone, which wasn't like him.

"Yeah, well. The little catfight in here made its way back to the station. Craig came by and everyone talked, and it's all smoothed over. What's going on with Dad?" I asked, hoping she'd let me change the subject.

She sighed. "It's gala season."

"Oh jeez. The gala. Isn't it soon?" As the big cheese at Daybreak General Hospital, my dad was responsible for all kinds of serious things. The annual end-of-summer gala, though not a matter of life and death, was still one of those serious things because it brought in a ton of money for the hospital's operating expenses each year. It helped keep programs like the LifeStar helicopter service going, in case anyone needed to be airlifted off the island. So it was super important. But usually he didn't need to be involved in the organizing of it, given his position.

"Yes. Two weeks from tonight."

"Isn't Dad a little high up to be involved in the planning? Is something wrong?"

My mother glanced around to make sure he wasn't listening. "The board is putting a lot of pressure on your father this year. They've raised the amount they're expecting to net considerably higher. Dad's assistant usually organizes most of it, but she's had some personal problems and has been out a lot." She dropped her voice lower as Dad drifted closer to us, still glued to the phone. "I'll tell you more later. But he's very worried about it. And it's taking up a ton of his time."

"Why didn't they hire an outside planner to do it?" I asked.

She shrugged. "I suggested it, but you know Dad. And it's a little late now."

I did know Dad. He was a bit of a control freak. It was where I'd gotten the tendency, although I'd been trying hard to let it go of late. Not sure I was succeeding, but at least the effort was there. "But still," I said. "If there are things going wrong, someone else who can worry about it full-time should come in and sort it out."

I stopped talking as Dad ended his call and put his phone in his pocket. He looked at us curiously, probably sensing we were discussing him. Or at least, his problems.

"Brian. Turn that thing off," my mother said, going over and slipping her hand into his. "We're going out to dinner and I want your full attention."

"You got it," Dad said, giving her a hug. "I'm sorry, Sophie. This event may just kill me this year."

"It's not worth it," my mother declared. "Let's go eat. And you can make it up to me by letting me talk you into adopting Moonshine." She winked at me.

"We'll see," Dad said with a smile. "Maddie, congratulations. What a lovely job you've done."

I beamed at the praise. "Thank you, Dad." I wanted to ask him about the gala, but I could tell Mom didn't want him to get sucked back into that vortex so I let it be. I saw them out and locked the door behind them, then headed to the kitchen in desperate need of some wine.

"Want me to make us some dinner?" Grandpa asked, slinging an arm around my shoulder. "Or should we order something?"

"Let's order something. You've been on your feet all day too." I studied Grandpa Leo. Sometimes I had to remind myself he was seventy-four. True, his thick head of wavy hair had turned whiter over the past couple of years and he didn't walk as fast as he used to. But compared to the state I'd found him in when I'd arrived at the beginning of summer when my grandmother died and a local shyster was trying to take this house from him, he looked a hundred times better. He had a purpose again, as a co-owner of this fine establishment. After being police chief for so long, as well as a devoted husband, to have both those roles terminated over the past five years had been devastating. All that, topped off with the possibility of losing the home that had been in his family for generations, made me worry Grandpa wouldn't be around for much longer.

But the anonymous benefactor who'd saved his house, with the stipulation it be used to help care for the island cats, had changed all that. The birth of the cat café seemed to have given Grandpa new life, too. My mother swore having me back was the bigger piece of it, but I thought he just needed something to which he could put his mind again. I'd never known him to be a cat person, but he'd taken to the whole thing like a natural. I think JJ had helped. He loved my big orange guy. Although I needed to find Grandpa a job at the café that suited him. We hadn't quite figured that piece out yet. Right now he did a bit of everything—and usually left a few things undone when he moved to the next.

JJ rubbed around my ankles now, reminding me that it was his dinnertime also. He didn't want to wait until I ordered food. "Let's get some pizza or something easy," I said, looking at Ethan, who was silently cleaning up the kitchen. "You good with that?"

"Sounds like a plan," Ethan said. I hid a smile. I could've said, let's go outside and dig up some clams from the beach and steam them, and he'd go along with it.

"I'll call Sal's," Grandpa said. "Two large. What toppings?"

After a few minutes of healthy debate, we decided on one mushroom and olive, and one pepperoni. Grandpa placed the call while I poured wine for all of us and spooned

JJ's food into a bowl. He attacked it with a vengeance, despite the fact that people had been slipping him treats all day. They hadn't wanted him to feel left out when they'd fed them to the "real" café cats. I was going to have to keep my eye on him during open hours. One, to make sure he didn't get fat, and two, to make sure no one slipped off with him. I'd had about six people ask if they could put in an application for him today.

While we waited for the pizza, we sat around the table and rehashed the day.

"I think Tommy Gregory will be your best customer," Grandpa said. "He loves cats. His wife is deathly allergic and he's never been able to have one. I always thought he'd divorce her in a second if someone offered him a cat."

"That's so romantic." I wrinkled my nose and sipped my wine.

"Well, now he doesn't have to. He can have an affair with a different cat every day." Grandpa winked at me and turned to Ethan. "So, Ethan, did you leave a lady behind in California?"

Ethan clearly wasn't expecting that question. "Um. No," he said, a light pink color rising up his neck.

"I see." Grandpa nodded. "So are you hoping to date my granddaughter? Or are you already doing that?"

"Grandpa!" I nearly dropped my wineglass. Clearly he hadn't gotten the memo about me and Lucas. Or seen The Kiss today.

"What?" Grandpa Leo fixed me with the even stare he'd probably used on countless suspects over the years. "I have a right to ask. You're both living in my house."

"Oh, for Pete's sake." I dropped my face into my hands. "No, Grandpa. Ethan and I are not dating, nor were we planning on it." I raised my head and shot Ethan my best *please forgive me* look.

Grandpa looked from me to Ethan and back again, then shrugged. "Okay," he said.

"Okay?" I stared at him. "That's it?"

"Well, of course. What, did you think I was going to argue with you? I was just curious, that's all." He picked up the newspaper from the table and flipped to the sports page.

Before Ethan could run screaming from the house, the doorbell rang, thank goodness. "I'll get it," I muttered, and made a beeline for the front door. I was starving. And I hadn't had Sal's pizza in ages. My mouth had already started to water in anticipation as I yanked open the door.

But it wasn't Sal's delivery guy. It was Sergeant Mick Ellory from the Daybreak PD. And probably the last cop I ever wanted to see on my doorstep again. My memories of the last time he'd been here weren't pleasant. I held the door half open warily. "Yes?"

He nodded. "Maddie. Is your grandfather here?"

"Why?" I asked, immediately on the defensive. Silly, I knew. Grandpa didn't hold a grudge against him for doing his job. But I couldn't help it.

"I need to speak with him." Ellory's gaze leveled with mine. "He's not in trouble, Maddie."

"Well, I don't see why he would be. He hasn't done anything," I said, but pulled the door open wider. "Come in." I went down the hall to the kitchen and stuck my head in the door. "Grandpa. Can you come out here for a second?"

He glanced up from the paper. "What's wrong? You need money for the pizza?" He reached for his wallet.

"No. Someone's here to see you."

He raised an eyebrow, then stood and followed me. When he saw his visitor, he stood a little straighter. "Mick," he said, and held out his hand.

Ellory shook it. "Sorry to interrupt, Leo. Can I speak to you outside?"

Chapter 8

Sergeant Ellory let Grandpa go through the door first, then nodded at me before following him out. I stewed for a minute in the hallway, then crept over to the closest window. Unfortunately, Grandpa had left up the sheer curtains Grandma had loved so much that let the light in all over the house. They were pretty, but they didn't conceal eavesdroppers. I debated dropping to the ground and crawling over to lie under the window to listen, but that seemed a little excessive. I stood to the side of the window where I could still see them, watching body language and trying to guess what they were talking about. I couldn't figure it out, but now I was getting worried.

Ellory spoke for a couple minutes while Grandpa listened impassively. Then Grandpa spoke, presumably to ask a question or two. The whole thing looked very civil. It infuriated me. I thought one of the greatest skills anyone could have was holding a cop face. These two—not surprisingly—could win awards for it.

I hurried back to the kitchen. Ethan glanced up. "Everything okay?"

"I'm not sure," I said, picking up my cell phone. I pressed

the button for my mom's cell and was relieved when she answered, sounding completely normal. "Hi, Mom."

"Hi, sweetheart." She spoke loudly against the noise of the crowd in the background. Guess they were at their dinner. "What's going on?"

"Are you out with Dad?"

"Yes. We came to the new Indian restaurant in Turtle Point. It's packed! Is everything okay?"

"Yes, just checking to make sure Dad didn't get pulled into work and took you out to dinner. I'll talk to you tomorrow." I hung up and called Sam. She didn't answer, but a text message came through right after the phone went to voice mail.

I'm in yoga class. Call you back in a bit.

Phew. Val was my last family roll call, but just as I scrolled to her number, Grandpa returned. He looked troubled, but not the kind of trouble that meant someone close to us was hurt or worse.

"Grandpa?" I went over to him. "What happened? Is everyone okay?"

"Everyone's fine," he assured me. "Can you come out here for a minute though?"

Puzzled, I followed him back out to the hall. Ellory was still there. He nodded at me. I wanted to tell him to find a new way of communicating—like maybe speaking—but didn't want to sound hostile.

"Sergeant Ellory needs to ask you about something," Grandpa said, keeping his hand protectively on my shoulder.

I frowned. "What?"

"Your cat toys," Ellory said.

That was certainly not what I expected. All this drama over a cat toy? Why didn't he just come over and ask to buy one? I didn't know he had cats. "My signature café toys? They're great, aren't they? One of my volunteers makes them. Did you want one? How many cats do you have?" I started for the basket of them I kept in a cabinet in the hall, but Grandpa held me in place.

"No, I don't want one. I need to know who makes them," Ellory said. I could see him clenching his jaw in impatience.

I frowned. "Adele Barrows. Why?"

"And are they exclusive to your café? No one else has access to them?"

"Brand-new and exclusive to us, yes. Adele delivered the first batch yesterday. I mean, I think she gave some to Katrina and Gigi, the other people who work with the cats, but that's it."

He nodded. "Thanks. Leo, I appreciate your help tonight." He turned and walked to the door. Grandpa let him out and closed the door behind him.

"What the heck?" I asked.

Grandpa regarded me solemnly. "Maddie. I have to tell you something but you have to keep it between us for now."

I felt the slow somersault of dread in my stomach. Wordlessly, I nodded. This sounded . . . bad. I wasn't quite sure why, since we were talking about fuzzy cat mice, but it did.

But before he could say more, a car careened to a halt in front of the house, and then footsteps sounded on the porch followed by frantic knocking.

I was closer so I yanked it open.

It was Katrina. And she looked completely freaked out.

"Hey," I said. "What's up?"

"Maddie. Oh my God. I don't even—I can't . . ." She bent over, almost hyperventilating.

"Katrina? What's going on? What's happened?" Concerned, I grabbed her arm and pulled her into the house. "Do you need to sit?" I glanced at Grandpa, who sprang into action and took Katrina's other arm. We both led her to the couch.

She sank into it and covered her face with her hands.

"Seriously. You're scaring me. What's wrong?" I sat down next to her.

She finally looked up at me. "It's . . . Holly Hawthorne," she whispered.

"Holly Hawthorne?" Confused, I looked at Grandpa again. He avoided my eyes. "Why are you so upset about her?"

"She's dead," Katrina choked out. "And I'm afraid Adele finally lost it and killed her."

Chapter 9

My head was spinning, and it couldn't be from my long-forgotten glass of wine. I'd barely had three sips. "Dead? What? Katrina. Are you sure? How do you know this?"

Then my brain clicked the pieces together. Ellory's visit. He and Grandpa standing outside whispering. I turned and looked at Grandpa and knew I was right. He stared at Katrina with fascination. I could tell he wanted to ask her how she knew. Heck, so did I.

"She was found on her private beach tonight. Facedown in the sand. At her parents' summer house here in Daybreak. The one she and Heather share." Katrina swallowed. "They're questioning Adele!" She looked at Grandpa, fresh tears filling her eyes. "She's such a good person. But she has a temper. Oh my God, do you think she really did it?" She buried her face in her hands again.

I looked at Grandpa. "Is this why Ellory was here?"

"Come on," Grandpa said, reaching over and squeezing my hand. "Let's go in the kitchen. Katrina, we're getting pizza. You should eat something."

She started to shake her head, but Grandpa pulled her up and led her down the hall. "You need to eat," he repeated firmly. Sometimes he got into a real mother hen mode. "There's nothing else you can do right now. We all just need to calm down until this gets sorted out. Okay?"

I started toward the kitchen after them, then stopped and went back to the door. I flipped the dead bolt, something I hardly ever remembered to do here. Crime on the island was pretty minimal. Drugs, mostly. Some drug-related robberies. Usually in the more high-end areas. Although these days the island overall was considered high end, a place where the rich and famous came to spend their summers. Then you had your domestic altercations, which were more common in a place like this than one might think. Especially in the winter, when all the people were mostly gone, businesses were shuttered, and activities ranged from drinking at the bar to drinking in your house. Tempers were short. But murder? Aside from Chamber of Commerce President Frank O'Malley's untimely death a couple months ago, murders around here were basically nonexistent.

When I reached the kitchen, Grandpa was still trying to talk to Katrina. My mind worked overtime, trying to figure out why Katrina thought Adele had killed Holly. Sure, Adele seemed to be holding a grudge against her, but murder? Did that mean there were things about my star volunteer that I wasn't aware of? I didn't want to believe it. Not things of that magnitude, anyway. I had good people instincts, and I'd always trusted Adele. Still, I shivered, thinking of her vitriol-filled reaction to Holly's presence in the café earlier today.

The doorbell rang again. The pizza. I grabbed my wallet. Ethan scrambled out of his chair and followed me.

"What the . . ." he muttered when we were out of earshot of the kitchen. "Did they say that lady's *dead*? The one who got in the fight with Adele today?"

"That's what they're saying," I said grimly.

I yanked the door open and found Harry Peterson on

the porch. Harry worked for about five different places on the island. Sometimes in a given day. So it was hard to keep track of which hat he was wearing. Harry was somewhere between seventy and ninety. I thought he looked like Morgan Freeman. A little shorter though.

"Maddie." Harry presented the pizzas with a flourish.

I took the boxes gratefully. "Thanks, Harry. How much?"

He fumbled for the slip in his pocket, his rheumy eyes lingering on Ethan with unabashed curiosity. "It's $24.75. You Maddie's beau?" he asked, leaning forward as if Ethan was about to share a secret with him.

I wanted to knock my head against the wall. "No, Harry."

Ethan suppressed a smile. Harry shrugged. "Had to ask." While he counted out my change, he said, "Hey, you hear about the misfortune the Hawthorne lady ran into tonight?"

I froze. "What do you mean?" I asked carefully. How had this news spread so fast?

"I mean, Miss Holly Hawthorne's deceased. Someone finally decided they'd had their share of her antics, I guess." He shook his head and handed me a pile of ones. I counted five and handed them back for a tip. He thanked me and pocketed it. "Say, wasn't she here today causing some trouble for ya?"

"Thanks for the pizza, Harry." I closed the door before he could ask anything else, and slumped against the wall. From the open window, I could hear the street sounds. Harry making his way back to his junky old car and firing up the engine, people strolling by enjoying the summer night, either on their way back to the ferry dock down the street or maybe heading to the lobster shack for dinner. Normal people, doing normal things with their lives. I'd never wanted to be a normal person. Too boring. But lately, since moving back to Daybreak and dealing with seemingly endless insanity, I craved normal. Although I wasn't even sure what that meant anymore.

Ethan took the boxes from me. "Should we go back in there?"

"I guess we have no choice." I followed him into the kitchen, feeling like my flip-flops were attached to blocks of cement, making my feet drag. Katrina's eyes were still red, but she seemed a bit more under control.

Ethan dropped the boxes on the counter and pulled out some plates. I had no idea if anyone had any appetite at all. My stomach growled, but I felt like there was a giant boulder sitting somewhere between my throat and my chest that would make it impossible for any food to reach its destination.

"So what's happening to Adele?" I asked, unable to stand the silence any longer. "Katrina, did she call you? Is that how you found out about this?"

Katrina nodded. "The cops had just left her house. She was really upset when she called me. Just kept saying she knew it."

Well, at least they hadn't dragged her to the station. "Knew what?" I asked.

Katrina lifted her shoulders miserably. "She was pretty hysterical."

"Which cops went to see her?" I asked. Grandpa looked at me. I shrugged. "Just out of curiosity." I wanted to know if it was Ellory. He was usually the big shot in charge of these things. Well, at least the one other murder I had experience with. But if he'd been here and had sent, say, Craig, that was different. Craig was not as experienced, so if they'd sent him they may not be as serious about Adele as Katrina feared.

Katrina shook her head. "No idea. But it doesn't have to mean anything, right, Leo?" She looked hopefully at Grandpa. "I mean, maybe I got a little freaked out when she told me. Mostly because she was freaking out. The police have to question everyone who had an issue with Holly, right? Although that could take a long time, knowing . . . how everyone, uh, felt about her. But they're not going to arrest Adele or anything, are they?"

All eyes turned toward Grandpa, waiting for words of wisdom, or at least comfort.

Chapter 10

My cell phone rang, saving Grandpa from having to formulate an answer at that moment. I glanced at the screen. My sister Val. I picked it up. "Hey. Can I call you back? It's a little crazy here—"

"Maddie," she interrupted. "I need Grandpa."

"What's wrong?" Given the tone of her voice, I sensed this was not good news. This whole night was turning into crazy town.

"The police just came here looking for Cole. They wouldn't tell me what about. But it sounded serious, and I can't get a hold of him. I haven't talked to him since this morning. And no one's answering at his parents' house." She sounded completely panicked.

"Cole? The police?" I'd never liked my sister's husband much. He struck me as a guy with little ambition who got by riding Daddy's coattails. His father was a big-shot defense attorney who defended high-profile criminals in the Boston court system, and Cole had been absorbed into the family business. Still, I'd never had him pegged as someone who'd be in trouble with the police. I glanced at Grandpa, who was listening to my side of the conversation with an odd look on his face. "Val. Relax. I'm sure it's nothing. Especially knowing who his father is. But Grandpa's right here. Hold on." I handed the phone to him, raising my eyebrows in a silent question. He took it and left the room.

Katrina looked as dismayed about his departure as I felt. Ethan grabbed a piece of pizza and munched on it, his eyes darting back and forth between us nervously. Lacking something to do, I took a piece and chewed on it without really tasting it. "Katrina," I said, once I'd swallowed. "Why would you possibly think Adele killed Holly? I mean, you guys are really good friends, right? And you wouldn't be friends with a murderer." I laughed a little nervously, but she just sat there staring at me. I tried again. "Are you worried because of what happened here today?"

She barked out a laugh. "I wish it were as simple as that," she muttered.

"Then why?" I pressed.

Katrina hesitated, her eyes landing on Ethan. I sighed. I loved this island, but people were wary with anyone they considered an *outsider*. Which often meant people who hadn't been born fifth-generation Daybreakers or something ridiculous like that.

"If you're worried about Ethan, don't," I said bluntly. "If you trust me, you can trust him. End of story."

Ethan flashed Katrina a thumbs-up, still chewing on his pizza. I'm glad he was so zen nothing affected his appetite.

Katrina looked like she had no idea what to make of him—especially since he was still eating during a time like this—but turned back to me. "Fine. Holly and Adele have—had—a history."

"The cat last summer?"

"Among other things, yes. They . . . crossed paths often. And they really didn't like each other. And Adele, well, she can hold a grudge like no one you've ever seen."

None of that surprised me, from what I'd picked up in

the short time I'd known her. Still it didn't scream *murderer* to me. "Why did they cross paths often? Have there been that many cats?"

"Some," Katrina muttered. "Long story."

"Well, now's as good a time as any," I said.

Katrina squirmed a bit. Clearly she didn't want to tell me, which made me want to know even more. What other kind of history could Adele and Holly Hawthorne possibly have together? If Katrina wouldn't tell me, I was going to get to the bottom of it myself.

Grandpa came back in and all eyes turned to him.

"Hey," I said, letting Katrina off the hook for now. "Is Val okay?"

He nodded and took his seat, reaching for the pizza box. I waited while he selected a slice and took a bite.

"Well?" I demanded, exasperated.

He sent me a look that clearly said *Not now* and turned back to Katrina. "So you were asking me about the police questioning Adele," he said.

Katrina nodded. "Is that normal?"

"Yeah," I said. "Is it? It seems extreme to me if it's all because they had a disagreement today. Unless there's something that everyone here knows about but me." I shot Katrina a look but she avoided my eyes.

"Listen, doll." Grandpa reached out and squeezed my hand. "And you," he said to Katrina. "You listen, too. Adele has a reputation for being . . . a hothead. I know that's no surprise to you. She didn't try to hide the fact that she was upset with Holly. And in cases like this, any good cop worth his salt starts with the most recent problem someone had and works from there. It's all we can do."

It sounded rational enough. As much as I hated to admit it because it hit home, it made sense to start with the person who'd participated in a screaming match with the victim a few hours before. I still didn't believe Adele would go to that length to make a point. She'd won. Holly wasn't getting a cat, at least not from the only rescue place on the island. Plus the cats Adele took care of were her whole world. She fed feral cats—cats who weren't getting their meals from any other source, aside from what they could catch and eat on their own—all around the island, pretty much by herself. Gigi helped but Adele clearly led the charge. And she felt very strongly that the cats depended on her. So why would she jeopardize their ability to eat just to get back at Holly Hawthorne?

"So what happens next?" I said finally, when the silence in the room had stretched to the breaking point.

Grandpa looked at me. "The police investigate," he said. "And we let them do their jobs."

That was kind of funny, coming from him. He was probably the last person who would stay out of this. He couldn't really help it. Police work was in his blood, and sometimes he forgot he'd retired. Especially when things like this happened. I'm sure a little piece of him wished that if a murder or two had to happen, it would've happened while he could still officially be part of the investigation. Most days, Grandpa glossed over the minor detail of his retirement. Word on the street was that the new chief got a little prickly about Grandpa's involvement in official police business. I could've told the new chief to save his energy. Grandpa would find a way to keep himself in the know until the day he left the planet.

Katrina finally calmed down enough to eat a piece of pizza. Half of one, anyway. When she couldn't seem to choke down another bite, she excused herself. I walked her to the door.

"Are you going to tell me what's really going on?" I asked in a low voice, glancing behind me to make sure Grandpa hadn't followed me.

Katrina's eyes slid away. "I just worry about Adele," she

said. "She's been drinking a lot more. She gets so angry. I know she's overwhelmed with trying to save the world, and people like Holly really upset her. But I guess we'll see, right?"

I wondered why Katrina wouldn't confide in me. Had Adele done something in the past that would make Katrina worry like this? "Katrina. Is it . . . safe to have Adele working at the café?"

Katrina's eyes widened. "Oh my gosh. Of course. Maddie, I didn't mean . . . of course it's safe. She gets upset sometimes on behalf of the cats. It's harmless."

Then why was she a murder suspect? I cleared my throat. "Well, there are cats at the café. So I just want to make sure I have the right people here."

"She's perfect," Katrina said. "Trust me. I know this is all going to work out." She tried valiantly to infuse confidence into her words.

"Yeah. Okay, then. I guess we'll see," I said in response to her original question. I gave her a hug, then watched her walk to her car and drive away. Then I went looking for Grandpa to grill him about what was going on with my sister.

Chapter 11

Ethan saw the determined look on my face when I returned to the kitchen and made a hasty exit. He was probably still trying to process the fact that one of our first customers had been murdered. Among all the other things he was trying to process about his new life. I'm sure he didn't want to hear why the cops were visiting with my sister's husband to compound everything. I wasn't sure I wanted to either, but I felt like I had to know.

"So what's the deal?" I demanded as soon as Ethan had disappeared. "What did Val say? What's going on with Cole? And why was Ellory asking me about my cat toys?"

Grandpa calmly finished his piece of pizza, then wiped his mouth. I crossed my arms and tapped my foot, demonstrating my impatience. He cocked his head at me.

"Would you sit? I'm not going to tell you anything while you're standing over me like one of those nuns from elementary school." He grimaced.

"A nun?" I shook my head and dropped into a chair, tucking one leg under me. "I've been called many things in my life, but a nun is truly a new one. And stop trying to sidetrack me, Grandpa."

"I don't know why you didn't become a cop, Madalyn,"

he said. "You've definitely got the one-track mind for the job. Now. What I was going to tell you before that high-strung friend of yours busted in here like a bull in a china shop was why the police came to talk to me. Which has to do with why your sister called me. Which you cannot discuss with anyone else, am I clear?" He frowned, drawing his bushy white eyebrows together to illustrate his point.

"Yes, fine, clear." I leaned forward in anticipation, although a sense of unease had settled over me.

"Ellory paid me a courtesy call to tell me that Valerie's husband called in the dead body."

"The dead body." I sat back, letting my foot fall to the floor like a stone. "Like, Holly Hawthorne's dead body?"

Grandpa nodded.

My brain struggled to catch up. "But . . . how would he have known that she was dead? Unless he was at her house. Why would he have been at Holly Hawthorne's house?"

"Well now," Grandpa said. "That's the big question, isn't it?"

"So the cops went to talk to him about . . . what? Wouldn't they have talked to him when they came to see what was going on?"

"He left," Grandpa said. "He called it in and left. Or left first, and then called it in. I'm not entirely sure which. And apparently he didn't go home, because he wasn't at his house when they went over. Hence the call from Val."

"*Left?* How do you just leave a dead body?"

Grandpa shrugged. "Guess he thought he had a good lawyer he should talk to first. He must've gone straight to Daddy."

I let that sink in. "So is he in trouble for leaving the scene?"

"I'm not clear on all the details, but since he was the one who called it in, naturally they wanted to know why he was there, when was the last time he'd seen her, all the usual questions. Ellory only told me he was being questioned as part of typical procedure. He didn't tell me anything else. And he didn't want me to hear it from Val and come storming into the station demanding information. His words." Grandpa looked amused by this.

I thought about this. "Was he the only one at her house?"

Grandpa looked me in the eye. "It's not clear. There were other people around the house at some point. Evidence of a party. But when her body was found, I'm not sure who else was there. Ellory was vague." He hesitated. "And there's another piece."

"Great. Does it have to do with a cat toy?" I was being sarcastic, but Grandpa wasn't laughing.

"It does. What Katrina said was true. They found Holly on the beach, facedown in the sand. But . . . she'd been choked. With one of your cat toys."

"Choked? My cat toy? The fuzzy oversized mouse?" I dropped into a chair, not sure my legs could hold me any longer and regretting the few bites of pizza I'd had. My stomach was churning violently. Then another thought punched me in the gut. "Does Ellory think *I* did it? Is that why he came here?"

"You? Why on earth would he think you did it?" Grandpa asked.

"Because I have the cat toys," I said. But he only wanted to know who made them, I reminded myself. And if he wanted to arrest me, he would've just done it. He certainly didn't need Grandpa's permission. The whole concept of the toy confounded me though. Who choked someone with a cat toy? How did you even do that?

Talk about sending a message.

"Maddie. No one thinks you killed anyone. Unfortunately, the jury is out on Adele. That's why Ellory wanted to confirm who made them, and if they would be floating around the island freely. If only a few people have access to them, it certainly narrows down the pool. Especially since Holly didn't have a cat. So she wouldn't have had the toy on hand."

"So whoever did it had the toy with them? Or brought the toy specifically to use on Holly?" But then what did Cole have to do with all this? He certainly didn't have any of my cat toys. "Grandpa. Was Cole . . . seeing Holly?" I asked. "Do they think *he* did it?"

"I don't know, Maddie. That definitely wasn't part of the conversation." We were both silent for a bit.

"How's Val holding up? She sounded freaked," I said finally.

"She's worried. And it's not helping that her husband hasn't been in contact with her. What kind of man shuts his wife out and runs to Daddy?" Grandpa shook his head in disgust, then glanced at me. "Sorry." He didn't sound it though.

"Don't be sorry. I don't like him either. Never did." I'd be willing to bet most of our family felt that way too, even if my parents would never admit it. Well, that and the fact that Cole's mother was on the hospital board, which meant my dad had to play nice anyway, semirelated or not, since the board was technically my dad's boss. The simple fact was, Val was too good for Cole Tanner. The problem was, she didn't think so.

Grandpa smiled a little at that. "I know that, Maddie. Your poker face isn't as good as you think."

"Oh." I felt a little bad. I wonder if Val knew how I felt. Then I decided I didn't care. Clearly, Cole was even worse than I'd thought, if he was at some woman's house while my sister was home alone. "So wouldn't he be more of a suspect than Adele?" I asked, still trying to wrap my head around all this. "I mean, that's a little more suspicious than the fact that Adele made a stupid cat toy, don't you think?" I shut my mouth abruptly when I realized I was arguing for my brother-in-law to get locked up. Which would likely make my sister unhappy.

Grandpa didn't even seem to notice. "I don't know, Maddie. I do know the Tanners and Hawthornes have known each other for years, so it could have been quite innocent."

"Uh-huh." I crossed my arms over my chest. "If it was so innocent, why didn't Val know he was over there?"

Grandpa hesitated, then shook his head. "I don't know that either."

"Well, if all of it was so aboveboard, seems to me she wouldn't be in the dark," I said. "It also seems that Adele maybe doesn't have anything to worry about. But Val might."

I went upstairs a few minutes later and flopped down on my bed, covering my face with my pillow. I felt a light thump on the bed, then a loud purr sounded in my ear. JJ always knew when things weren't right. I peered out from under a corner of my pillow. "Hey, bud. Did you hear what happened?"

JJ regarded me with his big green eyes, kneading his paws deliberately and seriously into the blanket.

I nodded. "It is pretty serious. I mean, she didn't seem like the nicest person and all, but who the heck chokes somebody with a cat toy?"

JJ squeaked. It sounded reproachful. I remembered his insistence today in bringing me one of the cat toys and felt a chill. Then I realized how crazy that thought was and pushed it out of my head. JJ was smart, but that didn't mean he could sense a murder before it happened.

Could he?

Chapter 12

My alarm went off at seven the next morning. It felt like I'd only been asleep for an hour, but really I'd gone to bed around midnight and fell asleep right away. My sluggishness was probably a combination of the grand opening busyness and the crazy developments that happened later, but I still hated it. I needed coffee.

I rolled out of bed, trying not to jostle JJ. He hated being disturbed, especially first thing in the morning. I figured it was because he was finally able to sleep in a bed, rather than a patch of grass in the local cemetery. He was entitled to some comfort.

Still, he opened one eye and gave me a dirty look when I moved his pillow slightly. "Sorry," I muttered, then headed for the bathroom. After washing my face and sweeping my hair back into a ponytail, I went downstairs in search of coffee. And smelled heaven from the kitchen.

I poked my head in. Ethan was busy at the oven already. "What are you making? Smells amazing."

"Tropical fruit muffins and blackberry scones," he replied without turning. "I found some gorgeous mangoes at the farmers' market yesterday."

"Tropical fruit muffins? My God. I love it. We have a

new special of the day." I spied a full coffeepot and made a beeline. "I would've gone to the market with you. I haven't had a chance to get over to one lately. Is Adele here?" I prayed she was, because that would mean she hadn't been arrested overnight.

Ethan shook his head. "Haven't seen her."

That wasn't good. A stab of concern pierced my gut. I pushed it back and poured a giant mug of coffee. "Have you seen Grandpa?"

"I did earlier. I thought he'd started cleaning."

"Maybe he did. I came in here to get coffee before I could face any of that. I guess I'll go scope it out now and get ready for opening. Let me know if you need anything."

"Actually, I do." He glanced over his shoulder, then sighed. "But it feels weird to be talking about this right now. With . . . what happened last night."

"I know. But we can't do anything about it. We have to keep doing our thing and hope it gets figured out soon. So what do you need?"

"Well. I need an industrial-sized oven."

I blinked. "That was probably the last thing I was expecting you to say right now."

Ethan grinned. "Listen, I was thinking about this." He put his mixing spoon down and turned around to face me, his eyes bright with excitement. "We can set up the garage as our café area. Make it really festive with a counter and everything, and have ovens in the back, get a couple of fancy coffee makers. That will solve the problem of sharing the kitchen, and we won't need to create a whole new one in the house. People can go out there to get served, and either sit out there and eat or bring their food in here and hang with the cats. We could even accommodate the people who are maybe on a wait list for a time slot with the cats and want coffee, or even people walking by who see us and want a snack. What do you think?"

What did I think? That it was too early to be discussing much, let alone planning a construction project. Especially when we had a million other details to get sorted out. I'd barely gotten our café cell phone in time for the opening, and I was still working with our developer out in California on working the bugs out of our online registration system. But Ethan was more animated than I'd seen him in a while, and he did move across the country to humor me.

"I think that's a really interesting idea," I said. "Let's put it on our list to talk about. If we ever find a contractor, which I'm beginning to think will take an act of God."

He nodded. "Fair enough. It gives us time to sketch out what we really want and that way we only have to do the work once. Right? Besides, Adele was calling her nephew. Let's see how that goes."

He made a good point. As usual. I wondered if Adele had gotten to make the call before being ambushed with questions about Holly's murder. "Right. Okay. Let's sit down later and talk it through. Right now I have to scoop litter boxes."

"I'll have a muffin for you when you're done." He waggled one in front of me.

I plucked it out of his hand. "I'll take it now. For energy," I said, winking at him. I took a giant bite, balancing the muffin on top of my cup of coffee so I could wrench the door open. The muffin was heavenly. I went out to what used to be Grandpa's living room and looked around, devouring my food in about five bites. I could feel my energy returning as I assessed the work in front of me. There was evidence Grandpa had been there. There were new blankets on the window seats and the food bowls were full. The water bowls, however, hadn't been changed and the litter boxes, which I'd done my best to disguise using cat furniture, hadn't been cleaned. I could tell by the trail of cat litter around each of them.

I sighed. He'd probably gotten distracted by one of his friends wanting to go out for a walk. Which I shouldn't begrudge. I'd told Grandpa from the time our anonymous benefactor proposed this idea that he wouldn't need to do anything for the café except make space for it in his house. He'd insisted he wanted to be involved, and for the most part, he helped every day. But he was seventy-four years old, and he deserved to enjoy his retirement.

And this was why I needed dependable volunteers. Although Adele had a pretty good excuse to be absent today. I thought about calling her, but I needed to get ready to open. No sign of Gigi, either, since her vanishing act yesterday. Nothing to do but get to work.

An hour later, litter boxes were scooped, floors were mopped, laundry was in, and water had been refreshed. Treats had also been dispensed. It was a good way to take roll call of my charges. Moonshine, the cat my mother had her eye on, liked the salmon-flavored treats best. She'd roll around on the floor in front of me until I gave her a generous handful. Georgia, the cat at the center of all the Holly controversy, stayed in her cat tree and nibbled daintily at one or two of the chicken-flavored treats. I counted the rest of them. The gray and white tomcat still ate everything like he had no idea when he'd get another meal, which made me sad for him. Then there were my tabby twin brothers, another black cat, an all-white cat with blue eyes, a flame-point Siamese, and my three kitten siblings, all in varying shades of buff and orange, huddled together on a big cat bed on the floor, but ventured forward to scoff some treats. All ten were accounted for. The orange guy was the one anxiously awaiting his adoption screening, which I had a feeling Katrina had forgotten all about in the chaos. I made a mental note to take care of it myself tomorrow.

Ten was the number Katrina and I had agreed on when we discussed how many cats the café would hold at any given time. Any more than that and I would feel like the cats were taking over the house.

I went back to the kitchen for a refill. "Where's my muffin?" I asked.

Ethan turned and raised an eyebrow. "You grabbed it out of my hand already."

I shook my head. "That was the test muffin. Besides, I was so hungry I didn't taste it. I need another. Please?"

Feigning a sigh, Ethan handed me a steaming hot muffin on a plate. "Maybe you'll taste it if you sit and eat like a human," he muttered.

"You're amazing." I refilled my coffee and sat down, breaking the muffin open. Mango and strawberry oozed out at me. I slathered it with butter and took a bite. Heaven.

"Wow. These are . . . so good. I have no idea how to describe them." This time I ate slowly, savoring every bite.

"Glad you like them. Imagine how they'd look in our fancy new case?" He winked at me.

I laughed. "I got you. We'll figure it out." I glanced at the clock. Almost eight thirty. We weren't opening until noon. I checked the café's e-mails to see if we had any reservations for today. Until our online registration system was up and running correctly, we had to have people e-mail in for appointments. We tried to keep the ratio of people to cats even so as not to stress the cats out, and people paid for an hour at a time to spend with their feline friends. Yesterday we'd simply opened the doors because it was day one and we wanted people to check us out. But today we were getting into what would become our normal routine.

Our inbox had nearly fifty new messages. All requests for time slots either today or for during the week. "Holy crap," I said to Ethan.

"What?"

"We're booked all day. We actually have a wait list.

Jeez, I need to get that registration system working. I need paper."

He pulled a notepad out of a drawer and tossed it to me with a pen. I sorted out all the time-slot requests for the day and sent confirmations, wait-list notices, and alternate times back to the requestors. Then I sat back and grinned. "I think this is really gonna work," I said.

Ethan glanced over his shoulder. "You had doubts?"

"I don't know. It's kind of a hit-or-miss concept, especially out here. But we're off to a good start." I stood up. "Listen. I have a quick errand to run. Anything you need my help with before I go?"

He shook his head. "Do your thing. I'll be here."

I hugged him. "Thanks. Don't know what I'd do without you."

I scooted out the door before he could see the tears in my eyes and ask if they were happy or sad tears. I honestly wasn't sure.

Chapter 13

Grandpa was still nowhere in sight. I presumed I'd been right and he'd left for his morning walk. I grabbed his keys and headed outside, slowing at the sight of the newspaper on the porch. I'd purposely avoided turning on the TV or even looking at the news updates that go straight to my phone. But I couldn't avoid it all day.

I bent to pick up the paper and blinked when a camera flashed in my face. "Hey," I said, straightening up and glaring at the guy with the camera. "Who are you?"

"I'm with the cable news station. You're the owner, right?"

"Of what?"

The guy sighed, as if I'd proven I was too stupid to interview. "The cat café."

"Oh. Yes, I'm one of the owners. Are you doing a story on the café?" I self-consciously reached up and tried to straighten my ponytail. "If so, I'd rather schedule it than be surprised."

He grinned. "Kind of. It's more of a story about the murder."

It took a second for that to register, and I'm pretty sure

my mouth fell open. I snapped it shut and shook my head. "No comment. Please leave."

"Whatever," he said. "We'll just broadcast from the sidewalk." He whistled to someone. "Set up out there," I heard him yell.

I bolted across the grass and into the driveway. My hands were shaking as I unlocked Grandpa's truck and slid in. I drove away and turned the corner before I pulled over to slow my pounding heart. Why were they filming my café? It wasn't like she'd been killed there or anything. Why weren't they over in front of Holly's house?

Once I could breathe again, I grabbed the paper and unfolded it. Of course, the murder was page one news. *Island Socialite Murdered,* the headline shouted, while the subtext added, *Body found on private beach, police interviewing persons of interest.* According to the byline, it was written by the regular cops reporter. Becky was listed as a contributor to the story. I tossed it aside without reading it. I didn't have the stomach for it right now. I put the truck back in drive and took off.

I'd Googled Adele's address. She lived on the east side of Daybreak Harbor on a small residential street filled with tiny cabin-style homes. I drove slowly, looking for house numbers. Adele's was at the end of the street on the left. Her number, 414, was missing the last 4. Her beat-up van was in the driveway. I parked Grandpa's truck behind it and climbed out, making my way to the front porch. The house looked like it had once been a fresh green color, but it had faded to almost gray over time. The porch sagged. I saw a cat dart into the space underneath it. I wondered if she had her own feral cats on the property, or if it had been one of her house cats.

I rang the bell and waited. Nothing. I knocked in case the doorbell didn't work. Still nothing. Now I was getting concerned. What if she'd fallen and hurt herself? Or what if the cops had come and hauled her away overnight? I pulled out my cell phone and called her mobile, the only number I had for her.

And I heard the phone ringing.

I followed the sound off the porch and around the side of the house, where I found a gate leading to a small backyard. I pushed the gate open. Adele sat at an old-school picnic table, like the kind with the built-in benches my grandparents had when I was little. At Grandpa's, that picnic table had long since been replaced by new, more modern patio furniture made from weather-resistant wood or some kind of plastic or whatever. I kind of liked the old style myself.

Adele didn't turn when I opened the gate. I saw her cell phone on the table, still vibrating and ringing at the same time, next to a giant box of wine and a half-empty glass. My mouth dropped open. It was barely ten o'clock in the morning.

"Adele?" I made my way over to the table. She glanced up, but didn't seem surprised to see me. She didn't seem . . . anything. Her face had no affect at all. She held a half-smoked cigarette between her index and middle fingers but it appeared she'd forgotten to smoke it. Ash dropped off the end and drifted away on the morning breeze. The harsh smell of the cigarette warred with the comforting scent of salt air that permeated the island.

"Maddie," she said, picking up the glass again, but had to put it down as she dissolved into a coughing fit. This woman did not appear to take very good care of herself. "What are you doing here? How'd you know where I lived?"

"I Googled your address," I said. "I was worried because I thought you were coming to the café this morning."

Adele took a puff from her cigarette and ground the rest out. "Yeah, well, I didn't want to embarrass you when the cops show up to arrest me." Her voice sounded extra hoarse today. I cringed thinking of her poor lungs.

"Adele." I sat down, even though she hadn't invited me yet. "What's going on?"

"Oh, please." She shot me a look of pure skepticism. "Don't tell me you haven't heard. Your grandpa's still got an in with the cops."

I didn't tell her Katrina had come over with the news last night. "Why do you think the cops are coming for you? They already talked to you. They've been talking to everyone who had an issue with Holly. It's entirely normal."

Adele took a generous swig of wine. Another cat peered out from behind a toppled-over wheelbarrow a few feet away. Adele made smoochy noises. "Come here, Tux," she cooed, her entire voice changing. The cat crept cautiously toward her and sniffed the fingers she held out. "My babies," she told me, stroking the cat. "Everything I do, I do for these cats."

"I know. They're very lucky to have you."

"Yeah. And what'll happen to them when I can't take care of them anymore?" She looked away, furiously blinking back tears.

"Adele." I almost reached over and squeezed her hand, but I was not the touchy-feely type and clearly neither was she. It didn't seem like a good idea for either of us, so I refrained. "Tell me what's going on."

"Why do you care?" she snapped. "You barely know me."

It was true. But she'd come highly recommended by Katrina, and in the couple months I'd known her, she'd impressed me. Not so much with her winning personality—she was perpetually abrasive, even when people didn't annoy her as much as Holly Hawthorne—but with how big her heart was. Plus her deep knowledge of cats in general, and also how much she knew about the island and where to find all the strays and ferals. She'd told me in which neighborhoods the colonies lived, which people helped her feed the cats and which ones threatened to call the police on her when she showed up in the middle of the night to leave them food. And there was nothing she wouldn't do for a cat, day or night. I'd heard she got up at two A.M. at times to go out and feed the cats.

So I'd opened up our house and the café to her. And while it had only been a short time, I depended on her.

I sighed. "Listen. I want to help you if I can. That's what I do. You're part of the café family. Talk to me."

She was silent for so long I didn't think she was going to speak at all, but finally she looked at me. "They think I killed that witch."

"You mean Holly," I said, stalling for time while I figured out how to answer that.

"Of course Holly, unless you know someone else who got dead lately."

Thank goodness, no. "Why would they think that, Adele? Just because you guys had a . . . disagreement yesterday? Did something else happen between the two of you?" Maybe she'd let down her guard enough to tell me what else was up between her and Holly.

But she didn't bite. Instead, she jerked her shoulder in a defensive shrug. "How would I know why? Ask your grandfather. They didn't say it outright, but they asked about the cat toys I make, and when was the last time I'd seen Holly, and where I was yesterday evening." I could see her eyes fill, and she blinked furiously to hold the tears back. I felt like she'd rather die than cry in front of me.

"Adele. That's common in these kinds of investigations. My grandpa even said so. They came over to talk to us at the café, too. Don't make more of it than it is."

She didn't seem to hear me, or if she did, she chose to ignore it. "I'm not sure how wanting to do what's best for the cats automatically makes me a murderess, but I guess that's how it is around here," she said. "Or maybe it's your social standing that determines that. Anyways." She stood abruptly, almost upending the wineglass. "I think it'd be bad for your place if I came back right now. So if this ever sorts itself out, we can talk. Meantime, Gigi's your gal. I'll make sure she knows to show up. You'll have to help her along. She's a bit . . . fragile. Needs some direction. But she's not a bad kid. Just troubled these days."

I stood too, a slight panic setting in. It was admirable of Adele to think of me. My place was brand-new and even though I was a known commodity on this island, I was still new to the business community here, and people needed to trust me. If I was affiliated with a murderer, that would not be good for business. But I still needed her, and I didn't believe she'd done it. "But, Adele. I need you. And I believe you didn't do anything." I waited for her to agree with me.

She said nothing.

I went on anyway. "If you stop your entire life, people are going to think they've won. Or that they were right."

Adele pulled her pack of cigarettes out of her pocket, tapped the box twice, then took one out and lit it. "Oh, honey," she said, shaking her head at me. "You don't get it. They've already won."

Chapter 14

Despite my best efforts, Adele wouldn't be convinced. I finally left with a feeling of unease sitting in the pit of my stomach. I'd just turned off her street when my cell phone rang. Becky.

"Hey," I said.

"I need a quote," she said, forgoing even a hello.

"About what?"

"What do you think? Holly, of course. I assume you know more than I do at this point, but I'll settle for a quote about what happened at the café yesterday."

"Why? She didn't get killed at my café. There seems to be a lot of confusion about that," I said.

"What do you mean?"

"The local cable guys were out front taking pictures and getting ready to film this morning when I left."

She muttered a curse. "Did you talk to them?"

"Yeah. I told them to go away."

I heard her stifle a laugh. When she spoke again her tone was less manic. "Listen. We're covering the Hawthorne house and what we know about who was there, but we can't ignore what happened at your place. Especially since they're talking to Adele."

"What do you mean, who was there?"

"We know she and Heather were having a party."

"Well, I'm sure they didn't invite Adele, so that should kill that line of inquiry," I said. "But I guess it's out, then? That the police are talking to her?"

"It's out, but the police won't confirm people of interest."

I chose my words carefully. Becky hadn't mentioned Cole. If his part in this drama wasn't clear yet, I didn't want to tip her off and cause more problems for my sister. "The cops came to the house last night. I guess they're retracing Holly's steps from yesterday. But wouldn't there have been someone else they'd go to first? They're really working off the motive being a cat?"

"Hey, you never know," Becky said. "People have killed over less, right?"

"Yeah, I guess. Seems flimsy to me though. Unless there's something else between Adele and Holly?"

"Huh. I don't know," Becky said thoughtfully. "I'm actually surprised they aren't looking at her sister."

"Heather? You're kidding."

"Why? They're both nuts," Becky said. "And they've never been those twins who are joined at the hip. I don't think they've ever gotten along."

That was encouraging—at least for Adele. Although the potential level of family dysfunction was kind of horrifying.

"Talk about juicy, though, right?" Becky went on. "I mean, it's crazy and disturbing, of course. But I'm hearing all kinds of stories about what killed her. The cops haven't confirmed cause of death yet. Morris! Why aren't you out getting reactions from the neighborhood?" she yelled to one of the reporters.

I heard a muffled male voice trying to defend himself, but she cut him right off.

"Go. I need reactions online by noon the latest. God.

They need written invitations to do their jobs. So. A quote?" she asked me.

I sighed. "I'm shocked and saddened by the news," I said.

"That's it?"

"What else do you want me to say?" I asked, exasperated.

"Fine. I have to go. I'll call you later."

I disconnected and tossed my phone into the center console. The fact that the cat toy down Holly's throat hadn't hit the news yet made me feel a bit better, though I wasn't sure why. If the cops weren't officially releasing the information about that bizarre fact yet, maybe they weren't completely convinced it was Adele. And maybe Becky was right and they *were* looking into her sister.

But why would Heather choose that method of death? She saw a cat toy lying around on the floor and suddenly decided it made sense to choke her sister with it? Doubtful. Plus there was the whole complication of having a cat toy with no cat to play with it. That alone would suggest the killer brought it with him or her, and would have a reason to have it.

I drove back home, thoughts churning through my brain. Something about that whole conversation with Adele bothered me. Maybe it was her fatalistic attitude. She definitely acted like her life was over, like they'd already proved her guilty and she was on her way to death row or something. Had she done it? My gut said no. Sure, she had a temper and would go to bat for anything she believed in, but that didn't make her a killer.

No, I think what bothered me was that she sounded like she'd given up. Like just because she didn't have the same social status or bank account as Holly Hawthorne, she wouldn't be given a fair shake.

I wondered about Holly's personal life. Was she seeing someone? Was she having an affair with Cole? If not, why had he been there? I didn't buy Grandpa's vague answer about the Tanners and Hawthornes being such good buddies. So many questions, and the answers seemed few and far between.

I pulled into our driveway. Luckily there was no TV crew in sight. Grandpa was out front talking to Leopard Man. It was hot today, so he had an abbreviated leopard outfit on: black Bermuda shorts and a leopard-print tank top, with leopard flip-flops. He had to have this stuff custom made.

I got out of the car, waved at them and headed for the house.

"Maddie!" Grandpa called.

Reluctantly, I turned. "Yeah?"

He motioned me over.

"I have to get ready to open," I said, but went anyway because that's what you did when Grandpa Leo beckoned.

Leopard Man smiled at me. "Good morning. And where is your sidekick?"

"JJ slept in today," I said. "You know how spoiled cats are. Although I'm sure he's now annoyed that he hasn't had breakfast yet. Unless Ethan fed him one of his tropical fruit muffins, which are out of this world, by the way."

Grandpa perked up. "Do we get to try them before you open? You know, to make sure they're good enough for the customers?"

"I'm sure Ethan will give you a taste," I said. "I've already had two of them. Quality control."

"Where were you?" Grandpa asked.

I hesitated. I wasn't sure I wanted to tell him I'd been to see Adele. I wasn't supposed to be talking about any of this. Although theoretically, I hadn't broken Grandpa's confidence. I hadn't said a word about Cole.

"I went to see Adele. She was supposed to be here this morning and never showed up, and I was worried."

That look passed through Grandpa's eyes. The one he'd gotten when he was a cop and his investigation had taken a turn he didn't necessarily like. "I see," he said. "And how is she?"

I shrugged. "Not too great, honestly. But that's to be expected, I guess. I'll see you inside." I made a beeline for the front door, feeling them both watching me as I went.

Chapter 15

Once inside, I did a quick walk-through of the main room to be sure no one had coughed up a hairball or anything. The cats had all been perfect angels while I was gone. Most of them were lounging in their trees or beds. Georgia sat in the window, oblivious to the chain of events she'd set off, tail swishing as she eyed a bird that had stopped at the feeder in the yard. Grandma had loved birds and had feeders everywhere, including a couple of hummingbird feeders. Grandpa and I took turns filling them every morning. I loved when the birds came. Especially the cardinals. I knew cardinals meant a deceased loved one was visiting, so now every time I saw one I imagined Grandma was sending us a message.

Ethan and I had pretty much opened the café on a wing and a prayer, wanting to take advantage of the last month of tourist season and a jam-packed island. Because of this, we'd set our hours as "introductory" and reserved the right to change them. Like today, we'd committed to opening for the afternoon, from noon to four. If people expressed a desire to have morning hours, we'd revisit that. Our hours over the winter months would be different anyway, and we'd have the whole season to do our work on the house/café and really get things in order. Right now, we had to take advantage of the end-of-summer crowds.

I could smell more lovely aromas from the kitchen. Ethan was falling into this role nicely. But he was right. We needed a real place to cook and bake. It was so frustrating. We had money to fix the place, thanks to the anonymous benefactor who had swooped in and saved Grandpa from having to sell the house. There were two stipulations, however. The first was that he did something to help the island cats here, which was where we came in. We'd satisfied that requirement. Now it was like the old adage about going shopping with no money and finding a million things you want to buy, but when you have money, you can't find anything. We had money to spend, yet there was no contractor to do the work. And I was impatient. Hopefully Adele's nephew would fit the bill. And have the time. I wish I'd asked her this morning if she'd called Gabe, but it hardly seemed the right time. I had his number still in the pocket of yesterday's jeans. I made a mental note to call him myself when I had a minute today.

The second stipulation was that the benefactor remained anonymous. There were no consequences, the attorney explained, but it was more of an honor-system thing. He or she wanted to remain anonymous, and we needed to respect that.

This one was harder for me. I was dying to know. Grandpa never spoke about it—a pride thing, I thought—but I knew he wanted to know as badly as I did. I wouldn't be surprised if he was using his investigative hat on this project, but he'd never say anything. So making a few gentle inquiries to see if I could solve that mystery was also on my to-do list. I didn't want our benefactor to be upset, but curiosity was winning out. Maybe I'd get Becky to help me.

Lord knew she loved playing investigator. I'd just have to convince her not to publish the story if she found out. Although she might be tied up for a while with this murder.

A knock on the screen got my attention. We weren't open until noon and it was only eleven thirty, but I smiled at the woman standing on the porch and went over to unlock the door. Since I didn't have a porch with a double door yet as the main entryway for the café, I had to keep the door locked at all times so I could make sure none of my residents slipped out. "Hi, there. Did you make a reservation over e-mail?"

She froze. "Oh gosh, no. I just wanted to see you for a minute. Should I come back?"

"Of course not. Come on in." I held the door wide.

She stepped in, looking around as I locked the door behind her. She appeared to be about my mom's age. She wore a blue skirt that looked expensive but dated, and a black tank top designed to look like strings of pearls hung from the top. The lines around her eyes suggested her life might not be easy. She held an old-style picnic basket over one arm. Her blond hair was streaked with silver and fell just past her ears in waves. The ends were split. "Good morning." She fluffed her hair with nervous fingers. Her eyes darted around the room, taking in the decor and the relaxing cats. "I'm Felicia Goodwin. Gigi is my daughter?"

"Oh! Hello," I said, offering my hand. "I'm Maddie James. So nice to meet you."

"Same," she said. "What a lovely idea for the cats."

"Thank you," I said. "They seem to like it. Come on in. So you wanted to see me? Or were you looking for Gigi? She's not here yet. Well, I don't actually know if she's coming today."

Felicia Goodwin twisted her fingers together nervously. "I'm here to see you. I won't take much of your time."

"Sure. Would you like to sit?" I waved at one of the

small bistro tables I'd found at a flea market a couple weeks ago. So far I'd decorated the place in a bohemian style of sorts. No matching furniture but everything was fun and colorful. I loved flea markets and garage sales. You could find such great stuff. "Do you want coffee and a muffin? We have some amazing tropical fruit muffins today."

Felicia followed me over to the table. "No, thank you. But I'm glad you mentioned muffins." She sat and took a deep breath. "Gigi has spoken so highly of you and what you're doing here. I'm not sure if you know that I run a catering business." She rooted around in her small white purse and pulled out a business card. As she pushed it across the table to me I noticed her hand was shaking slightly. "I hope you don't mind me being so bold to ask you this, but I wanted to see if you were interested in having some food for the café catered. I can do any type of food you want. Breakfast, lunch, light snacks, anything. I have recommendations I can give you. My business is only a few years old, but we have a fabulous reputation. And I brought samples." She laid a hand on the picnic basket, her eyes hopeful.

"Samples?" I eyed the basket.

"Yes. I figured you'd need to taste the food in order to make a decision, so I wanted to make it easy on you. Now, I have a few things with me that would do well as breakfast fare." She opened the basket and rooted around, pulling out her wares and setting them in front of me. "I have a cinnamon roll with maple frosting that's a favorite. For your health-conscious folks, I can do small cups of oatmeal with their choice of fruit. Also yogurt parfaits, and I have milk alternatives. Almond and coconut milk."

It looked like she had a lot more food in there. "Mrs. Goodwin—"

"Felicia," she corrected automatically.

"Felicia. This is lovely of you. Really." I glanced at the

simple, light blue card. *Felicia's Fare* was printed boldly across the front in raised pink lettering. Pictures of cakes and fancy dishes of food provided an opaque background for the text. Felicia's name and a phone number were in the bottom corners.

Felicia was waiting—anxiously, it seemed—for my response. I wasn't sure what to say. Ethan was running the café. He might need help eventually, but I wasn't sure now was the right time. And we'd still not completely sorted out our budget. "Thank you so much for coming by. As Gigi probably mentioned, we're just getting up and running and figuring out what we're doing," I said. "We only have tentative hours at this point for the rest of the season, but we'll likely adjust them. We still need to make some changes to the house and get a real kitchen going to operate out of. And I'm sure you know I have a business partner who's currently running the food portion of the café."

"I can supplement whatever he's doing," Felicia broke in.

"It's entirely possible," I said. "We're still in planning mode. I'll speak with him and get back to you soon." I smiled at her. "Thanks so much for considering us."

Felicia Goodwin's face told me that wasn't the answer she wanted, but she offered me a wobbly smile and nodded. "Of course. If you'd like to do a different kind of tasting, say for lunch or snack offerings, I can bring food samples over whenever you'd like."

I wondered what was up with Gigi's mother. She seemed kind of desperate to work for me. Or maybe she was just desperate for work. If that was true, I felt sorry for her. Although a good caterer should be living large right now, given the amount of people who gave fancy parties around here all summer long. "That sounds fabulous. Let me talk to Ethan and I'll give you a call in a couple of days. Does that work?"

She nodded and rose. "Thank you for your time. And

please, take the samples. Let your partner try them too." She handed me her basket. I accepted it.

I watched her walk out the door, shoulders slumped, and made a mental note to see what I could get out of Gigi about her mother's situation. I really didn't think I needed more food in here, but it was worth a conversation with Ethan, at least. I looked back at the table where she'd left her samples. It would be wrong to let it go to waste. Especially that delightful-looking cinnamon bun. I know I'd had two muffins already, but I hadn't had lunch yet either . . .

I picked it up and took a bite. My goodness, it was amazing. I took another. Before I'd realized it, the bun was half gone. Maybe we did need to hire her after all. Or not, if I didn't want to die of a sugar overdose.

I sat down to savor the treat, reveling in its moist, cinnamony flavor. Ethan's tropical fruit muffins were good, but wow. I'd have to downplay just how good these buns were when I talked to him. He might get jealous.

Chapter 16

Gigi showed up ten minutes later. She rode her bike here, so I didn't hear her until she appeared on the doorstep. She looked like she'd gotten no sleep. Her black hair was tucked under a blue bandanna with skulls on it. She wore a pair of ripped-jean shorts and a tank top that looked like she'd had it rolled in a ball and shoved into her purse. The tank top offered me an unobscured visual of the tattoo on her left shoulder of a giant owl. I figured Adele had called her.

It occurred to me I needed to talk to her about setting some permanent hours. And Lord help me, it looked like I needed to tell her how to dress too, if she planned to be here when we were open. Cleaning in ratty clothes was one thing, but I did want us to look presentable otherwise.

But we got busy right away, so I didn't even get to ask her where she'd disappeared to yesterday. People lined up outside for their time slots. Everyone scheduled showed up for the first two hours. They all wanted food too. The cost for an hour with the cats was ten bucks, so the food was really where we were going to make the money. I'd have to do some serious cost-and-benefit analyses to see if even considering hiring Felicia Goodwin made sense.

While most of our visitors wanted to focus on the cats,

there were a bunch who wanted to talk about Holly. Even nonresidents who didn't know her had heard the news, and how the murdered woman had been at the café not long before she died. I felt like there was some weird desire out there to see the last known place she'd had a temper tantrum.

JJ wandered in at some point, and decided he liked the three kittens. He was curled into a little ball sleeping in the middle of their bed, and they crowded around him like he was their dad. It was adorable. I took a few pictures for the Facebook page that I still wasn't great at updating regularly. A social media person was definitely on my list to add to our budget.

During one quiet moment when the cats were lounging with their visitors, Gigi sat down on one of the floor pillows and pulled Jimmy onto her lap. She petted him, staring off into space. I figured it was as good a time as any. I went over and sat next to her.

"Hey," I said.

She glanced at me, her eyes wary. "Hey."

"Was everything okay yesterday? You kind of just left."

"Oh. Yeah. I'm sorry. I wasn't feeling well."

Police disease? "Are you okay today?"

She nodded.

"Good. So how are you liking the café?"

"I love it," she said, immediately relaxing. "It's so great. The cats love it too. I can tell. They really like being here instead of in that awful animal control place."

"Yeah. It's a pretty great setup for them," I agreed. "So you think you want to volunteer regularly, then?"

Gigi nodded. "If you'll let me, I'd love to."

"Please. I need the help. We'll need to settle on the hours though. I need to know when I'm going to have help, you know?"

"Okay," she said vaguely.

"Do you work anywhere else?" I asked. "What hours would be better for you?"

She gave me a blank stare. I wondered how old she was. I thought Katrina had said something about her being in college, but she seemed much younger than that to me.

"Gigi? Do you have another job? Like, with your mother?"

Gigi visibly recoiled. "No."

Whoa. What was that about? "Oh," I said casually. "I thought you'd sent your mom here. You know, with her samples. She came over this morning. Delicious food."

"My mom came here?" Gigi clutched the cat so tightly he meowed, then bolted from her grasp. Seemingly lost without a cat to hold, Gigi crossed her arms over her chest and hunched over miserably.

"Yeah. She seems anxious to cater for us." Odd reaction. But then again, I was one of those lucky gals who always had a good relationship with my mother. I guessed this island could be pretty small if you didn't get along with a family member.

"Are . . . are you letting her?"

"Ethan and I still have to talk it over to see if we can make it work in the budget. But the food was amazing. Does she have a lot of jobs?"

"I guess," she said.

"Has she been catering long?" I asked.

She jerked one shoulder in a shrug. "A few years. Since my dad died."

Ah. It was starting to make sense now. Maybe Felicia Goodwin hadn't needed to work up until that point and was now struggling to find a way to stay afloat. "She must have a lot of customers, especially this time of year," I said, trying not to sound like I was digging for info.

Gigi shrugged. I was dying to know if they simply didn't get along, or if she seemed so uncomfortable for another reason. Really, I wanted to know if her mother was dependable and drama-free before I even considered hiring her. But maybe her daughter wasn't the most reliable witness.

"Do you know where else she caters?" I asked. "I forgot to ask her for references. My brain is so full of cats." I smiled apologetically.

"I really don't," she said. "She gets around though."

I wasn't sure what to do with that statement. "Would you still volunteer here if your mom was part of the deal?" I asked. Blunt, maybe, but I was a business owner. I had to figure out what was best for my café.

She looked at me, eyes as wide as a deer in headlights. "Of course. I love the cats. And Adele . . . wants me to."

"As long as *you* want to," I said.

Silence. I was starting to get a headache. I wasn't so sure I was cut out for this part of the business-owner life. Counselor had never been my thing. Ethan was much better at dealing with the people who worked in our juice bar. He was chill enough, while still being the leader he needed to be. I, on the other hand, had little patience for people's minidramas.

"Well," I said, when the silence grew awkward. "So you don't work with your mom. Where else do you work?"

A look of panic passed over her face. "Why? Are you not going to let me work here if I work somewhere else? I wouldn't, but I need some money—"

"Gigi," I interrupted. "Of course that's not why I'm asking. I just want to make sure your hours are realistic given your other commitments." What was up with this girl?

"Oh," she said. "Okay. Then I'm part-time at the dry cleaners over in Turtle Point. But my hours are flexible."

"Well, great. I'd love the help in the mornings with the cleaning," I said.

"Is Adele coming in the mornings?" she asked.

I hesitated. "I'm not sure of Adele's schedule right now. That's why it's really important I get your hours solidified. Make sense?"

Gigi nodded.

Encouraged, I pulled my phone out of my pocket and opened up the notes I'd written about café hours. "So I was thinking of being open six days to start. It may change once I get a contractor in here to do some work, but we'll figure that out later. We're doing trial runs with the hours for what's left of the season. I was thinking a mix during the week of days and evenings. Closed Mondays. Longer hours Saturday, and probably keeping noon to four on Sundays. I need to staff cleaners for both the morning and evening, as well as someone to oversee the café itself when it's open. Ethan and I will be here, of course, and Grandpa will help out when he can, but we can plan that better if we know when we'll have volunteers."

Gigi nodded. "I understand. I can be here pretty much every day for a bit. How about if I come early three mornings and clean, and then I can come back when you're open the other three days and help with the customer stuff?"

"Works for me. Here, I printed out a calendar." I casually leaned over to the coffee table and grabbed the manila folder I'd set down. "Do you want to write your hours in for me?" I uncapped a purple felt-tip pen and handed that over along with the calendar. Gigi chewed on her lip as she pondered what to write, as if she'd never be able to change her mind if she put it down on paper.

The girl made me nervous. I wasn't sure if it was because she was acting like a skittish barn cat, or if there was something off about her. She filled in her hours for the next two weeks, then handed the calendar and pen back.

"Thanks. So," I said, unable to avoid the elephant in the room any longer. "I'm guessing you heard about what happened last night."

Gigi stared at me, then nodded. Tears filled her eyes. "Is Adele going to get blamed?" she asked in a small voice.

"Why do you say that?" I asked.

"Because . . . she told me she probably would."

"When did she tell you that?"

"This morning. When she called me to come over and help you." She looked back at me, wiping at the tears. "She didn't do it."

I looked at her carefully. She seemed really sure of that. "I don't believe it either," I said.

Gigi nodded, encouraged. "That woman was nasty. Just plain mean. She—" She stopped abruptly.

"She what?" I asked.

"Nothing." Whatever she'd been about to say, she thought better of it. She looked at her phone. "I have to get going. Is that okay?"

"Of course."

"Okay," she said, and fled out the front door. I watched her go, wondering how involved she'd been in Adele's ongoing battle with Holly.

Chapter 17

Ethan's muffins were a hit so he kept them coming, which left me alone on the café floor after Gigi left. I hadn't seen Grandpa since I came inside, but I suspected he'd gone in the side entrance and down to the basement once he and Leopard Man had finished their conversation. I had a pretty good idea that he was up to something relating to Holly, and I itched to confront him about it. So after I showed the last guests out just after four and locked up, I hurried downstairs to his man cave. It struck me as funny that Grandpa didn't get his first man cave until seventy-four, but it was the perfect alternative to losing his living room. We'd moved his old furniture down there, and he'd even set up a little office for himself for the private-investigator work he'd been doing on the side. I wasn't sure what, if anything, he investigated on a daily basis, but it came in handy to have the gig up and running during times like this.

My suspicions were right, because as soon as Grandpa heard me coming I heard him hang up a phone call. I stepped into the room and took a moment to inhale the comforting scent of his pipe smoke. "Hey," I said, appearing in the doorway of his office.

"Hi, doll. Done for the day?" He was trying too hard to

look like he'd been doing nothing, straightening random things on his desk.

"Yep," I said. "What are you up to?"

"Nothing much," he said, a little too innocently. "Wanted to give you some time to bond with your guests."

"That's nice of you. Are you working?"

"Working?" he repeated.

"Yeah. You know, with your PI stuff. I figured you'd maybe be working for Val trying to figure out this Cole thing."

Ha. Busted. He tried his best to keep pure cop face on, but he failed this time. "I don't know what you're talking about," he said. It was hardly convincing.

"Come on, Grandpa. You wouldn't just sit back and wait to see how this played out, even if it didn't involve Val." I dropped into a chair and crossed my legs. "You've even changed out of your fun clothes and put on your serious clothes."

Grandpa glanced down at his jeans and black shirt, clearly surprised I'd noticed. "You're keeping track of my outfits?"

"Grandpa. You've been so excited about your café clothes." It was true. He'd gone out and bought outfits bordering on the ridiculous. Shirts with cats on them, even a pair of Bermuda shorts with cats doing yoga. He definitely wanted to play the part of the café proprietor. I thought it was adorable, and he'd gotten tons of compliments yesterday at our opening. But today he looked ready for a different type of work.

Grandpa rubbed his hand over his hair. "I'm just talking to a few people. Seeing if I can ascertain what went on last night. Nothing official."

I nodded. "Are you looking to get Cole off the hook?"

He frowned at me. "I'm looking for the truth. You know I wouldn't do it any other way, Madalyn."

"I know. Sorry. I didn't mean it like that." I sighed. "I'm worried about Adele."

Could Cole's influential father have enough power over the justice system that he could redirect the police investigation? The naïve side of me wanted to swear that could never happen. The realistic side knew there was a gut-wrenching possibility it could be true.

"I don't know much yet, Maddie. You know as much as I do," Grandpa said. He calmly went to his little fridge and pulled out two waters, handed me one. He looked at me curiously. "You sound like you want Cole to be guilty." His tone held no judgment, it was simply matter-of-fact. An observation.

I flushed and looked away. "Of course not. That would kill Val. But I don't believe Adele did it. Do you?"

"She drinks a lot and has a temper," Grandpa said bluntly. "Those two things combined could've gotten the best of her. Now that's not to say," he went on, holding up a hand as I started to protest, "that Cole Tanner couldn't have found himself in a similar situation. Especially if he was at the Hawthorne house on some . . . illicit business. Who knows, maybe there was something going on and Holly threatened to tell Val. He got mad, acted rashly. But . . ." He hesitated.

"What?"

He was silent for a few seconds. "The way she died," he said finally. "My gut tells me that if Cole—or any male offender—had done this in the heat of the moment, it's more likely he would've simply strangled her. This cat toy thing." He shook his head. "It seems more . . . like sending a message. That's the only reason I'm willing to look at someone other than Cole. And it's a clinical one. God knows he's not my favorite person. Or that self-important father of his."

Grandpa still held a bit of a grudge about needing Erik

Tanner's services when Sergeant Ellory, in charge of Frank O'Malley's murder had put him on the suspect list. But I had to admit, what he said made sense. And he certainly had the experience to back up his analysis.

Now he sat too. "Just be careful with Adele, even if this works out in her favor. You don't know her that well, Maddie."

"What does that matter? I know she isn't a killer."

"Are you going to hire her permanently?" Grandpa asked.

"She's a volunteer," I said. "She's got a job, and I'm not hiring staff yet anyway. Do you have an issue with her?"

"Not directly, no." He sighed. "I just don't want you to have any problems. Especially with the Frank situation still on everyone's mind."

"I'll be fine," I said. "But I want to make sure I've got the right people working here. So if you know something about Adele, please tell me. Although on second thought, I need to make sure I have people in general. So maybe don't tell me." I pressed a fist to my temple, aware of a sudden headache.

"It's just . . . she's a bit of a militant, no?"

"A militant?" I repeated. "How so?"

"Well, with cats." Grandpa seemed uncomfortable now that he'd brought the subject up. "She's very . . . adamant about everything. I mean, I remember we used to get calls about her when I was at the PD. She was always trespassing in people's yards, looking for cats or trying to feed them. She'd get verbally abusive if they tried to make her leave."

"Really?" That news didn't surprise me. And I kind of admired her for it. "Listen, Grandpa. Feral cat care and rescue is hard work, and most people get burned out fast. She's just really dedicated. I wouldn't be able to do what she does. It's not a bad thing. And everyone has their own method, I guess."

He didn't look convinced. "I still don't see why you can't do it without getting crazy."

"Because sometimes other people are acting that way and you have to hold your own," I said. "It doesn't mean she's a murderer."

"Then why did her friend think she did it?" Grandpa asked, referring to Katrina.

"I don't know," I said. "But it seems awfully convenient. Becky said she's surprised they haven't looked at the sister yet."

"Holly's sister? Why?"

"They apparently hated each other."

"Lovely," Grandpa muttered.

"So what kind of investigating are you going to do?"

"Who said I was investigating? I'm just talking to people," he said.

"That's investigating," I said.

"Maddie. You've got enough going on. Don't worry about this," he said firmly.

"But I'm already involved," I pointed out. "The cable network was here trying to take pictures and interview me this morning!"

"They were?"

"Yep."

He pondered that. "Did you talk to them?"

"Of course not. I have nothing to say."

"Good. Keep it that way. I mean it, Maddie," he said when I opened my mouth to protest. "Stay out of this. You have enough going on, and you don't need to be associated any more than you already are. For your own good."

Chapter 18

I went upstairs, annoyed by Grandpa's directive and trying not to show it. I had no intention of listening to him though. If he could look into it, so could I. I went up to my room and called Katrina.

"Tell me about Gigi Goodwin," I said when she answered.

"What? Why?" Katrina sounded distracted. She hadn't been in the office, so she was likely out picking up some kind of stray. Or rescuing some wildlife. I still giggled every time I pictured Katrina facing off with a possum.

"Because she's volunteering with me and I don't know anything about her," I said.

"I honestly don't know much. Adele said she lives on the beach."

"On the beach? I didn't get the sense she's rich." Of course, I shouldn't judge by her outfits. Plenty of people with lots of money dressed like they shopped at flea markets.

"No, I don't mean a house on the beach. I mean, she lives on the beach. Like in a tent."

"You're kidding. By choice?"

"She didn't want to live with her mother when she moved

back. I think she dropped out of school, or something," Katrina said. "And hey, while it's nice out, why not?"

Why not? Because any drunk person could wander into your tent. Or a violent thunderstorm with lightning could kill you. There were a million reasons why not. Or perhaps I'd become too citified out in San Fran. "Is she . . . okay though?" I asked. "Like, mentally? She seems troubled."

I heard a crash and a muffled curse at the other end of the line. "Hmm. I didn't think anything was off with her, but I don't do psych evals for my volunteers. I just take what I can get. Listen, can I call you in a bit? I'm in the middle of something."

"Sure. Have you heard anything else from Adele?"

"Nothing." Katrina's voice turned somber.

"I went to see her today. She's pretty down," I said.

"But she was home?"

"This morning she was." I didn't mention the wine, remembering Grandpa's words about her being a drunk. I didn't want to perpetuate that perception.

"Well, that's encouraging," Katrina said. "Okay, I'll call you back."

"Sure. Speaking of volunteers, though, I need more," I reminded her. "Are you going to hook me up?"

"Yeah, I know. I'll be back to you." She disconnected.

I made a face at the phone and went down to the kitchen. Ethan was at the table with a cup of his own coffee and a sketchpad. He looked up with a bigger grin than I'd seen in a long time.

"What's so funny?" I slid into a chair and simultaneously realized how tired I was. And distracted by the Holly Hawthorne/Adele/Cole ordeal.

"Nothing's funny. Just drawing out our new café." Beaming, he slid the sketchpad over to me, tucking one bare foot under him. "What do you think?"

I studied the sketch. He'd taken Grandpa's garage and

transformed it into a little kitchen, complete with a double oven and a giant coffee machine. A bar separated the cooking area from a tiny space with a few high tables and funky hanging lights.

"Wow. I didn't know you could draw so well," I said.

He winked. "There's plenty you don't know about me. So come on. You like?"

"I do," I said. "But do you think there's enough room out there?"

"Heck if I know," he said with a laugh. "I figure the contractor can help with that part. But I've already thought of that."

"You have?"

"Yep." He looked pleased with himself. "If we expand it a bit, we can put in a real kitchen, have room for the counter, and maybe have a little area to sell things. We can offer juices again," he said, knowing that would sway me. There wasn't a decent juice place on this island and it was getting to me. Ethan was making juices for us, but it was another need I saw and itched to fill. "We can bottle some to have on hand too. And I know you mentioned wanting to get some JJ memorabilia. Are you still planning on that?"

I grinned. "Of course. JJ would not be happy if I reneged on putting his face on a T-shirt now." JJ looked up from the floor where he was sprawled on his side, paws drawn up to his chest. He looked like a baby seal. The look he gave me said I better not.

Plus, JJ was a huge hit on the island since we'd rescued each other and he'd come into his stardom. He was a big part of the draw of the café. People loved that he walked around with me on a harness and leash, and I loved to stop and let kids and adults alike pet him. JJ was the impetus for the café, after all. The whole conversation had started when people began asking me to bring him to places like the senior center to let him visit with people. And since the place was named after him, I figured we should offer some souvenirs for people to take home. Mugs, T-shirts, bags—I had a whole slew of ideas on how to raise more dollars, some of which would go to help the island rescue efforts.

"So? Have I convinced you?" Ethan asked.

I snapped back to the topic at hand. "I think the price tag will convince me. And the zoning board's opinion." Grandpa had had to jump through some hoops to get the land classified for mixed use before we could open, a process that moved a lot faster once we pointed out that Frank O'Malley had gone through some back-alley channels to ensure the land could be commercially zoned if his evil scheme went through. Given that near debacle, I didn't think we'd get a lot of pushback, even if we made the garage bigger. But I didn't want to get Ethan's hopes up. At least our family was tight with the town selectman, Gil Smith. Who also happened to be dating Frank's widow, Margaret. Maybe he could make things easy for us.

I studied the drawing again. "What about the inside of the house? Did you draw that out too?"

Ethan's head shake was sheepish. "Sorry. Just really fixated on the kitchen."

"Understandable. I hope I can articulate what I want well enough to not destroy Grandpa's house. I worry about that." I passed the sketchbook back and studied him. "So how do you like it so far?"

"The café? I love it. It's a great idea, and people seem to dig it."

"They do," I agreed. "But I don't mean only the café. The island, the house." I waved my hand around. "I wonder how you really feel about staying here."

"I think it's great," Ethan said. "How could it not be? It's a fantastic house on a gorgeous island and we get to live here and run our business. What's not to like?"

I think if I'd parked Ethan in a tent out back he'd be equally as enthused. But thinking of a tent made me think of Gigi again.

"I'm glad," I said. "I was worried."

"Hey, as long as there's water I'm good. And you can even swim in this water." His eyes lit up. "It's amazing."

The San Francisco Bay was beautiful, but supercold. Only the most diehard ocean lover—and surfers wearing wet suits—ever braved it. Swimming in the ocean had been one thing I'd missed out West, which seemed like an odd reality in California, but true for the northern part of the state.

"So back to the café. Are we going to get more volunteers?" Ethan asked. "I'm not sure two will be enough if we get really busy. And it's looking promising. I sold out of all my muffins today." He beamed with pride.

"That's awesome. I knew those muffins would be a huge hit. I'm waiting on Katrina for more volunteers. She said she'd try to funnel some more people our way. Oh, and hey. Speaking of muffins. Gigi's mother stopped by this morning. She wanted to offer her catering services. I told her we were doing it ourselves for the time being, but . . . she sounded like she really either wanted or needed the job. I'm not quite sure which. I felt kind of bad for her."

Ethan thought about that, tapping his long fingers against the table. "What kind of food does she want to bring in?"

"It sounds like she can do whatever we'd like. She brought some samples," I said casually, trying not to let the dreamy look into my eyes when I thought about that cinnamon bun. "They were in the basket I left in here." I'd conveniently stashed it when Ethan was out of the kitchen, so I could have some more time to think about how to approach the topic with him. "She can do pastries, other breakfast items, even some lunch stuff. Unless you think it would be a waste of money, or stepping on your toes."

He grinned. "Mads. I found the cinnamon buns. They're pretty amazing. Listen. If the woman needs the work, why don't we give her some? I could still do some baking, like you said. At the very least, keep the coffee flowing. And that way it would free me up to help you more with the cats, or even do some of the work on the expansion or improvements." Ethan was a man of many talents. He could make a mean juice, but he could also do hard labor pretty well. He'd grown up working with his father doing odd construction jobs.

"You think?" I was relieved he hadn't taken offense about the pastries. "But what about the budget?"

"We'll figure it out. We're not footing the bill for any of the construction work, right? It's covered by the trust for the house?"

"That's true." When I really thought about it, there was no reason to say no. We could use all the help we could get.

"So let's do it." His confidence was inspiring. That was truly his superpower—he was always so sure of the right thing to do. Maybe it was all the meditating he did. And I knew he'd been going to Tai Chi lessons with Cass.

"Okay. I'll call her tomorrow." I made a mental note to do some Google searches on Felicia's business, just to be safe, then checked my watch. "I'm starving. Let's go get an early dinner. And a drink. Lord knows we deserve the drink."

Chapter 19

Since Ethan was new to New England, he'd missed out on years of summer island fare. Which meant he was trying to make up for thirty years of no authentic lobster rolls, fried clams, or real New England chowder. I decided we needed to rectify that as often as possible while all that deliciousness was in season. We were going to Moe's in downtown Daybreak.

Moe's Fish Place served the best fried seafood and French fries on the island. His place had been overlooking the water in Daybreak Harbor probably since the beginning of time. I usually tried to stay away from fried foods, but Moe's . . . called to me. It was even more dangerous now that I lived here again. When I was only visiting I could justify it, but I was going to put a ton of weight on if I didn't watch myself. I consoled myself with the thought that it had been a dramatic weekend full of highs and lows, and a few fried scallops wouldn't kill me.

We took Grandpa's truck. He'd gone out on foot anyhow and I preferred that over Grandma's car. I needed to think about if I wanted to get a car of my own. I supposed for now it was fine to use Grandpa's, and it was silly to buy something with Grandma's still sitting here, but it felt kind of wrong to be using it yet. She'd only been gone a couple of months. As an alternative, bikes were good in the summer. But not if it got too hot. Then it just ruined your hair. Sometimes island life was more complicated than it sounded. Ethan had the right idea. He just skateboarded around everywhere.

It took us about fifteen minutes to get there, mostly because the evening crowd wasn't out in full force yet, but the late-lunch crowd still packed the streets. Moe's dining room was still pretty empty when we arrived, which was a relief. I didn't want to have any more conversations about Holly Hawthorne today. We got a seat near the window, overlooking the water, and I was totally looking forward to my food as Ethan and I launched into a working session. We rehashed the weekend, studiously avoiding the fight and its aftermath. We talked about where we could make improvements, what we could do differently, and what had gone really well. I'd reached behind me into my bag to take out my notebook when I realized that one of the only other occupied tables had my old classmate and nemesis seated at it. Debbie Renault.

We spotted each other at the same time. She was with her husband, a former football legend at our high school. Debbie had decided she hated me for life when this same dude had abandoned her at the prom to dance with me. But that had been his idea, not mine. She'd never let it go, even after I'd moved away and he'd married her. She'd been more than happy to be the Realtor representing the people trying to buy my grandpa's house out from under him earlier in the summer. The depth of people's silly grudges never ceased to amaze me. Maybe it came from living in the same place all your life and never expanding your horizons.

As for her hubby, like most high school football players, he hadn't aged well. Where there'd been brawn and muscle before, now there was a layer of fat. He didn't look as bad as some, but it would only get worse. I thought of how adorable Lucas was and allowed myself a small smile.

Debbie noticed me catch her eye, said something to her husband, and made a beeline over to our table just as the waitress delivered our food. I muttered a curse under my breath.

"What?" Ethan glanced up from his own notebook, where he'd been jotting down notes.

"Nothing. Just keep your head down, for your own good." I pasted a fake smile on as Debbie swooped over in her four-inch yellow stilettos, coming to a wobbly stop at my side. "Debbie. How are you?"

"Maddie! I'm great, thank you. So good to see you." She'd turned the saccharine on full blast. Which meant something was coming. I braced myself. "And who is your friend?" She gazed at Ethan with unabashed curiosity and a gleam of nasty in her eyes. I watched her appraising every inch of him.

"This is Ethan Birdsong, my business partner. Ethan, Debbie Renault." I offered no further description.

Debbie stuck her hand out. "Lovely to meet you," she said. "I'm a Realtor on the island." She shoved a card into his hand. "Have you found an apartment or a house yet?"

"Uh, no," Ethan said, glancing at me with a questioning look in his eyes.

I opened my mouth to respond but before I could she laughed. "Please don't tell me you're all living in that old house with all those cats."

"As a matter of fact, Ethan and I are both staying at my grandfather's house," I said coolly.

Her smile faded, replaced by a triumphant gleam. I could only imagine the stories she'd be passing around town about this.

"Well. I'm sure you just haven't had time to look for a

place, right, Ethan? Don't worry about it. That's what I'm here for. Please call me." She winked. "I can hook you up."

"Uh, thank you," Ethan said, pocketing the card.

It took all my willpower not to throw my fried scallops at her. But that would've been a waste of good food, so I refrained.

When she got nothing further out of Ethan, she turned her attention back to me. "How was your first weekend with your little cats? Eventful, I heard?"

I sighed. Of course she'd want to talk about Holly. "We had a very good opening weekend," I said.

"Aside from the catfight. Literally. Right?" She giggled at her own joke.

Disgust flooded my body. "That's pretty tasteless, Deb. Considering what happened to Holly."

She flushed. "Of course; that was unfortunate. But it was your crazy cat lady who killed her, wasn't it?"

"I'm sorry, who would the crazy cat lady be?" I stared into her eyes, unflinching.

"Well, Adele of course," she said with a huff. "Your friend. The one who threatened Holly."

I stood, closing the height gap between us. She wasn't that much taller, even with her stupid shoes. "Adele isn't crazy," I said. "Nor did she threaten Holly. She wants what's best for the cats." Adele didn't deserve that label. And she certainly didn't deserve an automatic reputation as a murderer. *Unless she did it,* that annoying little voice reminded me.

Debbie nodded earnestly, entirely too willing to see my side of things. I was immediately suspicious. "I can see your point. After all, the big question is really Cole Tanner, right? How *is* your sister holding up? Poor thing. To find out like that."

I froze. How did Debbie know about Cole? And what did she mean, for my sister to find out like that? Did she mean finding out that he was at Holly's and calling in her body, or was she confirming there was an ongoing affair? I worked hard to keep my face blank. I would not give this cretin the satisfaction of knowing she was getting to me.

"My sister is fine," I said. "I'm sure everything will get sorted out and there'll be a good explanation."

"Mmm." Debbie made a noncommittal noise. "I'm sure too. Please tell Val I'm thinking of her." She squeezed Ethan's forearm. "*So* nice to meet you. I have an open condo overlooking the water right in Duck Cove. You should really come see it." With one last wink and smile, she sashayed back to her husband, who hadn't looked up from his phone once to see what his wife was doing.

Gritting my teeth, I turned my back on her.

"What was that all about?" Ethan asked.

"Nothing," I murmured. I wished I could keep my sister out of the gossip mill, but in a place like this that was impossible.

Chapter 20

I dropped Ethan at home with the leftovers, put JJ's harness on and led him outside. We set back out in Grandpa's truck. I needed to see my sister and find out what exactly was going on. I was halfway across the island—which would normally take about ten minutes, but in the height of summer it ended up being more like forty—when my cell phone rang. I hit the speaker button and answered, uttering a curse as the guy in front of me jammed on his brakes for the third time in as many seconds. A bike veered through the traffic. Its operator would get wherever he was going a heck of a lot faster than the rest of us.

"Maddie," my mother said. "Where are you?"

"Mom? What's wrong? I'm driving."

"Where are you?" she repeated.

"I was heading to Val's house, actually," I said.

"Oh, thank goodness." My mother sighed. "I was going to ask you to go over and talk to her. She's completely withdrawn from all of us and I have no idea how to help her. I've half a mind to go find that son-in-law of mine and tell him what I really think. Of course that won't help Val, so I won't. She won't answer the phone though, and I'm getting worried. I knew you'd be on it. If anyone can get through to her you can."

I wasn't sure why my family thought I had this superpower. I would try, but Val and I weren't even especially close. I knew it should make me feel good that my family depended on me. And I sort of knew coming back home would put me right back in my ongoing role of Family Fixer, a job I'd accepted early on as both the oldest daughter and someone who naturally liked taking charge. But really, I hadn't expected there would be so many problems since coming home.

"Not sure what I can do, but I figured I'd at least see how she is," I said, trying to keep my tone light. "I brought JJ with me. He can help."

"Maybe," my mother said doubtfully. "I'm not sure what's going on, Maddie. She won't say a word."

"Then how do you know about Cole?" I asked.

"Grandpa, of course," Mom said. "You think he wouldn't tell me? I'm his daughter."

"Well, he told me not to discuss it with anyone," I said.

"I'm sure he means outside of the family."

"I guess," I said.

My mother was silent for a beat. "You know, I always kept my opinion to myself," she said finally. "About Cole. Val's a big girl with a good head on her shoulders, but I always thought she sold herself short with him."

"You did?" I knew I wasn't the only one, but I was glad to hear her finally say it. My parents had put on the happy faces when Val announced she was marrying Cole, but they weren't stupid. I knew they could see through him.

Val and Cole had started dating when they were in high school. He was two years older than her, which made him a year younger than me, and when they'd first started going out he'd taken her to the prom. And then he'd spent the entire night, except for one or two dances, with every other girl in the room. He'd made a sheepish excuse to Val, saying that his parents expected him to dance with their friends' daughters. As if that wasn't bad enough, he took some other girl out to the afterparty because Val had a curfew. Val defended him. I thought it was crap. My mother agreed with me. Val didn't care what we had to say about it and decided she was in love.

Then, instead of pursuing her own dreams after they got married—Val had always wanted to design clothes—she shelved her plans to move to Boston. No one ever heard for sure that Cole told her to forget working, but I was convinced he had. My mother had brushed those concerns aside.

"I did. I guess I did a better job of hiding it than I'd thought," my mother said with a chuckle.

"I'm surprised you never said anything to me," I said.

"It hardly would've mattered if I'd told you, Maddie," my mother said. "I knew you didn't like him, and I thought if I said anything it would fuel the flames. If Val felt like we were ganging up on her, she might have gotten very distant from the family. We didn't want that."

She was right. I'd been silent too, even when I'd noticed upon my return for Grandma's funeral how unhappy my sister seemed. And it was only two years into the marriage. I'd initially attributed her mood to what was going on in our family, but I'd recognized it was more than a situational unhappiness. Plus Cole had barely been around when Grandma was dying, even though Val could've used the support. I'd had more support from Craig, my ex-boyfriend.

"And Dad? Does he feel the same?" I asked.

"You know your father. He rarely says a harsh word about anyone. And he has to be extra careful, since the Tanners are large hospital donors and Mira is on the board. Plus they have such status around the island."

I made a face. People like the Tanners rely on their status more than anything else, and in cases like this—especially where my family was involved—it aggravated me. "Well, it sounds like their relationship might play itself out," I said. "I'm guessing that whatever reason Cole had for being at the Hawthorne place, it wasn't a good one. Grandpa said there may have been a party or something there, but still. Why wouldn't he have brought Val?"

"A party?"

"Those are my words. I guess the cop gave Grandpa some vague answer about other people being at the house, but they weren't sure if those people were around when Cole called in the death. Anyway, Mom, I'll call you when I've seen Val, okay? I have to go."

I disconnected from my mother and told Siri to call Craig. He answered on the fourth ring, sounding distracted. "Tomlin."

"It's Maddie."

"Hey. What's up?"

"Question. Do you know who was at Holly Hawthorne's house the night she was found dead? Ellory made a comment to Grandpa about other people being there, but he wasn't sure if they were there when Cole called in the body. Was it just her sister, or other people like a houseful of crazy partiers?"

A pause. Then, "Do you really think I'm going to answer anything about the investigation? I'm not that much of a rookie."

I sighed. "Come on, Craig. I'm on my way to see my sister. I know Cole found the body. If they were having a party, it won't look as bad that he was there, right?" I counted on Craig's loyalty to my family. He knew how much this would hurt all of us, not just Val. Just like he knew when my grandpa was going through that rough time how much it was killing me to watch. I had no shame in certain situations—this was one of them.

Still, silence from the other end of the phone. But I heard footsteps and then the creaking of a door. Then street sounds. He must be at the station and had gone outside to talk freely.

"I shouldn't be telling you anything, but it's not like it's a secret. Plenty of people saw who was over at the Hawthorne house that night." He sounded like he was trying to convince himself. "I'm not sure who was there the whole time, but there were enough people at that house to make our lives difficult."

"Really?" I felt hopeful for the first time. That might make Val feel better, and it might actually explain why Cole was there. Maybe he hadn't been doing anything bad, and really had just stopped by a party. Even more promising, if there was a houseful of rich people, someone would have had to notice Adele Barrows sticking out like a sore thumb, if she'd been there. So maybe both of them were off the hook. "So this could've been just a terrible accident, right? A bunch of drunken people playing stupid games?"

"Maddie. Beer pong is one thing but what the hell kind of game would that have been? Who can swallow a catnip toy whole first? That doesn't even make sense."

I sniffed. It wasn't the best explanation, I had to give him that, but it felt way better than anything else they were thinking. "Maybe you should look at all the guests, then," I said haughtily. "And not just Cole. Or Adele, who wasn't even a guest."

"Thanks for the tip," he said, unable to hide the sarcasm. "Did you want to pass any helpful job secrets on to Sergeant Ellory too?"

Ellory. Ugh. "No, thanks," I said.

"Great. I have to go." And he disconnected.

I made a face at the phone before tossing it back into my cup holder.

Chapter 21

My sister's house was dark when JJ and I pulled up, but her car was in the driveway. Val lived on the west side of Duck Cove, in one of the wealthiest neighborhoods on the island. I assume Cole's daddy had bankrolled the place. Not that Cole didn't earn money for putting in an appearance at his father's office, but he couldn't make this much before he hit thirty. Could he?

With a heavy sigh, I dragged myself out of the car and up to the door, JJ tucked under my arm. I hadn't called first. Not that she was answering the phone, apparently. But she might not even let me in. I rang the bell and waited. Rang it again. Finally, it opened.

My sister peered out at me from the dark hallway. "What are you doing here?" Even in the dark I could see she looked very un-Val-like, wearing a pair of baggy gym shorts and a T-shirt. She looked like she'd lost weight, and she barely weighed anything in the first place. Her reddish-brown hair was pulled back off her face with a headband, and it looked limp. The headband had dragonflies on it.

"I wanted to see how you were. Can I come in?" I picked up JJ's paw and waved it at her. "JJ wanted to see you too."

She sighed and swung the door wide to let me in. I

stepped into the dark hallway. It felt different in here. The museumlike decor was the same, but there were shoes piled up near the door. A sweatshirt was balled up on the floor. Totally unlike my sister. I toed it out of the way. "Um. So how are you?" I asked.

Val frowned at me. "Great. How are you?" Without waiting for an answer, she turned and walked back into the living room where the giant TV that was as big as my bureau was paused on some show. It looked like *Orange Is the New Black*. Aside from the still images from the TV, this room too was in complete darkness. I put JJ on the floor, reached over and switched on the light.

"Do you have to do that?" She held a hand up to her face as if she were a vampire.

I could see her red eyes and pale face before she covered them with her hand. "Val. Talk to me."

"What do you want to talk about?" She flopped onto the couch and crossed her arms over her chest. JJ immediately jumped into her lap and settled in. She gave him a startled look, but didn't attempt to move him. Instead, she awkwardly petted his head. "Did you come over to ask me stupid questions? Shut off the light. I'm watching something."

She was worse off than I expected. I had to think. There had to be something I could do to help her. While I thought, I wandered over to the TV. "This is cheery," I muttered, the irony of the show not escaping me.

Val must've realized it too, because she jabbed the remote at the TV. It went dark.

"Val. Seriously?" I got up and switched on a softer lamp, turning off the larger light. "I know Cole called in Holly's death. What's going on with him?"

She crossed her legs as best she could with JJ on her lap and jiggled one foot, staring straight ahead.

I moved so I was in her direct line of sight. "Ignoring me isn't going to make me go away."

"I don't want to talk." Her petulant tone gave way to a quiver at the end of the sentence. I could see tears welling in her eyes.

I felt sorry for her. She must be feeling like absolute crap. Whatever happened to put Cole at Holly's house the other night, I'm sure a thousand things led them to this point—things that caused my sister pain. My anger flared up, swift and hot. I hated when people messed with my family.

I slid onto the couch next to her and hugged her. JJ, who'd apparently had enough of being jostled around, moved to the other end of the couch. "So. Have you talked to him?"

She sniffed. "No. He does this. Runs away and hides like a little boy when things don't go his way, or when they get scary. It doesn't matter that he dialed the stupid phone. That's the least of the story. He shouldn't have been there in the first place. But that's typical of Cole. Everyone on this stupid island is talking about me, do you know that?" She handed JJ to me, got up and paced the room.

I watched her, not sure what to say. Debbie Renault's hateful comments still rang in my head. I could only imagine what the rest of the snotty rich crew were saying.

"I'm sure you know that," Val said, answering her own question. "I'm sure you've heard it all."

"Val," I cut in before she could go off on another tangent. "Why was he there? Was he—"

"Sleeping with her?" she finished. "Probably. Or maybe her sister. Or both! Why not? He'd been spending a lot of time with the evil twins lately. He tells me he's working all day, then going out with the partners at the firm for drinks. Then he ends up at that little tramp's house and next thing you know she's dead? That's like a bad movie. Or one of those domestic suspense novels with the absolutely ridiculous endings. Now that loser is going to get arrested, probably. Maybe he even did kill her. I guess it depends on how long he was sleeping with her and what was going on. I heard she loves to find different guys every week and unceremoniously dump whichever poor loser she was with. So maybe she had a long list of people who wanted to kill her. But it figures my idiot husband would be the one caught in the spotlight." She stopped to take a breath.

My ears perked up. Holly had multiple boyfriends? Even if Cole was one of them, that certainly widened the suspect pool. I interrupted. "Where's Cole now?"

"I don't know, and I don't care. Probably with his daddy. Preparing his defense."

"Did you throw him out?"

She glared at me. "I didn't get the chance. The little wuss hasn't been back since the night of the party."

I wish she'd had the chance to throw him out. But this—this wasn't healthy for her. Sitting here in the dark, wondering if her husband had cheated on her and, even worse, if he was going to be arrested for murder. "You really haven't talked to him at all since this happened?" I tried to keep the judgment out of my tone.

She shook her head. "Nothing."

"Val. Come on. You can't stay here," I said, standing up. "It's not good for you. Let's get some things. You can come stay with me and Grandpa. Help out at the café for a few days. What do you say?"

She turned and stared at me as if I'd just suggested she dance naked down Main Street during the annual Lobster Festival. "You want me to leave my house?"

"Yes! That's exactly what I want. You don't seem like you're happy to be here right now." I looked around. The house was nice, but it wasn't homey at all. It was like something out of an interior design magazine. Which was fine if you liked that sort of thing, but I much preferred the feel of Grandpa's house. Mismatched, comfortable, lived in. Loved. This place felt like a museum. "Come on. I'll help you." I grabbed her hand and tugged her toward the stairs.

"Maddie. I can't just leave," she protested.

"Why on earth not?" I asked. "Screw him. If he comes back let him wonder where you went." *And when the divorce papers are coming,* I added silently.

Val let me pull her along. "Did Mom and Dad put you up to this?" she asked sullenly. "They've been trying to get me to go stay with them. I finally had to stop answering their calls."

"They have? No, they didn't ask me to do that. If you'd rather stay with them that's fine. I just don't think it's healthy for you here, Val." That was putting it mildly.

She stared at me for a few minutes. I couldn't quite tell what was going on inside her head.

"I'll go with you," she said finally. "Come help me pack."

Relieved, I followed her up the stairs, JJ trotting along behind us. Val pointed down the hall as we reached the top of the stairs. "Go raid my bathroom for makeup. I might want to use it again someday, especially if you take me out somewhere."

Chapter 22

While Val collected some clothes into an overnight bag, I went through her makeup cabinet. Without much luck. As I sorted through eye shadows older than Grandma's car, I realized I needed to take my sister to Sephora on the mainland first chance I got. I also realized that her vain, full-of-himself husband had more hair products than she did.

I resisted the urge to throw them in the trash and slammed the cabinet door. Val stuck her head in. "All set?"

"Yeah. Once this is over we need to go makeup shopping. Let's go." I clipped JJ's leash back on his harness and grabbed my bag. I hustled Val outside, feeling like we were staging some big getaway. Which we kind of were. I pointed her toward her car and got in mine, waiting for her to pull out in front of me, then followed her.

When we got back to Grandpa's, he and Ethan were sitting out on the porch having a beer. Grandpa's eyes widened when he saw Val and her suitcase, but he didn't say anything. Instead, he got up and gave her a hug.

"Hello, sweetheart."

"Hi, Grandpa."

They observed each other for a minute. I knew Grandpa didn't really know what to say, and Val knew Grandpa well enough to know he wouldn't say anything. They both seemed to like it that way. They'd probably already discussed the terms of Grandpa's investigation anyway.

"Val's staying with us for a while," I told them.

Ethan waved at my sister from his seat on the porch. "We're glad you're here," he said, and I felt a rush of gratitude for him.

Val offered him a stiff smile.

I squeezed her hand. "Come on. I'll get your room set up and then we can make a giant bowl of popcorn and watch some corny movie. Okay?" I smiled encouragingly.

She followed me upstairs to the third floor. "Here. You can be near Grandpa's room." I pulled some new sheets out of the closet. "You can borrow any of the cats from downstairs if you want company too." Val wasn't a huge animal person, but some cuddles might do her some good.

Val sank down on the bed. "Thanks. Can I just go to sleep?"

"No. We're going to watch a funny movie. And eat popcorn. Or ice cream. Would you rather have ice cream?" I looked at her over my shoulder.

"I don't care. I'm going to shower." She grabbed some clothes and disappeared down the hall.

I watched her go, feeling totally helpless.

After I made up the bed, I went downstairs to find a movie and some junk food. Grandpa had disappeared. I figured Ethan would've gone out too, but he was still sitting on the porch swing. I wondered if I should worry about him. He didn't get out enough.

"Hey," I said. "We're going to watch a movie. Are you going out?"

Ethan shook his head. "Nah. It's nice just hanging here." He touched one foot down, setting the swing gently rocking. "So how's your sister doing?"

I shrugged. "Feeling pretty lousy, I think."

"Understandable. Anyone figure out what her husband was up to yet?"

"Not that I've heard from Grandpa, but who knows. He may have already cracked the case." I managed a smile, but I wasn't really feeling it. "And this island . . . I love it, but it's like Peyton Place. You know? Everyone knows everything, and talks about everyone. You heard Debbie tonight. That's just a taste of what Val's in for if this doesn't get quashed."

"What about Debbie?"

Neither of us had heard Val slip out onto the porch behind me, and we both jumped. I turned around. She stood in the doorway, arms crossed, wearing pajama pants and a ripped Keith Urban T-shirt.

"Nothing," I said. "We bumped into Debbie Renault tonight. You know how she is." I tried to brush it off.

"Was she talking about me?" Val asked.

I hesitated, not sure what to say. But it was Ethan who came to the rescue.

"Actually, I think she was talking about me," he said with that gentle smile. "I'm the new guy, right? They're trying to figure out if I'm one of those West Coasters left over from the hippie days, which means I'm on drugs, or if I'm one of those plastic people who's really eighty but's had enough work done to make me look thirty. Plus they're wondering about my skateboard." He winked at Val.

Despite herself, a ghost of a smile touched her lips.

"Why don't you go in and pick out your junk food," I said, taking advantage of the moment. "I'll be right in."

Miraculously, she didn't argue with me and went back inside. I looked at Ethan. "Will you watch a movie with us? Please? You seem to defuse her." I sent him a pleading look.

He laughed. "Sure."

"Really?" Relieved, I leaned over and hugged him. "Thank you."

Val stuck her head back out the door. "We do need ice cream. There's only a tiny bit of chocolate chip left." Her tone indicated that was as serious a crime as any that had been committed over the weekend.

I looked at Ethan. "Shall we go get some ice cream?"

Chapter 23

"I can't believe I'm walking around like this." Val glanced down at her ratty clothes. She'd insisted she wasn't getting changed when I told her we were all going to get ice cream, and now it seemed like she was regretting her decision. Although when the island was hopping like this during the last days of summer, people in pajamas were hardly the worst you'd see.

I thought it was progress that she at least noticed how she was dressed. We'd decided at the last minute to forgo the trip to the grocery store for a few pints of Ben and Jerry's and instead get real ice cream at Mac's Dairy Bar downtown. Ethan had discovered their gorilla genius flavor—chocolate and peanut butter with caramel swirled inside it—a couple weeks ago and I think he was making daily stops here to get his fix. I didn't mind. I was partial to their strawberry cheesecake flavor.

"You going to try something fun today?" I teased Val. It was a running joke—she and our dad were the Boring Ice Cream family members. Some days they might live on the edge and get chocolate chip instead of plain vanilla. Or in my dad's case, coffee. Which I had to admit was one of my favorites too, but usually with something chocolatey or mocha-flavored mixed in.

But neither of them usually strayed from their typical kinds. And sometimes, it seemed like such a waste.

"I might get chocolate," she said, unenthusiastically.

"They have coffee mocha crunch!" I said, jabbing her arm in my excitement. "Or caramel turtle swirl." For those combos, I might stray from my usual favorite.

She rolled her eyes at me. "So get a scoop of each. I want chocolate."

"Then that's what you'll get," Ethan declared. "Maddie? Is that what you want? A scoop of each?"

I nodded. It seemed a little like overkill, but it had been quite the weekend.

"Cool. I'm going to try the almond coconut," Ethan decided.

Major decisions made, the three of us stood in silence in the long line snaking around Mac's parking lot. Pretty much every dairy bar on the island was like this beginning in late June, right through the start of the chilly days in September. People hated to see the ice-cream shops close down. It was like the last nail in the summer coffin.

Usually I hated when the summers ended. More so when I was a kid, and it meant the wild and crazy days of being out on bikes with my friends, or at the beach all day, were ending soon. This year though, I felt like we all could use the downtime of the fall and winter months to regroup and relax a bit. For me and Ethan, to really dig into the business side of the café and how we were going to operate. Get construction done on the house— and the garage.

My thoughts were interrupted when I heard my name being called. I spun around to find Lucas on the sidewalk, waving at me. "Save my spot," I told Ethan and Val, and hurried over to where he stood with a chocolate Lab pacing restlessly back and forth.

"Hey." He bent down and gave me a kiss.

"Hi," I said, when our lips finally parted. We looked at each other for a second, then I stepped back. "Who's this?"

"Jasper. I'm bringing him home. He was my last grooming appointment."

"You do pickup and delivery too? Impressive." I smiled, reaching down to pet Jasper. He licked my hand.

"How'd the rest of your opening weekend go? I heard about what happened." He dropped his voice and looked around to make sure no one was listening. "I wanted to come by today but we got slammed and I was down a groomer."

"No worries. The weekend went fine. Well . . . you know what I mean." I didn't want to talk about Holly. "You want some ice cream? I'm here with Ethan and Val."

He glanced at his watch. "Sure, I can do that." He followed me back to the line.

"Look who I found," I announced. "You know Ethan. Val, this is Lucas. Lucas, my sister Val."

Lucas shook her hand. "Nice to meet you." He was kind enough not to mention her pajamas.

"You too," she said listlessly. I hoped the ice cream improved her mood a bit.

By the time we reached the front of the line, Ethan and Lucas were engaged in a serious conversation about the lobster roll at Damian's place right near my grandpa's house, or at the other lobster stand near the beach entrance. Apparently Ethan had been getting around. I was glad to hear it.

I stepped up to order the ice cream, but Lucas slipped in front of me, placed the orders and paid for all of them, waving me off when I tried to stop him.

"Thank you," I said finally. "You're very sweet."

He smiled, a lopsided grin that always melted my heart. "You can go get us some napkins."

I set off to the little cart with napkins and spoons on it over by the picnic area. As I gathered a hefty supply—I was a messy ice cream eater—my gaze drifted through the piles of people sitting at the picnic tables and on the various benches scattered around the small property.

And my eyes widened. I blinked once. Twice. It couldn't be. I squinted, focusing on a bench at the farthest end of the lot near the parking area. Was that Cole? My sister's husband? And was he sitting with Heather Hawthorne?

I'd recognize her anywhere, especially after my up-close-and-personal visit with her sister. Her hair was different, but it was definitely her. And definitely him.

Someone trying to get napkins jostled me, then gave me a dirty look for standing there in the way. "Sorry," I muttered, moving aside. What were they doing? Had I been wrong? Maybe Cole wasn't seeing Holly. Maybe he was seeing Heather. The married sister. That would even the playing field, for sure, and be even more complicated. Maybe Holly had found out and threatened to expose them both, just for the fun of it. Maybe they'd conspired to kill her together. And now they were . . . what? Discussing whether or not they'd get away with it? Laughing at poor Adele? I watched Cole take a bite of ice cream and felt the mad start to slide up my neck and turn my face red.

I debated my options. Go over there and confront them? That would cause a huge scene and embarrass Val even further.

"Maddie?" Lucas waited for me, holding my cone up inquisitively.

With one more glance at Cole and Heather, I turned toward him. "Coming."

I'd have to think about this later, when I got home. Until then, I guess I'd keep it to myself.

Chapter 24

Monday morning. I opened my eyes and squinted at the sun streaming in through my window. A beautiful summer island morning. I got up and went to the window, peering out at the ocean. The tide was out, and the water lapped calmly at the shore, twinkling in the undisturbed morning sunlight. It was almost pretty enough to make me forget all the ugliness going on around us.

Almost.

I still couldn't shake the image of Cole and Heather Hawthorne, sitting on a bench at the dairy bar eating cones like her sister hadn't just been murdered and he hadn't found the body. And, oh yeah, hadn't been in touch with his wife in two days. What the heck was going on there? Luckily, Val hadn't spotted him. I'd managed to convince everyone to bring our ice creams back here. Too crowded, I'd said. Nowhere to sit. No one had been inclined to argue with me. Val had led the way back to Ethan's car. I'd let them go and gone with Lucas, who agreed to come back with us after dropping off Jasper the lab.

I hadn't said anything to him about what I'd seen. I needed to process it first. Maybe talk it over with Grandpa.

Heck, Lucas didn't even know the story about Val and Cole yet. So best to keep quiet.

When we got back, Val and Ethan were already inside. Lucas and I lingered on the porch for a bit. One of the best parts of Grandpa's house—aside from the book nook on the third floor—was the wraparound porch. We'd walked to the side where we could see the moon glinting off the water. Lucas had slipped his arm around me while we stood and looked at it. Neither of us said much. Then he'd kissed me. So much so that I hadn't wanted him to go. But since I lived in a virtual commune these days and there was so much insanity going on, it hadn't seemed like the right time.

But those few minutes had been the highlight of the night. The whole day, actually.

I took one last, longing look at the water, wishing I was heading out to the beach today. Or better yet, heading to the beach with Lucas. I shook that off. I had a business to run. A new business that needed a lot of attention. I turned around and surveyed my sidekick. JJ was sprawled on my pillow, paws crossed in front of him in his famous seal position. He wasn't ready to get up either; he had fewer responsibilities than I did. At least we weren't open today, so all I had to do was clean and feed the cats. Well, I had plenty to do behind the scenes, but nothing public-facing. Which meant JJ was off the hook too.

I left him to it and went downstairs, planning to get some of Ethan's excellent coffee and start the cleaning process. My thoughts drifted to Adele again. I hadn't heard anything else from her. I hoped she was okay.

I mentally ticked off my to-dos in my head: call Felicia and tell her we'd like her to help with the catering, spend some time thinking about how to structure Grandpa's work in the café, call Adele's nephew in case she hadn't gotten around to it. Talk to Grandpa about Cole and Heather.

But when I got downstairs, I stopped short. Both Adele and Gigi were there, and they looked like they were almost done with the heavy lifting. "Hey!" I exclaimed, going over to give Adele a hug after I recovered from my surprise. She froze, then reluctantly hugged me back. Guess she wasn't used to people hugging her. "I'm glad you guys are here."

Adele shrugged. "Sitting home isn't doing much good, and school's not back in session yet so my first job isn't paying right now," she said. Which I guessed was her way of saying she was glad to be here too, and had obviously changed her mind about staying away. "And I convinced Gigi that she wanted to help out and then do some feedings with me after we leave here."

Gigi smiled at me and tucked a strand of hair behind her ear. She still fidgeted, but I was starting to learn that was her natural presence.

"Well, that's amazing. I really appreciate it. Both of you. Did you guys get coffee?" I asked. "I'm sure Ethan has some made."

"I'll take some," Adele said.

Gigi shook her head. "I don't drink coffee."

I blinked at her. "Wow. And you're standing?"

She looked at me blankly.

Guess she didn't get my humor. "If you want a juice or smoothie we can arrange that too." She looked like she could use something green and healthy.

"I'd love a juice," she said. "Ethan makes the best juices." It sounded like she had a bit of a crush on Ethan. I was waiting for her to say something like how dreamy he was. Thank goodness she didn't.

"Well, we did run a juice shop." I headed to the kitchen, where he was already ensconced in his new "office" behind the counter. "Your reputation precedes you," I said to him.

He glanced over his shoulder at me from where he stirred blueberries into some mix. "Hmm?"

"I think Gigi has a crush on you. Or at least your juice. She'd like one. Adele and I need coffee. Did you know they were here?"

"No, actually. I've been focused in here. Your grandpa must've left the door unlocked when he left for his walk."

I'd told Grandpa a million times he couldn't do that. He was still getting used to how to live with cats, but it would be really bad if one of them got out. "I need to get this house finished," I muttered. "We need a café entrance so people aren't just walking into the house. Is Val up yet?"

Ethan grinned. "I'm not the warden. I haven't been taking attendance. But no, haven't seen her." He handed me two mugs. "Coffee is ready. I'll make some juices."

"You rock." I filled both mugs and went back to the café. I handed Adele her mug just as someone rapped on the screen door. I didn't recognize the man standing there. "Hi. Can I help you?"

"Gabriel!" Adele rushed to the door, almost spilling her coffee in the process. "Come in, come in. Maddie, this is my nephew, Gabe. Remember, I told you I'd call him to give you a quote on the work you need done?"

I couldn't believe she'd remembered, with everything going on with her. "Hey. Of course, come on in," I said. "I'm Maddie James. Nice to meet you."

Gabe held out his hand. "Gabe Quinn. Thanks for letting me look at the job." He didn't look anything like I would've pictured Adele's nephew. Not that I was exactly sure what that meant. But he was good-looking, tall, fit, with an outdoorsy vibe to him. He had broad shoulders and big muscles and a perpetual tan. He looked exhausted, though, which did remind me of her. Like he took on way too much and it was catching up with him. There was a sadness in his eyes, too, that his halfhearted smile simply couldn't hide. His voice was deep and scratchy, kind of like Keifer Sutherland's.

"No problem. I'm delighted. Trying to find a contractor during the summer season is like trying to find the answer to the meaning of life. Want some coffee?" I asked.

"No, thanks."

I picked up my mug. "Let's go in the kitchen. My business partner has a bunch of ideas too. And some sketches," I said, remembering Ethan's garage-turned-kitchen. "Then I'll show you around."

"This is a great place," Gabe said, craning his neck to try to take everything in. "It's a single family?"

"Yup. Been in my grandfather's family for generations. Perfect place for the cat café, but we really need to split the business from the rest of the house." I led him into the kitchen. "Ethan. This is Gabe, Adele's nephew. He's here to look at the work we want done."

Ethan smiled. "Excellent. Can we start with the garage?" He pointed to his stack of drawings, like he'd been waiting for the moment someone would come and start working on it.

"No," I said.

Ethan sighed. "Fine."

"So what exactly are you looking to do?" Gabe asked.

I outlined the thoughts I had about how we could remodel the first floor to better accommodate the café. "I want to not cut off so much of the main house. I want a separate entrance with a porch, as an added layer of protection against the cats running out. And the other problem right now is the kitchen. I'd like to reclaim it. If we can turn the garage into the kitchen where we make the café food like Ethan wants, that'll solve that problem. But we need to get the house and café part done first," I added, to make sure everyone was clear on that point.

Gabe nodded, looking around. "I don't blame you. Do you mind if we walk the floor so I can get a better idea?

I'm guessing you have other entrances that we could work around?"

I nodded. "We have a back door and a side door that leads out to the driveway. Where the garage is."

Gabe followed me around the first floor as I pointed out where I thought we could make better use of the rooms for the café. He listened mostly in silence until I was done, then said, "Can I make a couple of suggestions?"

"Of course," I said.

"What if we took these few smaller rooms"—he indicated the den where my grandmother used to work on all her hobbies and my grandpa's home office—"and made these into the café rooms? That way you're not losing the biggest living area you have, and you've got a way better setup for a private entrance here. You can put the café tables in this open space. You also have great spaces for cubbies for the cats. You'd be on the same side of the house as the garage, so if you do end up going that way for a kitchen, you're not having to walk around the entire house with all the food a million times a day. And if you have cats who don't love being with all the other cats all the time, they'll feel like they can sneak away and have another space to be in."

I'd never considered this side of the house before for the café. But the more I thought about it, the more I loved the idea. "That's brilliant," I said, breaking into a grin.

"You'll have a bathroom for the patrons right here too." He motioned to the small bathroom by the side door. He was really getting into it now, rapping on the wall with his knuckles to test the wood, stepping back to gauge sizes for entryways.

"You sound like you're familiar with cats," I said.

He grinned. "My aunt wouldn't have it any other way. I have three cats. They all came from her. I won't say she twisted my arm, because I love them, but I wasn't really in the market for cats when they arrived."

That sounded like Adele. "This is great," I said. "So what's next?"

"Show me the garage. Then I can work up some quotes."

"Fabulous. Let's go." We headed outside and had just crossed the driveway past Gabe's dark blue van with the name QUINN BUILDERS emblazoned on the side doors when another car pulled up to the curb. A police car. With Craig and Sergeant Ellory getting out of it.

Chapter 25

My heart immediately plummeted. Were they here for Val? Did they have bad news for her? They couldn't be. No one knew she was here. Did they?

"Maddie," Craig said with a nod as they got closer. He was so formal when his superiors were around. I guess it was because they all knew we used to date.

I folded my arms across my chest. "How can I help you?"

Ellory looked at Gabe, then back at me. "Is Ms. Barrows here?"

How did they know to come here looking for her? On second thought, I guessed it wasn't really that hard. She wasn't home or driving a taxi, she was probably here. Warily, I nodded. It would've been senseless to lie about it since her car was parked in my driveway. "Why?"

"We need to speak with her." He didn't wait for an answer, but headed up the steps. Craig averted his eyes as he passed.

"Hey," Gabe said, following them. "What do you want with my aunt?"

Ellory paused and looked back at him. "Your aunt?"

He nodded. "Adele is my aunt. I'm Gabe Quinn."

Ellory didn't answer him. He went into the house.

"You've got to be kidding me," Gabe muttered.

Craig paused on the steps. "I'm sorry about this, Maddie. I wish we didn't have to do this here, but we have no choice."

"Do what?" I asked, that sinking feeling in the pit of my stomach rushing back.

He didn't answer. I made a move to go inside, but Craig reached out a hand and laid it on my arm. I debated tossing it off and going anyway, but in the end, I gave in. We stood there in uneasy silence for what seemed like an hour. Gabe clearly didn't know what to do. He shifted from one foot to the other. At one point he started toward the door then turned around and went back to his shuffling.

It probably wasn't more than two minutes later, even though it felt like forever, when Ellory came out holding Adele's arm. Her face was mottled red and I could see tears tracking down her cheeks, but she stared straight ahead, head high, as she passed us. I noticed with relief she wasn't handcuffed or anything, but it didn't look like she had a choice in whatever was happening.

Gabe stepped in front of them, his face turning a dangerous red. "Wait just a second. Where do you think you're going with my aunt?"

"Gabe, sweetie. It's okay," Adele said, but she didn't sound okay. She sounded small and afraid. Very un-Adele-like. "Maddie. I'm so sorry. This is what I was afraid of," she said, her voice breaking on the last word.

"Where are you taking her?" Gabe demanded, ignoring her.

Ellory ignored him and led Adele to the police car, opening the back door for her.

I looked at Craig. "Are you seriously *arresting* her?"

Craig glanced over to see if Ellory was paying attention. He wasn't. "I'd call a lawyer, if you know one," he said to Gabe in a low voice, and then followed Ellory to the car. They got in and drove away.

People on the street had stopped to watch. I wanted to crawl into a hole.

Gabe stood there, looking absolutely shell-shocked. "Did they . . . just arrest my aunt?" he asked in disbelief.

I didn't answer. I had no idea what to say. Had they found more evidence against her? I barely noticed Gabe running down the driveway toward his van. He jumped in and pulled away from the curb, tires spinning, leaving skid marks on the street in front of our house. The crowd started to disperse. I didn't want to hang around and hear what they were saying. I made a beeline back inside. Ethan was in the living room, his arm around a crying Gigi.

"I can't believe this happened," I said. "Ethan, what did they say?"

"They asked her to go with them to answer more questions. That's all I heard," Ethan said.

Gigi swiped at her eyes with her hands. "I feel so awful!" She started crying again in earnest. "Like this is all my fault."

I frowned and looked at Ethan. He shrugged.

"Your fault? Gigi, why would it be your fault?"

Gigi shook her head, as if she couldn't bring herself to answer me. Then she abruptly stood up. "I have to go," she whispered, and bolted for the door.

"Gigi, wait!" I followed her out, but she was already gone. I could see her hair flying out behind her as she pedaled her bike furiously down the street, dangerously close to the cars. I turned and looked back at Ethan. "Why would she think this was her fault?"

"I have no idea," he said, but his face was pale.

"Craig told Gabe to find a lawyer. So it doesn't sound good. I need to talk to Grandpa."

"About what?"

We both turned to find Val in the doorway. I hadn't even heard her come in the room. She looked from me to Ethan and back. "What happened? Is something else wrong?"

"No. Well, yes." I sighed. I couldn't keep it from her. She'd find out eventually, especially if this meant her loser husband was off the hook. "The police just took Adele away."

"You're kidding." Her eyes got really big. "So does this mean . . ." I could hear the hope in her voice and it killed me. I know she wanted to believe her husband had nothing to do with this. And why wouldn't she? Even if he was a cheater, I guessed that was better than a murderer.

"I don't know what it means," I said.

"Can't Craig tell you? He'll do anything for you. You know he's still in love with you."

"Val," I began, but turned when I heard someone at the door. Lucas. Crap. How long had he been standing there? Long enough, I supposed, given the look on his face.

"Hey." I hurried over to the door and let him in, trying to work a smile in place. "What are you doing here?"

He held up a tray full of coffees, his eyes searching mine. "I wanted to make sure you guys were okay."

God, he was sweet. "Thank you. So much. Come in," I said. "I'm sorry, it's a little chaotic in here this morning."

"I'll say," Val muttered.

"I gathered." Lucas followed me in and set the coffees on the coffee table, stooping to pet one of the cats rubbing on his legs. "What's going on?" He handed a coffee to Val and Ethan.

"Thanks, man." Ethan raised the cup in a salute, although he had plenty of his own in the kitchen. "I'm going back to work. Val, want something to eat?"

I sent up a silent prayer of thanks when she followed him into the kitchen, then turned my attention back to Lucas and filled him in on what had happened. "I can't believe they took her. God, this is awful." I paced the room, rubbing my forehead. I suddenly had a violent headache. "I wish Grandpa would get back."

"But doesn't that mean that your sister's husband is off the hook?"

I dropped my hand and turned to him. "Honestly, I don't know what this means. I know this is hard on my sister, but I don't really believe Adele would kill this woman."

"How well do you know her?" Lucas asked.

I hesitated. "Not very, but I just don't get the feeling . . ." I trailed off, knowing how that sounded.

"So you'd rather it be him? Wow. Is he that bad?"

"No. God." I shook my head. I was a terrible person. I wished it was neither of them, that the police would discover it had been some twisted vagrant who had stumbled across Holly on her private beach and choked her with a random cat toy when she tried to order him off her property. But I think we all knew that wasn't going to happen. "I just think my sister is too good for him. And I know he was up to something over there, even if he didn't kill Holly." I took a breath. "I saw him last night. When we were getting ice cream. He was with the other twin."

Lucas's eyebrows shot up. "Seriously?"

I nodded.

"But you didn't say anything because you didn't want Val to know."

"Right again."

"Wow." He thought about this, pacing slowly around the room. "Should you tell her?"

"I have no idea."

"Does Val love him?" he asked.

I looked away, out toward the street. A couple was walking their dog, a baby husky. I loved his little face, with the eyes that looked like a mask. "I don't know," I said, still watching the dog prance along the sidewalk. "Or maybe I just don't want to."

Lucas was silent for a bit. "Hey, Maddie?" he said finally.

I looked at him.

He hesitated. "I know this isn't the best time, but I have to ask you. This thing with us. Are you . . . do you . . ."

I waited.

"I like you," he said finally. "A lot. And I'm wondering where you're at. Like, is there someone else for you?"

Like Craig. "I like you a lot too," I said. "And no, there isn't someone else."

He looked relieved. "No? Not even . . ."

"If you're asking about Craig, no," I said firmly. "Look. Craig and I dated in high school. He asked me out when I first came back. We'll always be close, but just because we dated when we were kids doesn't mean anything."

"Okay. Well. Good," Lucas said, rubbing his hands together nervously. "So does that mean—"

"Maddie!"

We turned to see Grandpa hurrying up the walk. "I just heard what happened to Adele."

I stood up and went to greet him, wondering about the relief I felt at not having to continue this conversation with Lucas right now. "I'm glad you're back. Can you find out what this means?"

"I don't know that they'll tell me, but I'll do my best. I'm going to make some calls. Good morning, young man. I didn't mean to interrupt," Grandpa said to Lucas.

"No problem, sir. Good morning," Lucas said. "Maddie, call you later?"

"That sounds perfect. Thanks." I gave him a quick kiss, then followed Grandpa into the house.

Chapter 26

Grandpa hurried down to his office to make some calls. Val was still in the kitchen with Ethan. He was probably force-feeding her. I wandered the café checking on the cats, straightening blankets and moving the furniture a few inches back and forth, fluffing my floor pillows. Obsessive-compulsive always worked for me in the face of unnerving and traumatic situations.

When I'd run out of things to move, I tried to get some work done. I had some voice mails on the café cell phone, which I realized guiltily that I'd turned to silent yesterday and never turned back to loud. I checked messages and called back the ones I needed to. I did vet checks and reference checks for my kitten who was waiting on his new family. All good news, so I called his family to tell them they could come get him tomorrow. I grabbed my computer and checked e-mails again to see if any registrations had come in for the rest of the week and sent another e-mail to my Web developer to prod him along with the registration site. This manual keeping track of things wasn't working for me. I would love to find someone to do it for me. Maybe Val would. It might take her mind off everything. Annoyed, I shoved my computer aside. I couldn't focus. I needed to get out of this house for a bit.

"Come on, JJ," I called, picking up his harness and shaking it. Just like a dog, he bounded over.

I slipped JJ's harness on and led him outside. I thought about walking, but it was superhot and we'd probably run into more nosy people that way. We got into Grandpa's truck and drove slowly down the street. Damian Shaw was leaning on his counter at the shack when we cruised by. He waved and pantomimed eating, pointing at JJ.

I pulled over. JJ would never forgive me for passing by his treats. Damian always gave him scraps from the lobster or whatever else he was serving, and today was no exception.

"There's my boy," he said with a grin, coming around with a dish that he placed on the ground. JJ immediately attacked it.

I smiled. "Thanks, as always."

"Anytime. So how's it going?"

"I'm fine. How are you? How's business?"

"Business is good. Great, actually. All that marketing stuff you helped me with really made a difference."

When I'd met Damian, he'd just moved to the island and taken over the shack from a local couple. He'd also been practicing saying *lobstah* with a Boston accent. Which, to a guy from the Midwest, did take some work. I'd given him some tips on how to attract not only the vacationers going to and from the ferry, but also the islanders who were harder to win over. Grandpa thought he had a crush on me. But Grandpa thinks any boy who talks to me has a crush on me. "So what was going on over there this morning? I saw police cars," he said casually.

I grimaced. His flagging me down hadn't been for totally unselfish reasons. "Ugh. I don't want to talk about it."

He laid a sympathetic hand on my arm. "I know. I'm sorry. Is it about the woman who works for you?"

So much for not talking about it. "Yeah. The police seem to think she had something to do with the murder. They're wrong," I added, in case there was any question.

"So who do you think did it?" he asked, leaning in.

"I have no idea! And I don't want to talk about it anymore. For real."

"Okay, okay. I'm sorry." He looked properly ashamed.

"Don't worry about it." I glanced down at JJ, who'd cleaned out his bowl of treats. He looked up at me and squeaked, his signature sound. For a rough-and-tumble cat like JJ who'd lived on the streets for who knew how long, the sound was almost comical. But he got very offended if anyone commented on it. "We'd better go. We have some errands to run in town."

"Have a good rest of your day," he said. "Keep me posted on, well, you know."

"Sure, Damian," I muttered. "Be happy to. Come on, JJ." JJ squeaked and followed me back to the truck. We drove on, passing the ferry docks. A boat had just come in, and it disgorged its passengers in a throng. Tourists, mostly, people who were starting their vacation. And doing it with a vengeance. The island attracted folks who were serious about a real summer experience. They wanted the whole nine yards—beautiful beaches, junk food, overpriced shopping. The quest for bad food was one of the reasons why it was hard to find a decent juice bar here. There were a few places that dabbled in juices, but nothing like mine and Ethan's place out West. The locals were convinced that places like that would die in a month here, that people only truly wanted the milkshakes and frappes. But I didn't buy that. Anyone who paid attention could see the subtle shift in the types of people who came to the island. Of course people wanted the frappes and giant sundaes. Usually the families. But there was also the crowd that wanted to keep up whatever healthy lifestyle they lived off-island. Or at least touches of it. And I wanted to be there for that crowd.

I hadn't said as much to Ethan yet, but the wheels had already started turning about an East Coast branch of Goin' Green. Once the cat café was up and running, all the glitches worked out, it seemed like a logical venture to pursue. I'd already spotted some storefronts that could work, both here in Daybreak Harbor, as well as in Turtle Point. The latter town wasn't as big as Daybreak Harbor, but it had a nice downtown with classy shops and restaurants. It was a bit quieter, but I think it attracted a more serious clientele. Which could also work.

I could feel the adrenaline course through my veins just thinking about it. I loved new business ventures. Plus, it took my mind off Cole, Holly, Val, and Adele. Setting up shop, creating business plans, marketing, all of it excited me. Well, when I wasn't dealing with murders at the same time. The sight of a group of people with TV camera equipment getting off the ferry quelled my thirst for a new adventure, at least for the moment. Word was out on the mainland about Holly. Becky would be hyperfocused making sure the paper was getting first dibs on any and all information coming out about the murder. She got really defensive about her turf.

We hurried into town and straight for the pet store. JJ perked up as I pushed the door open. He liked this place. The owner, Mish, was behind the counter with her Yorkie in her lap. Mish and I had gone to school together. She waved at me.

"Hey, Maddie! How are you? Hello, JJ! Oh, I have to come over there and scratch his chin." Placing her dog on the chair, she bolted out from behind the counter and bent to JJ's level, cooing ridiculous baby talk to him. I hid a smile. JJ was so not that cat. I feared he might take a swipe at her, but he withstood the degradation. He was no dummy. He knew his favorite treats came from this place. Mish ordered all the treats from a woman down in Connecticut who ran an operation called Pawsitively Organic. All her pet treats were homemade, with locally sourced ingredients. I'd actually been thinking about stocking some myself to sell.

"I'm good, Mish. You?" I tried to head back to the treat aisle before she started talking, because I knew what the topic would be. But she just followed me.

"I'm good, but wow, I can't believe this whole Holly thing! Can you?"

I shook my head, pretending to be engrossed in finding the right flavor of crunchy snacks.

"I mean, I know she wasn't the nicest gal. She was a total jerk to me in high school. Or maybe that was Heather," Mish said thoughtfully, tapping on her chin with a long, pink nail. "Either way, what a way to go. At least she died on the beach. If I have to die, I want to be on a beach. You know?"

"Mish . . . I don't really want to talk about it," I said. How many times was I going to have to say that today?

She was instantly contrite. "I'm sorry. I understand. It has to be difficult, since it was your grand opening and all where it started."

"That's a bit of a jump, don't you think?" I said. "No one said anything *started* at my place. She and Adele had a disagreement. It's early to link the two events, no?"

Mish gave me a skeptical look. "I heard the cops are questioning Adele at the station this time. I'm sure they've got plenty of reasons to suspect her. I mean, she wasn't shy about how she felt. I remember one time last summer at the pet fair down on the green. I don't even know what she was mad about, but she threatened to slash Holly's tires. Right in front of a huge crowd. And she's got that younger gal running around acting crazy with her." Mish shook her head. "Maybe the two of them were in it together."

"Younger gal?" My brain lurched into gear. "You mean Gigi Goodwin?"

Mish nodded. "Adele has her all fired up. Crazy cat-lady-in-training," she said with a laugh, then immediately sobered. "I shouldn't joke. This is serious. There was some incident where they were caught prowling around Holly's car at the other Hawthorne house. The one where the parents live. I don't think they did anything, but the police came. They said they were feeding cats or something."

Before I could ask her when this was, the bell on the shop door jangled. Mish went to see about her new customer, leaving me with my cat treats. But warning bells were dinging in my brain. Had Gigi and Adele really been feeding cats on the Hawthorne property? It made sense, given what I'd heard about Holly turning cats loose outside. Or had they been up to no good? And Gigi had seemed so upset this morning when Adele was taken away. Which was understandable, given how close she was to Adele. But I remembered her words. *I feel like this is all my fault.*

Why would Adele's being questioned by the police be Gigi's fault . . . unless she had something to do with Holly's death and Adele was taking the blame?

Chapter 27

I hung around for a half hour waiting for Mish to finish with a woman agonizing over the right tutu for her tiny Maltese. When Mish finally returned to ring up JJ's food and treats for the week, she looked like she had a headache. I hated to add to it but I really needed some intel.

"So. This thing you mentioned with Adele and Gigi," I said, as she bagged up my stuff. "Do you remember when it was?"

Mish thought as she passed the bag over the counter to me. "I guess last summer," she said finally. "Why? Do you think it's a motive?" She looked excited, caught up in the real-life drama like everyone else. I wanted to remind her that real people were involved, but suddenly I didn't have the energy.

"I don't know," I said. "I was just curious, I guess. Thanks, Mish." I grabbed my bags and JJ's leash and made my way over to the market, still lost in thought about Adele and Gigi.

I'd missed the farmers' market this weekend, which was a bummer. One reason I loved summer in New England was the fresh fruits and veggies. Don't get me wrong, California had a plethora of them, and more farmers' markets than I could keep up with. But in New England, they seemed like a treat, a fleeting moment in a season that most everyone craved, one that passed with the blink of an eye. To not take the fullest advantage of it seemed like a crime.

So I did the next best thing and went to my favorite place to food-shop, the local co-op. JJ liked it here, too, because the cashiers always slipped him some organic cat treats. I don't think he much cared about the organic part. He just loved to eat, and anyone who offered him food ranked pretty high on his list.

I was inspecting the kale for the best bunches for our juices when a woman stepped almost right in front of me without an *excuse me,* nearly stepping on JJ in the process. And she didn't even have the decency to apologize or even look at me, for that matter. I gritted my teeth and prepared to be the bigger person, walk away, then realized who I was looking at.

Heather Hawthorne. Holly's sister. Buying Swiss chard like her twin sister hadn't just been murdered a couple of days ago. Then again, last night she'd been eating ice cream with my brother-in-law, so I guess this wasn't really all that shocking.

Be nice, I ordered myself. *You have no idea what that was about last night.* But maybe I could find out.

"Heather," I said, forcing sympathy and a touch of sweet into my voice. "I'm not sure if you remember me. Maddie James."

She turned and faced me, still holding her bunch of Swiss chard. It dripped all over the floor, and all over JJ. He shook the water off and ran behind my legs. Heather's eyes narrowed and her lips thinned and for a second I could swear I was looking at Holly, even though Heather's hair was a lot longer and cut differently, with sloping bangs falling over her forehead and loose curls worked into her layers. Holly's hair was—had been—chin-length, cut into a fashionable shag that looked like she'd perpetually just gotten out of bed.

The irony of that wasn't lost on me.

"I know who you are," she said. "You have some nerve."

I frowned. "Sorry. What?"

"You have some nerve," she repeated, louder now, taking a step toward me. She waggled the Swiss chard like a weapon, and I had to blink water out of my eyes. "You don't talk to me or my family. Your *friend* murdered my sister!"

The last word rose to a shout, and the people around us turned and stared, their quests for the perfect fruit or vegetable forgotten with the promise of more drama. The entertainment factor on the island could be limited, even during tourist season.

"Heather," I said, keeping my voice as low and reasonable as possible, determined not to get sucked into this call for attention. "I'm very sorry about Holly. I'm sure you two were . . . I can't imagine losing one of my sisters," I finished. I'd been about to say *I'm sure you two were close,* but I knew they weren't. "Anyway. Please let me know if there's anything I can do for you."

There. Leaving it at that, I turned, put my kale in the basket, and prepared to walk off with JJ.

The bunch of Swiss chard hit me smack in the back of the head. More water sprayed down the back of my tank top. Beneath me, JJ squeaked under the shower of greens and drops of water.

I turned, slowly. "You have got to be kidding me," I said, as the crowd around us collectively held their breath.

And then suddenly an older man I'd never seen before rushed over and grabbed Heather's arm. He had graying, wavy hair and a neat, trimmed beard. He also had kind eyes.

"Come on," he said quietly, shooting me an apologetic look. "I'm sorry," he murmured as they passed us.

"I'm not," Heather shrieked, trying to wrench her arm away from his. He simply held on firmly, as if she were nothing more than a child, and led her out the door, depositing her full basket of produce on an end cap as they exited.

I wasn't aware I'd been holding my breath until I let it all out with a whoosh. The chatter started around me, low and excited, rising to a full-on buzzing within seconds. I picked up the Swiss chard from the floor and handed it to the co-op employee who'd stood silently in front of one of the displays, too stunned to defend his veggies. He took it without a word.

I abandoned my own basket, scooped up JJ, and left the store. Apparently both Hawthorne twins had anger-management issues. Either that, or they were just nuts.

Chapter 28

I left the co-op and stood on the corner with JJ, trying to wrap my head around what had just happened. But I couldn't, so instead I texted Becky that I was stopping by the paper. She texted back to come to the reporter's entrance and she'd let me in.

We hopped back in the truck and drove the few blocks to the newspaper office. But, of course, parking down here was abominable. I cruised the block twice hoping for a metered spot to open. When it didn't, I pulled down a side street and parked, hoping for the best. It was fifteen-minute parking, but I hoped any cops that came by would recognize Grandpa's truck and skip the ticket.

The *Daybreak Island Chronicle* still lived in the same building it had years ago when Becky and I were growing up. We used to ride our bikes there most days so Becky could stand outside with her notebook and pretend to be interviewing people. She was one of those kids who always knew what she wanted to do, and never wavered in her pursuit of it. Even better, she knew *where* she wanted to do it. Right here on the island. Unlike me, she'd never been inclined to wander. She'd gone to college at Salem University, then promptly moved back home. And like it had all been planned by a higher power, a reporter position opened up pretty much the week she returned with her degree. She'd been at the paper ever since, working her way up.

I grabbed JJ and hurried around the corner, buzzing the intercom. She must have been waiting there for me because as soon as I rang the bell, the door to the reporter's entrance buzzed open. I climbed the stairs to the newsroom. She poked her head around the corner as I made my way up.

"Oh, good. You brought JJ," she said. "I'm going to feed him the fish that one of my copyeditors keeps leaving in the fridge. Stuff stinks up the whole floor."

"Great. You know, you don't need a gym with these stairs," I said, huffing and puffing slightly as I reached the top. The *Chronicle's* staircase was twice as tall and steep as any normal staircase. Either that, or I needed to get back into my exercise routine. It was one of the things that had fallen by the wayside during this transition period. I did miss rollerblading down by the pier, something I did nearly every day when I lived in San Fran. I needed to find something to replace it here. Rollerblading in the summer, with these crowds, could end up being more of an extreme sport than an enjoyable exercise routine.

"Yeah, well, you get used to it," she said.

I followed her into the newsroom, which buzzed with activity. Reporters were crammed into nearly every cube. The newsroom assistant, Miranda, glanced up and waved at me.

Becky led me to the empty meeting room and shut the door. I dropped into a chair and settled JJ on my lap.

"What's going on?" she asked.

"Heather Hawthorne just threw a bunch of Swiss chard at my head."

She stared at me, then burst out laughing. "What? How?"

"At the co-op. Lunatic. I told her I was sorry about her

sister and she attacked me with vegetables. It's as random as a cat toy. You were right. They should be looking at her." I tried to shake off my annoyance and refocus. "Speaking of that cluster. Any news?"

She cocked her head at me. "Other than the Boston newspapers and TV people having nothing else to do but worry about my island? Not much. Nothing I can use, anyway." She paused.

"Ah. You heard they were here."

"Heard? They've been coming in shifts." She shook her head. "Vultures."

"Why are the Boston papers so interested?" I asked instead of answering.

"Their mother has ties to the area. They have a place in the Back Bay. And Heather works in some high-powered job in finance up in Boston. So of course it's big news in their high society circles."

"Did Holly work up there too?"

"I don't think Holly worked at all, but she lived up there part of the year," Becky said.

"Where'd she live the rest of the time? Here?"

"That I don't know. Hang on." She rose and opened the door to the conference room. "Jodi!" she yelled, leaning out the door. "My society-page person," she explained. "She's been doing a lot of legwork on this, given Holly's *standing*." She rolled her eyes at the term, clearly not hers.

A woman with red hair wrapped in a bun and more freckles than I'd ever seen appeared a moment later. "Yeah?" She glanced at me suspiciously.

"Come on in. This is my friend Maddie. The fight with Holly and the cat woman happened at her place."

"The cat woman?" I shook my head.

Becky shrugged. "It's kind of what Adele's known for. Anyway. Jodi. Remind me what Holly's ties to Boston are?"

Jodi came in and sat in the chair next to me. "She has

a town house in Beacon Hill but doesn't use it year-round. Lives—lived—off her trust fund. Couldn't be bothered to work. Her sister is the one who wants to be investment banker of the year or some crap like that. But they both do the whole party scene up there. And the parents have a place too. So they're part-time old-money Bostonians and part-time Daybreakers. The Boston media loves them because they're always having some kind of brawl."

"You're kidding," I said.

Jodi shook her head. "Those two sisters hated each other. Like, with a passion," she said. "Their parents try to make them like each other. It's why they share that house here. Neither of them would be allowed to use it if they don't spend some time there together over the summer."

"So what happens if one of them is gone?"

Jodi shrugged. "I guess the other would own it free and clear."

"Is it the same deal in Boston?"

"No. They have separate places. Heather is married. But they always end up at the same parties because, really, they hang around with the same people. There was one party last year where Holly apparently thought Heather was hitting on some guy she wanted to take home that night. Even though Heather is married. Though I'm not sure that matters much. Anyway, Holly threw her drink at her sister and started calling her nasty names. Of course it got caught on camera. Our very own Kardashians." She smirked.

It must have been her husband who dragged her away from the Swiss-chard assault. "Wow. They do that in public?" I asked. "Were the parents there?"

Jodi shook her head. "No, it wasn't a party for the parents. But someone actually got a shot of the drink getting thrown. I guess she gave enough warning that she was about to lose her mind and the cameras were at the ready."

I glanced at Becky. "Why haven't they arrested her

sister, for crying out loud? How badly does she want that summer house?"

Becky raised her hands, palms up. "Who knows. Jodi, did you hear anything more about what kind of party was going on over there that night?"

Jodi nodded. "Some end-of-the-season party. They do it every year."

"Were the Tanners invited?" I asked casually.

"I haven't seen the guest list, but I assume so," Jodi said. "The Hawthornes and the Tanners have been competing for years, but they pretend to be friendly so they can keep an eye on each other."

"So they weren't friends?"

"The parents weren't. The sons and daughters are friendly." She glanced at her watch. "I have to get back. Got a phone call with one of Holly's neighbors in a few minutes."

Becky nodded. "No worries. Keep me posted." After Jodi left she focused on me, and I could tell she wanted to say something.

Chapter 29

"What?" I said.

"Did you ask about the Tanners because Cole called in the body?"

So much for my slim hope that hadn't made its way entirely around the island. "I guess that's pretty well known at this point, huh?"

She shot me a look. "You think? How's Val holding up?"

"She's staying with me and Grandpa. That piece of crap hasn't even been in touch with her since he was brought in to talk to the police."

"You're kidding."

I shook my head. "And I saw him last night. At the ice-cream place. With Heather."

Becky's eyes widened. She sat back in her chair. I could see her mind working its way through that. "Really," she said finally.

"Yep."

"What were they doing?"

"Talking."

"He see you?"

I shook my head. "Val was with me, so I didn't want to call attention to him. What do you make of that?"

Becky thought again. "Either they are friends, or they were in it together," she said.

I could've laughed if the situation wasn't so dire. "Good to know we still share a brain. Hey, what do you know about Gigi Goodwin?" I asked.

Becky shook her head. "Who's that?"

"She's another one of my volunteers. She was there the day of my opening. The younger, slightly insane-looking girl?"

"Oh right." She nodded. "I remember."

"Apparently Adele is her . . . mentor." I hesitated to use Mish's words about crazy cat-lady-in-training. We weren't all insane single ladies wearing cat sweatshirts and hoarding a hundred cats in our homes. Well, most of us weren't that. The single part aside. "I heard she was part of the . . . altercations Adele had with Holly outside of what happened at the café."

"Hmmm. Good question." Becky scribbled a note on her steno pad. "I'll ask my cops reporter to do some digging. Hey, Miguel!" she called out the open door. "See what the cops will tell you about any history between Holly and a Gigi Goodwin. Has to do with the Barrows lady."

"Got it," Miguel called over his shoulder from the cube nearest the conference room.

"When was this?" she asked me.

"It started a few years back, actually."

"Great. That'll make it hard to find. It might be a needle in a haystack," she called over to her reporter.

Miguel raised a hand over his head in acknowledgment without turning around. Guess he was used to her crazy requests.

"So tell me about Cole," Becky said.

"Not much to tell. I wish I knew what he was up to, but I'm guessing his father has him pretty insulated from the whole thing."

"Were they having trouble?" Becky asked.

I shrugged. "Val never said. She wouldn't have confided in me anyway, I don't think. But she didn't talk to anyone else in our family either."

She glanced at her watch. "I have a meeting in ten. What else?"

"Isn't this enough?" I shook my head. "Seriously, why does this stuff always have to happen around me?"

"I have no idea, but our murder rate has doubled in the two months since you've been back to town," Becky said. "Maybe I should do a story on that."

"Funny."

"How's Lucas?" she asked.

"Fine," I said.

"That sounded convincing. Have you been out lately?"

"Last night. He came to get ice cream with me, Val, and Ethan."

"How many times have you actually been out? Are you guys, like, official?" she pressed.

What was it with everyone needing this to be official? I liked Lucas. We had fun. I might want it to be official, but we just hadn't gotten there yet.

"We've been out a bunch of times," I said, ticking the dates off in my mind. There was the night I'd gone to see his band play and sang with him, that ended with me in the hospital. I still liked to think of that as our first date. Then we'd gone to a party at the beach that one of his friends threw. We'd had dinner a couple of times, and then we'd gone out with Ethan and Val last night. I wasn't sure if all of those counted as dates.

"Do you not like him, then? Why is this taking so long?"

I frowned. "Of course I like him. Everything's been so crazy—"

She rolled her eyes. "Oh, Maddie. Come on. We've

known each other since we were like, three. I know your MO."

"My MO?" I said skeptically.

"Yup. You go after the jerks. And when they don't treat you right you get upset and swear off men, then you do the same thing again six months later. The nice guy comes along, it's not so interesting."

"That is so not true." Well, mostly not true.

"It so is. Lucas is hot. And if he's nice and can rock, you should be all over that."

I squirmed in my chair. I didn't want to admit Becky was right, but there was something I was holding back. I kept saying it was because of these murders, but now I wondered if that wasn't just a foolish excuse.

"Is it Craig?" Becky asked. She was nothing if not persistent.

"Is what Craig?"

"The reason you're not jumping in with Lucas."

"Not at all. No way. Craig and I dated in high school, for God's sake. That doesn't mean we're supposed to be together for life, just because that's how half the people on this island think." It was so infuriating. Most people who'd lived here forever thought they needed to marry the first person they dated, simply because the choices of those who actually wanted to live on the island forever could be kind of slim. It was an odd way to pick a mate, to my mind.

"No, but he's still totally in love with you," Becky pointed out.

"He is not, Beck."

"He is," she insisted.

"Well, heck of a way to show me," I said, trying for brevity. "First trying to pin a murder on my grandpa, and now arresting one of my only volunteers."

She smiled wryly. "You know what they say. When

boys want to get your attention they often do annoying things."

"Yeah, in fourth grade."

"Find me a man who doesn't act like he's still in fourth grade," she said.

Chapter 30

I left the newspaper office a few minutes later, my spirits a bit higher, but as soon as I thought of Adele, probably still at the police station, they plummeted again. I remembered her sitting at her picnic table just yesterday, telling me that she'd be blamed because of who she was. That didn't sound like a woman who was guilty. Or was that the booze talking? Had she convinced herself that she was innocent? Or maybe that Holly deserved it, and the only reason anyone cared was because she was rich and her family had big voices here?

Or was something else going on?

JJ scampered along at the end of his leash, waiting patiently when stopped by admirers. He always attracted attention. Partly because he was cute and partly because cats on harnesses running around the island weren't the most common sight. Usually I loved it, but today I had to force myself not to be impatient. It wasn't good for the café, plus no one should be denied a dose of JJ's cuteness. But I seriously wasn't in the mood.

And to make matters worse, when I finally reached my car, a ticket sat under the left windshield wiper.

"Oh for . . ." I kicked the tire in frustration.

JJ looked up at me and squeaked, sensing my aggravation.

"Yeah," I said looking down at him. "I feel the same way."

Just then, Craig turned down the alley, heading back to the cruiser I just noticed parked farther down the alley. Craig. Of all people. Becky's words played through my head, an annoying sound track that had become an ear worm. Deep down I knew she was right—Craig was still interested in me—but what exactly did that mean? I couldn't figure out if he was hanging on to an old idea of us, or if he really thought that the people we'd both morphed into over the past decade would actually be compatible.

I wasn't so sure we would be. And I wasn't interested in finding out. My gut told me Lucas and I could really have something. So why couldn't I get my act together?

He saw me and lifted his hand in a wave. "Hey, Maddie."

"Hi." I lifted the ticket in a gesture imitating his wave.

"What's that?"

"A ticket."

Craig winced. "Really?"

"Really."

"Sorry about that. We have a couple new guys. They don't know Leo's truck." Craig reached out and patted the hood as if to reassure it. "Here. Give it to me and I'll take care of it."

I surrendered the ticket gratefully. "Thank you."

"No problem." He left off the *it's the least I can do*, but I saw it on his face. He pocketed the ticket, then leaned against the truck. The silence was awkward.

"How's Adele?" I asked finally.

Craig lifted a shoulder. "I'm not sure, Maddie."

"Craig. I know you guys have your reasons for looking at Adele, but can you consider that there might be other people to look at too? Listen." I leaned closer and put my hand on his arm. "I saw Cole and Heather all cozied up at the ice-cream place last night. Seems kind of odd, right, given the circumstances? Her twin's dead, he's not talking to his wife . . ." I trailed off, not wanting to give him too much info on Val's situation.

He didn't look impressed by this news. "So they were having ice cream together?"

"Yes."

"Well, I admit that I probably wouldn't be out having ice cream if my sister had been murdered, but people deal with their grief differently. That's not exactly an admission of anything, Mads. And what is it you think they did?"

"I don't know." I threw my hands up helplessly. "Look. I thought Cole and Holly were . . . together or something. But what if it was the opposite? Cole and Heather were? And Holly found out and threatened to out them?"

"So they conspired to kill her? And couldn't think of a better way than suffocating her with a cat toy? I think both of them are a little smarter than that."

"Okay, then what about Gigi? She made some comment about how what happened to Adele was all her fault. What do you think that means?"

"I have no idea. I don't know Gigi, but she looked a little unstable to me the other day." Craig squeezed my hand. "Maddie. Let us figure this out, okay? I know you're worried about Val and Adele, but we've got this under control."

I knew he was trying to be nice, but I never was much for the whole *I've got it covered, little lady* spiel. Still, I might need him over the next few days, so I held my tongue, told him I'd see him later and loaded JJ in the truck.

I turned out of the alley onto Bicycle Street. The usual summer traffic clogged our main drag, causing me to inch along at about one-tenth of a mile per hour. I'd had enough of being out in the world today. But I also had a raging headache and wanted a cup of coffee. I didn't feel like waiting until I got home. I stayed in the traffic until I reached Bean, the island's hip new coffee shop. At the risk of getting another ticket, I pulled into a metered slot and fed the one quarter I could scrounge up from the center console. Which gave me about three minutes to get a coffee. I grabbed JJ and raced to the door.

And almost bumped smack into Felicia Goodwin, who was exiting. Thank you, universe, I thought. Now I could cross off an item on my to-do list without having to remember to call her.

"Felicia! Perfect. Just the person I needed to see," I said.

She looked startled to see me, almost like a deer in headlights. Maybe she was nervous I was going to try to let her down easy. "Yes. Hello," she said.

I smiled, trying to look warm and friendly. "I wanted to circle back on our conversation from yesterday. About catering for the café?"

Warily, she nodded.

"I spoke with my business partner, Ethan, and we think it would be great if you could provide some food."

It seemed to take a second for that to sink in, but then she smiled, the guarded look lifting from her face. "Really?"

"Really. Do you want to come by tomorrow and talk about menus?"

"I would love that."

"Great. We close at four. Does that work?"

"Perfect." She reached out and clasped my hand. "Truly. Thank you, Maddie. This means a lot."

"You're welcome," I said, but she'd already turned and hurried away. Not before I saw that her eyes might be watering. I wondered what the deal was with the Goodwins. Did she need work that badly that my job made such a difference? Was her family having trouble? Maybe that was why Gigi was so neurotic.

Ah, well. At least I could help her a little. I went inside

and joined the line, keeping one eye on the street for cops or parking enforcement. My cell phone rang. I gritted my teeth and thought about ignoring it, but glanced at the caller ID. It was my dad. He never called in the middle of the day. I answered, setting JJ down so everyone clamoring around him could have full access.

"Dad? What's wrong? Is Mom okay?"

"Hi, sweetheart. Yes, your mother is fine. Everyone's fine." He paused. "Did I catch you at a bad time?"

"No," I lied. "What's up?"

"Are you available to come by my office today? There's something I need your . . . advice on."

"My advice? Sure," I said. "Is this about the gala?"

Another pause. "What do you know about the gala?"

"That it's next week, and you're stressed about it. Mom told me. At the café Saturday."

"Oh. Well, yes, it's about the gala. Can you come over shortly? We can have lunch."

I thought about saying no. This couldn't be good. But how could I turn down my father? "Sure," I said, trying to work up some enthusiasm. "I'll head over there in a few minutes."

"See you then. Thank you, Maddie."

I hung up, pressing my fingers to my temples. I'd just ordered my mocha with a triple shot when I saw the guy in the red shorts with his little red PARKING ENFORCEMENT cap, standing in front of my truck. Defeated, I turned back to the barista. "Better make it an extra shot," I said.

He looked at me dubiously. "You want four shots of espresso?"

"Oh, trust me. That's not nearly enough," I said. "But it'll have to do for now."

Chapter 31

I put my new ticket in my wallet and drove straight to the hospital. It took me about twenty minutes to slog through the remaining traffic and pull into the hospital parking lot.

I turned to JJ, who was taking the whole day in stride. "Well, you ready to see what this is all about?" I asked.

He squeaked his response.

"Good. Let's go."

I gathered him up and headed to the main entrance. Once inside, I took the closest elevator up to the third floor, where the executive offices were. My dad's door was open. I was surprised to find his assistant's desk empty. Anne Marie had been working for him since I was a kid. She was *always* here, and always one step ahead of whatever my dad needed. He depended on her like he depended on Mom. Sometimes more, if you want the truth. I remembered what my mother had said about her having some problems. I hoped she was okay.

Dad leaned forward in his chair from his inner office to see who it was, then waved at me. "Come on in, Maddie. And JJ. How nice to see you both."

JJ squeaked at him. He glanced at me. "Did you sneak him in?"

I shrugged. "We took the closest elevator to the door. Hi, Dad." I leaned over to give him a kiss. "Where's Anne Marie?" I took a seat in one of the chairs in front of his desk. "It feels weird not seeing her when I came in."

He sighed. "Well. That's actually why I asked you here. Can I get you some coffee? Or would you like to go have lunch downstairs?"

Oh no. I started to get a sinking feeling in my stomach. "Coffee's fine." I'd downed my mocha on the way over. "I'm not that hungry," I said, hoping to stall whatever was coming. Although my poor body wasn't going to last much longer living on coffee and sugar like this.

Dad got up and went to his Keurig machine. "Dark roast, I'm guessing?" he said over his shoulder.

"You bet. So what do you mean about Anne Marie being why you asked me here?"

Dad said nothing while he waited for the coffee to finish spurting into the little cup, then turned and handed it to me. "First things first. You were at the co-op today?"

"Yeah," I said, wondering how he knew that.

"And you bumped into Heather Hawthorne?"

"That's one way to put it," I said dryly. "Why, Dad?"

He sighed. "I'm sorry to have to say this, Maddie. You know how I feel about certain aspects of my job. But unfortunately there are people . . ." He trailed off. "Oh, this is crap. Look, just stay away from those crazy people, okay? They're not nice and everyone knows that, but unfortunately I have to deal with them because of my job. So no more food fights with any of them, understood? Sloan Hawthorne is on the hospital board. I don't need the headache."

"Wow. News travels fast around here," I said when I could find my voice. "Food fight? That lunatic threw Swiss chard at me!"

My dad made a strangled noise that sounded like he was

trying to disguise a laugh. "Did you throw anything back at her?"

"I should've thrown my fist at her," I muttered. "But no, Dad, I didn't. I actually felt bad that she'd lost her twin sister and I wanted to offer my condolences. Although I'm not sure I should've, since I heard she could very well have offed her own sister."

I thought my father was going to choke. His eyes nearly bulged out of his head. "Maddie! You can't walk around saying things like that!"

I crossed my arms over my chest and leaned back defensively. "Why? She's nuts."

"I don't disagree. But I'm in a spot here, Maddie. And you cannot say things like that."

"What, did she call Mommy or Daddy and tell them I threatened her?" I asked, indignant.

My dad cleared his throat. "Did you threaten her?"

"No!" I sighed. "Dad. Seriously, I was trying to be nice and she freaked out. She threw greens at me, for God's sake. And at JJ. I have no desire to have a repeat performance of that, so I don't plan on seeking her out next time I see her at the co-op. Okay?"

He tried to hide his smile. "That'll have to do. Thank you, Maddie. Now. On to the important piece of the conversation. Anne Marie's on leave," he said, returning to his chair without a cup for himself. "There are a few things going on. One, her husband died recently."

My hand flew to my mouth. "Oh! How sad." They'd been married for fifty years or so. Then a horrible thought occurred to me. "Please don't tell me he was murdered."

Dad looked aghast. "For the love of God, no. But she's going to be out for a while. She's not taking it well. He'd been ill for a couple of months, which understandably was taking up a lot of her time. And she'd been having some health problems of her own, which have been exacerbated by her situation."

"That's terrible," I said. "Poor Anne Marie. I'm so sad."

Dad nodded. "Me too."

"So what does all this have to do with me?" I asked, sipping my coffee.

"Well." Dad took a deep breath. "It's about the gala."

"Yeah. Mom said you were stressed."

"Yes. It's next week, and . . . well. I need your help, Maddie," he said bluntly. "Your mother said you suggested a planner, and we both thought there would be no one better at that than you."

I sat there, stunned. My first thought was, *Oooh, my mother is in for it, using my own words against me.*

"There are things Anne Marie always does for this event that just haven't been getting done," Dad went on. "Anne Marie tried to make allowances for her absences and recruit help, but no one is as good as her. Plus she has all the contacts, and she's been doing it so long she can do it in her sleep. People were happy to help when Anne Marie was asking." He shook his head. "Without her, I'm not having much luck. I have people doing some things, but they can't get organized. That's the downside of having an assistant who wanted to oversee this personally. She's fabulous at it, but when she's gone, we're paralyzed."

"Wait. You need *my* help? Like what kind of help?" I asked, suspiciously. "If it's next week, shouldn't most everything be done?"

Dad tapped his pen against a notepad on his desk. "One would think. But the caterer just quit, and most of the auction items haven't been confirmed yet, and no one's been working with the facility on setting up the room, and dear Lord, I shouldn't know any of this, never mind be concerned about it." He took a breath. "I'll pay you, Maddie.

And you'll have people. You just need to tell them what to do and be firm about it. I need a leader. Someone to rally the troops."

"Dad." I shook my head. "Isn't there an events team or something here? You're seriously telling me one woman did all this every year?"

"An events team?" He actually laughed. "We're a not-for-profit, honey. And Anne Marie is very good. She had help, she just led them tremendously well and made it fun for everyone. The woman she asked to cover for her has no leadership skills and she got terribly overwhelmed." He grimaced. "She went out on a medical disability leave. Stress."

I groaned. "Seriously? Why me, Dad? I'm trying to run a brand-new business." Why did everyone think they needed my help? Not only was I trying to figure out my own life—professional and personal—but now I was the party planner? Not to mention the one who had to figure out Val's life too, and give jobs to all the people who needed money, and try to convince Craig and the island cops that Adele hadn't killed anyone.

Remind me again why I moved home in the first place?

"Because you're good with details, you know people, and you get things done." My dad clasped his hands together and smiled at me.

"Val's better at details," I said. "She's just like you. You always say so. And she needs something to keep her mind off everything."

He shook his head. "Val's having a difficult time right now. I'm not sure she'd be able to focus."

My mouth dropped open. "What do you think I'm having?"

My dad raised an eyebrow. "Maddie. I know I'm not supposed to say this to any of my children, but you are the most together daughter I have. You're doing amazingly well making this transition back home. You're keeping your grandfather afloat and giving him a reason to live, which makes your mom happy. You're running a successful business. Two, actually, because I know your place out West is still running. And your cat café is already the talk of the town. I heard two people discussing it in the waiting room yesterday."

"Really?" I asked, feeling my chest swell with pride.

"Really. You make me proud every day." He smiled at me.

Wow. This was a lot of praise from my dad. Who I always knew was proud of me, but still. He wasn't the type to say it often. I might even cry. "Well," I managed. "Thanks, Dad."

"It's all true." He paused. "Which is why I know you'll be perfect helping me with these few details. Here." He reached into a drawer and pulled out a binder, handed it to me. Buttering me up, apparently, for the big sell.

"What's this?" I set JJ on the ground and took the book.

"Anne Marie's binder of what she usually does for the gala. Everything is outlined to a tee. You know how thorough she is." He winked. "Don't look so stressed. A lot of it's been cobbled together. Maybe not terribly well, but it's done. The big problems are the catering and the auction items. And maybe decorations. I can't remember."

The big problems? That sounded like basically the whole event to me. I searched for words, but they were escaping me.

My dad took my dumbfounded silence as agreement. "Thanks, sweetheart. Here." He scribbled a number on a piece of paper. "Call Charlotte. She'll get your team together. Now. I have a meeting in ten minutes and I have to prepare a bit. I'll call you later?"

I let him usher me out, feeling shell-shocked. And scammed. I didn't think my dad had it in him, but he was good. I went to Grandpa's truck and sat there for a few minutes, trying to figure out what had just happened. Finally I flipped open the binder and perused the contents. It contained pages for tasks including *Organize Mr. J's guest list* and *Make sure the caterer has vegetarian and vegan options*. The binder looked like it was a hundred pages thick.

I wasn't a freaking party planner. My dad was crazy. I pulled out my cell phone and dialed my mother at home. She didn't answer. I tried her cell. Nothing. Ugh. She was totally in cahoots with my dad. He'd probably told her not to answer the phone until I'd had a chance to process this. Which meant, resign myself to the fact that I was doing it.

Wasn't life supposed to get easier, not harder?

Chapter 32

It took all my energy to drag myself out of bed Tuesday morning. The past few days all seemed like a bad dream. The last couple of sleepless nights had caught up with me, because I'd slept soundly until nearly six. Now I had a bunch of jobs to do, and no real ambition to do anything. I wondered if Adele was still sitting in a holding cell at the police station. If they'd arrested her or let her go, or were keeping her in limbo. Now I wondered if I'd be able to pull this party together for my dad. And if life would ever get back to normal.

What was normal, anyway?

What finally propelled me out of bed was realizing I had a missed call from Lucas from late last night. I'd fallen asleep early and hadn't heard my phone. I listened to the message. He wanted to have dinner tonight.

"Yes," I said out loud to the message. "I would love to." I was about to call him back when I realized it was way too early, so I shot him a text instead. That made me feel a bit better. But I knew I was going to have trouble facing the day—and even the date—unless I got some much-needed perspective. We weren't opening until noon today, so I had some time.

I threw on some clothes, rounded up JJ, and drove to Jasper's Tall Tails, Cass's bookstore/healing center/Tai Chi studio/tea bar/general place of awesomeness. I pulled into the secret little parking lot around back. It was one of the only buildings on Bicycle Street, the main drag in Daybreak Harbor, that had one. The building used to be a two-family house, which allowed it parking spaces. Cass lived upstairs and didn't have a car. He'd given me permission to use the spaces whenever I needed.

I peered inside. Lights were on. Silly me. I didn't know if Cass ever slept, but he certainly wouldn't be asleep at nearly seven. I tried the door. Unlocked. I'd taken one step inside when I heard his voice. Like the voice of God or something.

"I knew you were coming. Lock the door."

I looked around, spotting him at the back of the store in his tea bar, heating up his various kettles of water and adding them to mini teapots. Without looking up, he said, "Come. I have tea."

JJ squeaked and ran to him. He loved Cass. Cass bent down and stroked his head.

I locked the door and approached. "I was hoping you would."

Cass finished his musical teapots then came around and wrapped me in a true Cass bear hug, his grip warm and comforting. I hugged him back around the waist because that was really all I could reach.

He stepped back. "Let me see your tongue," he instructed.

I stuck my tongue out obediently. This was some ritual Cass had to determine what kind of tea people needed. I didn't pretend to understand how he did it or what he was looking for. I just knew I usually felt a lot better when he gave me tea, so I didn't question it.

I sat in one of the chairs while he heated water and

poured it over the tea, which usually looked like twigs and sticks and dried-up leaves. Whatever it was, it was magic.

Cass didn't speak until he'd brought over two teacups full of steaming tea, sat and took a mindful sip. He waited until I did the same, then nodded. "Now. What bothers you?"

"What doesn't?" I muttered. "Where to start?"

Cass regarded me through the steam rising off his tea. "The beginning?"

"Yeah, well, you know that part. Everything's been mayhem ever since Holly . . . died," I said. "My star volunteer is sitting at the police station being questioned, my sister's husband was at the scene of the murder, and Val's sort of falling apart. And I have no idea how to date normal people. Oh, and now I'm not only going to be running my own business, but I'm taking over my dad's annual hospital fund-raiser gala. Have I left anything out?" I paused for a breath.

He assessed me for a minute, taking slow sips of his tea. "I heard they are questioning Adele," he said.

"Yeah. It's wrong. She couldn't have done it."

Cass arched an eyebrow. "No?"

"I can't believe she'd really *kill* someone. I know she had a temper, and I know she hated Holly. But I feel like if she was going to kill her she'd have just walked up to her and smashed her over the head with something, you know? In a drunken rage. The whole way it was done feels wrong."

"We might never know why someone does something," Cass reminded me.

"I know, I know. Maybe I'm crazy. But what about Cole?"

"Your sister," Cass said. "That worries you most."

It did. And I had no idea how to handle the problem.

"Yeah," I admitted. "I mean, either way it's a bad

situation. Either he was over there because he was having an affair with Holly or her sister, or he was involved in this somehow. That's all it can be, right?"

Cass didn't offer an opinion.

"She won't really talk to me. Or anyone." I sighed. "You know Val. She's so . . . closed off. God, I knew I hated Cole Tanner." I drained my teacup. "I don't know what to do about her."

"Ah." Cass nodded, his silver rings clacking against his cup as he picked it up again. "So what do you want to do?"

"I want her to talk to me."

Cass smiled a little. "Is there anything in particular you want her to say?"

I stared at him for a second, then started to laugh. Cass could always cut to the heart of the matter, and he knew me so well. "I want her to tell me she wants to divorce the jerk so I can call a lawyer for her."

"And if she doesn't?"

I wasn't really sure. I hadn't thought that far ahead. I'd thought at the very least the fact that Cole had clearly lied to her about his whereabouts would send Val to divorce court. Combined with the reason for that lie, well, she'd be a fool, right?

But what if that wasn't enough for her? Val hated change. I hadn't given much thought to what would happen if Cole was cleared and she went home to him. I'd been happy she might finally be rid of him.

"I don't know," I admitted. "I mean, nothing, I guess. I just . . . wish she'd see the light."

"Why?" Cass asked. There was no judgment in the question, just curiosity.

"Why?" I repeated. "Because he's a jerk."

Cass smiled again. "But you are not your sister."

"I know, but—"

Cass cut me off by holding up his index finger until I

went silent, then he rose from his chair and vanished into the stacks of books. I waited, resigned. Cass returned a few minutes later holding a book. "You're not meditating," he said. It wasn't a question.

I sighed. "I'm trying. I haven't spiritually evolved enough to sit still for ten minutes without my mind flooding with a million other things though."

"Doesn't matter. The point is, you bring your attention back when it wanders." He handed me the book. *365 Tao Daily Meditations.* "Every day, one meditation," he said.

I didn't see how this was going to help me handle this mess today, but I knew better than to argue with Cass. "Okay," I said. "But—"

He held up that finger again. A ring covered nearly the whole thing, an oval design with spirals covering it. "Just sit with it."

"Sit with what?"

"Your problems," he said. "You can't solve everyone's. But you can solve your own if you figure out what they are."

"That'll be a heck of a lot more than ten minutes a day if I need to meditate on each of my problems," I grumbled, but I accepted the book and flipped it open. Each page had a quote with a couple paragraphs below it. "How long?" I asked Cass. "I mean, how long do I sit for?"

He smiled. "As long as it takes."

Aargh. Sometimes he lost me. I looked up at him. He watched me, that tiny smile still on his face. He knew he was challenging me. I wanted him to know I was up for it.

"Got it," I said breezily. "Now. Can I have more tea?"

Chapter 33

I left Cass's feeling infinitely better, as usual. His tea always made me feel better. Heck, his presence did that. And even though I had homework now to add to my list of things to do, I felt calmer thinking about the little book of meditations in my bag. That man was good for my soul. And good for everyone around me, because when I felt peaceful like this, it meant I wasn't trying to force everything to go my way. Val should be thanking Cass because I wasn't going to go home and harass her to file divorce papers. I wondered how long I'd be able to hold on to this feeling.

But since I hadn't actually done any of the meditations yet, and my habit of problem-solving wasn't going to dissipate overnight, I felt like I needed to *do* something.

The problem was what. It was hard to make sense of any of this, so figuring out what to do was even harder. Talking to Heather Hawthorne was out, and I figured Cole was holed up at his parents'. Or maybe he'd gone back to his house now that it was empty. Either way, I didn't think it made sense to ambush him right now.

So that left Adele and her history with Holly. And Gigi,

whatever her part in that was. Maybe I could find out what the deal really was with her. I didn't know a lot of people who could give me that information, but I did know one.

So JJ and I drove to the animal control center. Katrina had to know more about Adele and Gigi and whatever was going on with Holly than she'd let on. And I was going to make her tell me one way or another. I wanted to get to her early because I knew once she hit the road, she tended to be out most of the day.

When I pulled up in front of the pound, she was out front doing something in the back of her van. I parked at the curb, picked up JJ, and went over to her.

She glanced up from adjusting cages. "Hey." She looked like she'd been up all night too. Her eyes were bloodshot and her clothes were wrinkled.

"Hey," I said. "Got a few?"

"I was actually on my way out to a call," she said.

"I'll ride with you," I offered.

"Yeah?"

"Yep. As long as you have me back by ten."

"I'll tell the raccoon I have to catch and relocate that he best cooperate to fit your schedule," she said dryly.

I grinned. "Appreciate it. Come on, JJ." We hopped up into the van.

Katrina finished organizing, slammed the van doors, and climbed into the driver's seat. She pulled out onto the road and turned left, heading toward the east side of town. Out here, the houses were less crowded together and the beaches were in full view from the road. I was content to just sit for a few, watching the scenery slide by and inhaling the salt air.

Finally she looked at me. "So what's up?"

"Tell me about this history between Adele and Holly. I know you know more than you're telling me."

She concentrated on driving around a hairpin turn, chewing on her lip the whole time. "I wish I didn't know half this stuff," she muttered. "I don't want to think Adele did this. But then I think of everything that's happened with Holly."

"Why did she hate her so much?" I asked. "Just because she's wealthy and she has no idea how to treat cats?"

"Pretty much," Katrina said, but I could hear in her tone there was more. I decided to wait before I latched onto that and see what else she had to say first. "Holly knew one of the women who worked at the rescue organization before they shut down. This stupid woman used to humor her and let her have cats. It started a few years ago, when Holly started coming back for the summer. Heather was usually the one who spent summers here, and it sounded like she was happy to do it without her sister. But then Holly started coming back. And she *needed* a pet." Katrina rolled her eyes. "The first time, no problem. But then she returned the cat. Adele got her back up about that. Then the woman let her take another one home. This one got killed. Holly let it outside and it got hit by a car. And it was one of Adele's favorites from the shelter, so she lost it."

"Wow," I said. "Not a great track record. I can see her point."

"Oh, there's more," Katrina said with a sideways glance at me. "Then Holly went back to the shelter for another cat. She didn't find one she *bonded* with"—she made air quotes around the word—"so she went on Craigslist and answered an ad for a free kitten. Came home with two of them and never got them fixed."

"Ouch," I said, sinking lower into my seat. I could tell what was coming next.

"Yeah. Ouch. Boy and a girl. By the time she got a clue, there were two litters. And she didn't know what to do about it—or didn't care—so she let them outside. By the time Adele found out about it, there were about twenty cats from those two kittens."

I winced. No wonder Adele had been so nuts about Holly not getting a cat. "So did Adele confront her?"

"There were a couple of incidents. She tried to trap them and get Holly to donate money for their care, and Holly wouldn't. Then Adele got mad and, being Adele, told Holly what she thought of her. But she still wanted to help the cats, so she decided to trap them all and fix them. But Holly threatened her with trespassing charges when she tried to go on the property."

This kept getting better and better. "So, what happened?" I asked finally when Katrina went silent.

She sighed. "Adele got Gigi involved. They got most of the cats, but I never asked how. I had to stop listening to the stories, I felt like I was about to get in trouble just by proximity." She glanced at me. "I do know that the police had to pick them both up once. They went on the property right in front of Holly and it was a whole big thing."

"Why didn't you tell me any of this before?"

"Because I didn't want you to think badly of her." She glanced at me. "Silly, considering . . . everything."

"Not silly at all. So that's it? It really is all about the cats?"

"As far as I know," Katrina said, but I still got the sense she was holding something back.

"What about Gigi?" I asked after a moment. I wondered if her quiet, fragile demeanor was authentic or not. If she was running around with Adele and getting picked up by the cops, she had to have some spunk in her. And she and Adele seemed really tight.

"What about her?" Katrina slowed and peered out the window, looking for some landmark.

"What do you know about her?"

"Not much, like I told you. She left college. I think she ran out of money. She's camping out at the beach. She likes cats, and found Adele, who brought her along to volunteer. Where the heck is this place?" She craned her neck to look at the address on a mailbox.

I felt like Katrina was telling the truth about not knowing much about Gigi. But there was still something she hadn't told me and I wondered how far I could push her.

"Hey, listen," she said, hitting the gas again before I could decide whether or not to press her. "While you're here, I do have to ask you something. Kind of a huge favor." She widened her eyes with her best puppy-dog look.

"Oh boy," I muttered. "Now that I'm trapped, you mean?"

She pretended to be hurt. "Come on. You'll love it. This is perfect for you. And it's really gonna help me out."

I held up a hand. "Katrina—"

"Just hear me out." She took a deep breath. "I started this new program. A pet pantry on wheels to help out the people who want pets—like seniors—but can't get out to get them food, or the people can't afford food. It's a way to keep the pets in their homes if there's some problem, and get more of the pets adopted."

"It sounds great," I said warily. "What's the catch?"

"Adele was going to be my driver." She sucked in another breath. "Obviously that's not happening now. Maddie. Can you please help me? Even just temporarily?"

"Me?" I stared at her. "Katrina. You're supposed to be finding *me* volunteers. I'm pretty strapped right now. I have one in jail and one who shows up when she thinks of it. I mean, Grandpa Leo has been helping, but that's not fair to him."

"Please, Maddie. It's only temporary." She sent me a pleading glance. "I have three routes every week. That's it. I have four people signed up here in Daybreak Harbor, three in Turtle Point, and one in Fisherman's Bay so far."

I rubbed my temples. That headache was back.

"Please. I have no one else," she said, her voice small. "The people on the list really need the food for their pets."

God. She knew exactly where to get me. I couldn't resist if it was for the animals, despite my insanely full plate. "Fine. I'll help you for a couple of weeks, but it'll have to be around the café hours," I warned. "And you have to be actively looking for someone else. Maybe Grandpa. He might like the job."

She squealed and hit the steering wheel. "If I wasn't driving I'd hug you right now. Thank you so much. You are amazing. Truly. I love you!" She hit the gas a little harder and visibly relaxed. "The first route is scheduled for this Friday. Now that that's sorted. What's going on with you?"

I leaned my head back against the seat. "Know any good party planners?" I asked.

Katrina sent me a funny look. "No. Why?"

"No reason."

I grabbed onto the dashboard as Katrina swerved over near an old farmhouse. "You can stay here," she said, and got out of the van. I heard her rummaging around in the back before she emerged with a net.

Of course, I didn't. I rolled down the window and placed JJ on the seat, then got out and followed her. I really wanted to see her in action.

"What are you doing?" she asked, catching sight of me behind her as she headed toward a barn on the property.

"Watching our tax dollars at work." I grinned.

She rolled her eyes at me.

"What are you trying to do?" I asked as she approached the slightly open door.

"I'm supposed to relocate this raccoon. He's eating all the chicken feed."

"Relocating. Does that mean . . . ?"

"Letting him free in a different location," she said. "Of course I wouldn't just kill anything!"

"Jeez, I hope not," I said under my breath.

She sent me a filthy look and handed me the net. "Make yourself useful."

Chapter 34

Once we'd stalked, captured, and re-homed the embattled raccoon in a wooded area—nearly an hour later—Katrina dropped me off back at my car with a promise to be by later to drop off my new café residents. JJ thought the whole thing was pretty boring. He'd slept in the van the whole time. Now, I hauled him into the car and he barely opened one eye before curling back up.

Oh, to be a cat.

But I had to go open the café. All my slots were booked today, and I had two more cats, along with my little kitten, being picked up by their new families. Then I had two new cats coming later tonight to replace them. I allowed myself to feel good about that.

My cell rang, taking me out of the moment. My dad. The gala. I groaned and thought about letting the call go to voice mail, but I didn't want to be responsible for my own father's heart attack. "Hey Dad."

"Good morning. Just checking on your progress."

"My progress," I repeated. "Well, so far today I've gotten out of bed."

Silence.

"I'm kidding, Dad," I said. "I mean, I did get out of bed.

But I know what you mean. I'm getting to work in a bit. I had some things to do this morning. I still have to go through your binder."

"Oh." I could hear the panic on the other end of the phone. "Okay. Well, any leads on a caterer? Because there's a meeting set up with the hotel to talk to the caterer tomorrow."

"But you don't have a caterer," I pointed out. "So how is there a meeting?"

"Well, we need the meeting to make sure things are on track."

I wanted to pull out my hair at this illogical logic. "Fine. Sure, Dad. I have a lead," I said. "I'll get back to you later. What time is the meeting?"

"Three o'clock."

"Great." I hung up on him, muttering to myself as I turned the truck toward home. I did have a lead on a caterer. The only one I knew. But if she needed the money that badly, maybe she'd jump in and help me out. And do it incredibly well so my father didn't disown me.

When the phone rang again I almost didn't answer. Until I saw it was Lucas. Then I snatched it up.

"So we're on for tonight?" he asked.

"Yes. Absolutely. I can't wait," I said.

"Good." He sounded pleased. "I'll pick you up at seven."

"I'll be waiting," I promised. I drove home with a smile on my face, despite the fact that I expected I'd have to do a whirlwind cleaning job. And I was starving. Aside from Cass's tea, I hadn't put a thing in my stomach yet. I hoped Ethan had made something yummy.

When I got there, I pulled into the driveway and paused. Something looked off. It took me a minute to realize what it was.

Adele's van was gone. It had been left here, abandoned, when the police had taken her away yesterday. Had Gabe come to pick it up for her? Or had she been released? For the first time, I felt hopeful.

We slipped in through the side door. I let JJ off his harness. He took off for the café, waiting at the door to the dining room for me to open it. Once inside, he headed straight for his kitten pals. They greeted him like their long-lost dad. I wondered if he would miss the little guy who was going to his new home.

I looked around, sniffing in appreciation. I could smell pastry, but also the scent of a candle. Someone had cleaned already. The room was calm and full of cats. In fact, all the cats. No one was hiding. I went into the kitchen.

Ethan was organizing the fridge. Gigi was at the table sipping a juice. She looked miserable. "Hey. Looks great out there," I said, trying to raise the vibe of the room. Which was pretty low.

Ethan glanced over his shoulder. "Yeah, Gigi and Leo took care of everything." He looked sort of down and out too. I wanted to ask him what was up, but not in front of Gigi. I also wanted to ask him about Adele's car, but I wasn't sure if that would set Gigi off. I stifled a frustrated sigh. I wasn't good at treating people with kid gloves.

"Thanks," I said to Gigi. "I appreciate it."

She mumbled something that sounded like *No problem*.

I snagged what appeared to be a homemade doughnut off the counter and poured some coffee. "Hey, is Val around?"

"She was here earlier. I made her breakfast." Ethan kept his head buried in the fridge.

I wanted to ask how she was doing, but thought it might sound weird. And he didn't seem to want to talk. I went out to the dining room area to sit at one of my little tables and checked e-mails, reorganizing the schedule for the day based on a couple of cancellations and some wait-list confirmations. We only had one open slot left. I posted something on Facebook to that effect and took a few pictures of the cats to add to it.

And then it was time to open.

I went through to the living room, leaving the door separating the two rooms open. Gigi was about to let people in. I glanced out the door, surprised to find a crowd on the front steps.

"Wow. Morning, everyone," I said, ushering them in. "Can I get your names so I can check you off my list? Did everyone make a reservation?"

Grandpa's friend Tommy Gregory waved. "I did. Morning, Maddie," he said, looking around eagerly for a glimpse of a cat. "Where's my pal?"

"Morning, Mr. G. Which baby are you looking for?" I checked Tommy off my list.

"The black and white one. With the pretty eyes." I could swear he blushed. I remember Grandpa saying he'd be my best customer. It looked like he might be right. I just worried what would happen when all his babies got adopted. He might ask us if we could rent him a room so he could move in with the cats.

"I saw him in that cubby over there." I pointed to the far corner of the room, where I'd installed a cat tree with various levels of hiding places. Tommy made a beeline. I heard him a minute later making coaxing noises to the cat. I turned back to everyone else.

"We didn't make a reservation. We just really wanted to see the place," a woman with a leopard-print jacket that would've made Leopard Man jealous said, sounding anxious.

I separated them into two groups and gave Gigi the list of people who'd signed up, then turned to the extra people. I didn't want to turn away the revenue, and I figured I could be flexible since it was my first week.

"I appreciate everyone coming," I said. "If I could have

you sign in here. We've got more people than cats right now, so as long as we're all polite about it and making sure the cats aren't stressed, it's cool if everyone comes in. Okay?"

Everyone agreed, looking relieved. They signed in and paid their money, then began milling around checking the place out.

Grandpa, who'd wandered in from the kitchen, came over to me. "Pretty good, right?" he said with a grin.

"It's nice, but I want to make sure things stay calm for the cats," I said. "Hey, Grandpa. Adele's car is gone. Did you see anyone come get it?"

He nodded. "Adele did. Someone gave her a ride. She didn't come to the door or anything, but I heard them drive up and happened to look outside."

"So she's out," I said. "Wow. That's good!"

"Mmm," he said, noncommittal. "Ethan's making a snack, so I'm going to grab something to eat and then come out here to keep an eye on things." He patted my arm and returned the way he'd come.

I shook my head, amused, and went over to lock the door. As I did, a woman rushed up to me with three of Adele's catnip mice in her hands. Looking at them made me feel vaguely ill, but I swallowed it and smiled at her.

"Excuse me. Can I buy these?" she asked, her eyes bright.

"Of course. They're five dollars each."

She forked over a twenty. "Keep the change. These are the real things, right?"

"The real things?" I repeated.

"Well, yes, dear. The real mice. The one the murderess used to kill that woman. Do you happen to know which color was used?" She smiled sweetly, her tone so disconnected from her actual words that it took me a minute to catch up. "I want to tell my friends I have an exact replica of the murder weapon in my hands!"

Damian, who'd come up behind the woman, took a startled step back. I knew how he felt. My jaw had already hit the floor.

"Um," I managed. "I'm not sure what you're talking about, but I hope your cats like the toys." Great answer. So much for thinking on my feet, but she'd really just floored me. I pocketed the money and bolted for the kitchen.

"What's wrong?" Grandpa and Ethan asked simultaneously when I burst through the door. Grandpa had a half-eaten Danish in his hand. Ethan had stopped mid-pour of some fancy coffee.

I sank down into a chair. "I feel like this is becoming one of those murder houses where the tour buses drive by," I said. "If I see any trolleys come down this street I'm going to lose my mind."

"Word's spreading, eh?" Grandpa said, calmly finishing his snack.

"I would say so. A woman just bought some catnip mice. Wanted to know if they were the *real thing*. As in the murder weapon." People never ceased to amaze me. "I need coffee."

Ethan finished pouring the coffee and set the cup on a tray. "I'm sorry. Did you just say someone came in here to buy replicas of the murder weapon?"

I nodded.

Ethan shook his head. "Small-town thing?"

Grandpa and I nodded simultaneously.

"Makes sense," Ethan said, and went to deliver his coffee.

I got up to pour myself one of his dark roasts. "Grandpa," I said, turning back to him. "What am I going to do? People are going to come sniffing around here like it's the next Amityville Horror House!"

Grandpa chuckled. "You're being a little dramatic, Maddie."

I opened my mouth to let him have it, but was interrupted when Tommy Gregory poked his head in. "Excuse me, Maddie?"

I turned. "Yes?"

"There's, uh, a guy at the door to see you? I didn't let him in. Wanted to ask you first if it was okay."

Grandpa and I looked at each other. "What kind of guy, Tommy?" Grandpa asked.

Tommy shifted from one foot to another. "He's a tour guide. He wanted to know if he could bring some people inside to see the place. They're doing a tour of the town murders, and this is a spot that plays into both recent murders. So he wondered if they could come in, or if they should stay outside?"

Grandpa simply stared at him.

I was overcome with a ridiculous urge to laugh and cry at the same time. "Still think I'm being dramatic?" I asked Grandpa. "People need hobbies, I swear."

"That is a hobby," Grandpa pointed out. "People love those murder and scandal tours."

"I guess," I said. "I'd much prefer a pub tour, but that's me."

Chapter 35

After I'd made it clear enough that I wasn't willing to list the café on any spooky tour itinerary and decided to stick with my reservations only for the rest of the afternoon, things calmed down. We closed up at four on the dot. It felt like the longest four hours I'd spent in weeks. And Ethan and I still had to meet with Felicia, then I had a date to get ready for.

Felicia was right on time, which I appreciated. Because not only did we need to talk menus, but I had a proposition for her. Only she showed up before Gigi had a chance to leave. I heard the knock at the door but didn't make it out in time to get it before Gigi did. I peered out of the kitchen doorway to see mother and daughter staring across the room at each other as if they'd never seen each other before.

Felicia cracked first. She pasted a smile on her face. "Hi, sweetie."

"Hello," Gigi said stiffly, then walked past her mother and out the front door.

Felicia's face fell. She bowed her head, but not before I saw her cheeks redden at the slight from her daughter. I felt sorry for her. I waited for a beat to save her the embarrassment, then stepped out, smiling brightly. "Hi, Felicia!"

Her head snapped up and her smile was back in place. "Hello, Maddie. Is this still a good time?"

"Absolutely! Come on in." I beckoned her to follow me. We went into the kitchen.

Ethan placed a tray of leftover pastries on the table. "Welcome, Felicia. Coffee?"

"No, thank you," she said, pulling out a chair and perching awkwardly on the edge. "The kitchen is lovely. I remember coming here for dinner once. I really enjoyed your grandmother's company."

"You were friendly with my grandma?" I asked, surprised. Why hadn't I known that?

"My mother was," she said. "Your grandmother had dinner with her every couple of months. One night she invited me along. It was after . . . my husband died."

"That's lovely," I said. "My grandmother was thoughtful like that. I'll take some coffee," I said brightly to Ethan. "So. We were going to talk about menus."

"Yes," Felicia said, reaching into her bag. "I brought some samples for you to look at. Some are breakfast only, others are breakfast, lunch, snacks. I can work through the pricing depending on the variety you choose." She handed me a stack of laminated cards.

Ethan came and sat down next to me. I glanced through the pages, then handed them to Ethan. "These look amazing, Felicia. As long as the cinnamon buns are on here, we're good." I grinned at her. "On second thought, maybe they shouldn't be. I'll weigh three hundred pounds in no time."

"This is great. We should do a mix," Ethan said to me. "We'll go heavier on the pastries and breakfast items. I like the dairy-free options for yogurt too. Then we can do a small selection of sandwiches and chips. What do you think?"

"Perfect," I said. "You're the food guy. Whatever you think, I trust you."

He tugged at his beard. "She says that now," he said to Felicia. "She should trust you. You've been in business longer than us, I'm sure."

She froze. "Oh. Well. I don't know about that," she said with a nervous laugh. "You two have your juice place, don't you?"

Ethan glanced at me and nodded. "Yeah. We opened it up about four years ago."

Felicia's gaze dropped to the table. "You've got a year or so on me. I mean, I've been cooking forever," she hastened to add. "My food is top-notch, I promise you. But my business is fairly young. Three years. Since I lost my husband."

"I'm so sorry," I said.

"Thank you. Me too. Gigi's had a very hard time ever since, I'm afraid."

"At least you have each other," I said, aware that my words were trite and probably untrue. But I had no idea what else to say.

Felicia smiled, but it didn't reach her eyes. "My daughter rarely finds comfort in anything I can offer her."

"Oh." I looked at Ethan, who continued reading menus. I desperately wished he'd interject right now, but he was engrossed. "I'm sorry, Felicia. She'll come around. Every daughter goes through that with their mothers, right?" It wasn't for me and my sisters, but I had enough friends who went through it that it seemed like it could be true.

She looked at me as if she'd never seen me before. "No. I didn't. But ever since Gigi went off to school and came back thinking she's some political activist, she's been different. She prefers to do things her own way. She's hooked herself up with the wrong people. I guess she's following her own path. But honestly? I don't even know her anymore. She's angry and secretive and troubled. She won't even come home and stay with me. She'd rather live like a homeless person out on the beach. She stopped working for me. She'd rather work at a dry cleaner making minimum wage." Felicia shook her head, the frustration oozing out of every pore. "I mean, she doesn't even have any friends her own age anymore. She spends all her time with that woman. And she's picked up bad habits from her. I swear, she's become as jaded and cynical as Adele. Although now she's in jail, so I guess that's over."

Too late, she seemed to remember who she was talking to. "I'm sorry. I don't mean . . . I feel terrible about what happened," she said, nervously clasping her hands together. "And I think being here is good for Gigi. I hope you won't hold what I've said against her."

"Of course not. That's between you two. She's been helping us a lot here," I said. "Please don't worry about that."

"Okay. Thank you. I should be going. What time would you like me here tomorrow?"

"We're going to open at ten, so maybe nine?" Ethan said. "Let's go with these menus to start." He handed three back from her pile.

She nodded. "Perfect." She tucked the others in her bag and added a Post-it note to the ones he'd selected, then rose to go.

"Before you go," I said. "I need to ask you something."

She turned slightly pale, but sat back down. Mother and daughter were a lot alike. Both buckets of nerves. "Yes?"

"My dad needs help with his annual gala for the hospital and he's asked me to . . . sort out some details. I guess the major problem is they have no caterer. And the gala is a week from Saturday. Would you be interested in the job?"

Felicia's eyes widened. "The hospital gala? The annual event? The auction?"

I nodded. "The very same. What do you say?"

She burst into tears.

"Oh, jeez, Felicia . . ." I looked helplessly at Ethan. "You don't have to if you don't want to. Why are you crying?"

Ethan reached over and patted her arm. "This is a great opportunity, Felicia, don't you think?"

"It's amazing," she choked out. "Maddie, are you sure?"

"Of course I'm sure," I said, bewildered. "So . . . you do want it?"

"Yes!" She jumped up and threw her arms around me, almost knocking my chair over.

"Well. Great," I said, once all four chair legs were back on the ground. "I have to get some details in place, but I heard there's a meeting tomorrow at the venue. The Emerald Hotel downtown. Can you make it? It's at three."

"I can make it," she said tearfully. "I'm so overwhelmed that you asked me. Thank you!"

After about a hundred more thank yous, I ushered her out the door. I closed and locked it behind me and slumped against it, feeling insanely relieved.

One item crossed off the to-do list.

Chapter 36

I called my dad back. Thankfully I got his voice mail so I left him a quick message and told him I had a caterer on board, and that I'd call his person Charlotte tomorrow to get the rest of the team organized but I was unavailable tonight. I thought about shutting the phone completely off, but my type-A personality would never let me. But I had a date tonight and I didn't want the entire world intruding on it.

I did think about asking Lucas if we could have a quiet night in somewhere. I wasn't sure how I felt about being out in public. Maybe I could convince him to watch a movie at his place or something. Although I'd never even seen his place. He'd seen Grandpa's house, of course, not only because of the café but over the summer when he'd come over to fix the plumbing and pick me up for a couple of dates. I wondered what his place was like. I presumed he lived alone, but he'd never said.

I guess I'd never asked though. Which made me feel like a jerk. What the heck was wrong with me? I thought back to Val's and Becky's questions about whether or not Lucas and I were official, and why the heck we weren't. It all came down to one thing—me. I mean, I wanted to be, but things kept sidetracking us. Sidetracking me, actually. But I liked him. God, I *really* liked him. He totally made my stomach flip every time I saw him. And he kept asking me out, so I was hoping the feeling was mutual.

But I had to be better at letting him know I was just as interested as him. Starting with tonight, where I would *not* discuss Holly Hawthorne's deadness.

No. The only things we were talking about tonight were ourselves, so we could learn more about each other. And a nice outfit wouldn't hurt. I wasn't going to show up wearing jeans and a T-shirt. In fact, I needed to take some initiative. Instead of waiting for him to show up and ask me what I felt like, or expect him to have planned the evening, I was going to find somewhere nice to go and make reservations. Show him I was just as engaged as he was.

Going out in public was what we'd do, I decided. No hiding out for us.

And I was going to take my time getting ready and enjoy the process.

But first I checked in on the new cats Katrina had dropped off. A gray guy named Myron who hated the car and had been hiding ever since he'd come in because the trip had traumatized him. I managed to coax him out of his cubby with some of my best treats and got to pet him a bit. And a female tiger cat who was the friendliest gal I'd met in a while. I played with her for a bit then headed for the shower.

Unfortunately I didn't make it there before my cell phone rang. I glanced at the screen. My mother. No doubt wanting a Val update. But I had a bone to pick with her.

"Hi, Mom. I can't talk long. I'm going out tonight. And I'm kind of mad at you."

"Mad at me?" my mother asked, sounding surprised. "What on earth for? And who are you going out with? Craig or the cute dog groomer?"

"The dog groomer! What is it with this Craig thing? I don't want to date Craig!"

"Well, he wants to date you," my mother said. "It's clear to pretty much everyone. But at least you know what you don't want."

I didn't have much of an answer to that.

"I hope you have fun. Have you tried the new seafood place in Turtle Point?"

"No. What new place?" I asked, curious in spite of myself.

"It's amazing. They've been open for a few months now, and they're super popular. Saltwater is the name," my mother said. "I can make reservations for you. I know the hostess. What time?"

"He's picking me up at seven, so seven-thirty?"

"You got it." I heard her scribble a note in her ever-present notebook. Ever since my mother had decided she was writing a mystery novel, she carried notebooks everywhere she went. She wrote down phrases she overheard on the street, descriptions of people when she was sitting somewhere people-watching, and whatever random, crazy ideas popped into her head. And sometimes her grocery list. I hadn't seen the book yet and she was cagey about discussing her progress, but she was still going strong.

But right now she was messing with me. Trying to make me forget I was angry. "Stop trying to distract me. I'm still mad."

"Honey. What are you mad about?"

"You volunteered me to run Dad's gala! I have no time to run Dad's gala. I'm not a party planner. And I have a new business to run! What were you thinking?"

"Whoa. Hold up. What do you mean, run Dad's gala? I told him about your idea to hire a project manager, that's all."

"Well, apparently that project manager is me. Along

with the food coordinator and the auction-item figure-outer. He said you both agreed that no one is better at details than me! That's not even true. Val is way better."

"Oh no," my mother muttered.

"Yeah. Oh no," I said.

"Maddie. I'm sorry. I didn't mean for him to ask *you* to do it. I just told him he should think about getting *someone* to do it. I'm sorry. I can talk to him."

"No, forget it," I said sullenly. "I'm roped in now. And I already found him a new caterer."

"You did! That's amazing. Who?"

"Felicia Goodwin," I said.

She paused. "Really?"

"Really. Why?"

"No reason. That's great, honey. Let me know if you need help."

"Great. I do. I'm calling Dad's team of people tomorrow and setting them loose on the auction items. Maybe you can help." I smiled, feeling slightly vindicated. We could make this a family affair.

"Oh. Well, of course I'll help," my mother said, sounding less than thrilled. "Just tell me when you need me."

"I sure will."

"How's your sister?"

"She seems to be okay," I said. "Ethan is keeping her entertained."

A pause. Then, "Ethan?"

"Yeah, Ethan. Something wrong?"

"Not wrong, exactly." My mother exhaled. "I talked to Lilah Gilmore today. She called me." Her tone of voice suggested this had been the low point of her day.

I didn't blame her. Lilah was the island gossip. She knew everything long before everyone else did, and loved being the town crier, especially for the really good stuff.

I mentally cringed. "And?"

"Well, as expected, there's lots of talk floating around about the Tanners and what's going on." Mom hesitated. "She also said she'd heard Val was *cozying up* to some other man. Clearly digging for information. I told her to mind her own business."

"Good for you, Mom." Not that I doubted how my mother would handle a situation like that. She was the quintessential mama bear who would rip out someone's eyes before letting them say a cross word about anyone in her family.

"But Maddie—do you know what she's talking about?" The worry was there, sneaking into her voice even though she made an effort to sound casual. "Because it sounded like your partner. When she described him. Red hair and a beard."

"Ethan and I took Val out for ice cream the night we brought her to stay here," I said. "To cheer her up. And I should probably mention that while we were there Cole and Heather were all *cozied up* together having a snack."

My mother gasped. "What?"

"Yup."

"Did Val see?"

"No. And I didn't tell her either. But the double standard around here is kind of disgusting."

"Oh, believe me, I hear you," Mom said. "I just worry about Val because of this . . . life she chose. People are more apt to be watching her and having opinions and comments about all this as it develops. I hate that she has to deal with it. Just tell her to be careful, okay? She won't like it if it comes from me."

But she'll love it coming from me? I shook my head, promised my mother I'd broach the subject if the opportunity arose, then hit the shower.

Chapter 37

After spending a half hour in the hot water with a few songs from my *Get in a Better Mood* playlist, I felt like I could show up without too much crazy for this date. I focused on staying calm and getting ready. I dried my hair and added some loose curls. I dug through my clothes and discovered a dress I'd forgotten I had—a funky lavender-colored Betsey Johnson I'd scored at a designer discount store before I left San Fran. Turquoise beading around the neckline and a fringe of beads around the hem, it was fancy enough, but not too. I lined my eyes with a jade-green liner and added some neutral eyeshadow, put on my favorite red lipstick, found some silver sandals, and threw my stuff into a little black bag. Good to go.

I had some time, so I went up to see if my sister was around. I wondered if she had tried to call Cole. I doubted he'd been in touch, but maybe she'd reached out. I hoped she wasn't planning to go home tonight.

But there was no answer when I knocked. I took a chance peeking in, but it was empty.

I went downstairs. JJ followed me. He knew it was his dinnertime, after all. He was probably the smartest cat I'd ever encountered, and I'd encountered a lot of cats. I liked to think we were a good intellectual match. And I didn't want to wait until later, because with any luck I wouldn't be home tonight. I took out JJ's food and put it in his bowl, then set it down for him with some treats on top. I watched him eat for a minute, then went down to the basement to see if Grandpa was around. No luck there either. That was typical. He'd spent so many years out on the town, so to speak, in his official capacity that it must be hard to give that up. Even when he was chief, he rarely sat behind his desk. He preferred to be out in the action. And even though he didn't carry his badge anymore, he still kept to the same habits, infusing himself into the island, observing, assessing the scenarios he came across. I imagined he would do these things until the day he left the planet.

I checked in on the cats, who were all relaxing in various cubbies and beds.

I found Ethan out on the porch swing. With Val. They were eating what looked like lobster rolls from Damian's. I had to blink a few times to make sure my eyes weren't playing tricks on me when I saw Val actually smiling. Wow. Now I was impressed. Ethan just might be a miracle worker.

"Hey," I said. "What's going on?"

Val turned to me, still smiling. "Ethan was telling me about growing up in California. It sounds fascinating."

"With hippie parents," Ethan added, his eyes twinkling. "Val is enthralled with that concept."

I laughed. My sister hadn't ventured too far off the island, true, but my mother was a borderline hippie. And our youngest sister would've been right at home in a commune, much to my father's chagrin. But no sense in outing Val's hippie experiences while she looked so relaxed.

"Where are you off to?" Ethan asked.

"Hot date with Lucas tonight."

"Oooh," Val said. "Where are you going?"

"To dinner, and then I'm not sure what," I said. "But I'm hopeful."

"It's about time," Val said.

"Hey," I said. "Not cool."

Her cell rang. She fished it out of her shorts pocket. I watched the smile fade off her face as she excused herself and went inside to take it.

Ethan watched her go, a worried look on his face. "That's the second call she got today that made her get that look," he said.

"I hope it's not Cole," I muttered. "But hey, Ethan. You don't have to babysit my sister, you know," I said, lowering my voice so she wouldn't hear me if she came back out.

Ethan sent me a quizzical look. "Babysit? That's not what I'm doing. She's a nice person and she's having a hard time. I think she needs someone to talk to."

I perched on the edge of Grandpa's swing and rocked lightly. "She's talking to you? Like, about . . . stuff?" Ethan was very easy to talk to, but still. Val wouldn't even talk to me.

Ethan smiled. "She's getting there."

I raised an eyebrow. Something in his tone . . . did he have a crush on my sister? Good grief. I hoped not, for his sake. Her life was way too complicated right now. Plus she could be a true pain in the butt. Especially for someone as laid-back and relaxed as Ethan was.

"And I like her company," he went on, oblivious to my thought process. "She's interesting. And really smart."

Warning bells were going off in my head, but before I could probe any further, Lucas drove up and pulled into the driveway. I waved at him. This was gonna be a good night, I could feel it.

Lucas got out of the car and approached the stairs. "Hey, Maddie. You look great." He nodded at Ethan.

"Thanks," I said. "I'm just going to grab my purse." I

slipped inside. Val was nowhere in sight. I picked up my bag and a wrap in case the restaurant was freezing, ruffled JJ's head, said a quick good-bye to the café cats and headed out.

Lucas and Ethan were chatting. When I stepped onto the porch, Lucas smiled at me. "Ready?"

"Ready," I said.

"Have fun, kids," Ethan said.

We got into Lucas's car. "I wasn't sure what you were in the mood for," he began, but I held up a hand.

"Already taken care of," I said. "There's a great seafood restaurant—well, I've heard it's great, anyway—over in Turtle Point. It will be quieter than this part of the island too. I made reservations."

He glanced at me. "You did? That's cool," he said. "I'm totally in the mood for fish."

"Good." I gave him the address, then settled back in my seat for the short ride into the next town. Traffic wasn't too bad, surprisingly, mostly because people were going in the opposite direction. Looking for the excitement of Daybreak Harbor's summer nightlife. Usually I would be right there with them, but tonight I was looking forward to a quiet, romantic evening with Lucas. Nothing was going to screw up this night.

Chapter 38

When we arrived at the restaurant, Lucas took my hand as we walked inside and didn't let go until we were sliding into our booth. I'd asked for a table with a circular booth, in hopes we could get into the snuggling mood. So far, so good. He slid up close to me, his thigh touching mine, and gave me that smile that could knock me over.

I smiled back and we did that goofy staring into each other's eyes thing for a minute, until the waitress came over and totally hijacked the moment.

"Welcome! Can I get you something to drink?" She beamed at us, handing us each a menu.

I looked at Lucas. "You like whiskey?"

He nodded.

"We'll have two old-fashioneds," I said. "And the oysters."

She flashed us a thumbs-up and headed off to the bar. Lucas looked at me with admiration. "I like a lady who takes charge," he said with a grin.

"Good," I said. "I like a guy who'll drink whiskey with me."

We took a few minutes to peruse the menu. When the waitress returned with our drinks, I ordered the mahi-mahi tacos. Lucas ordered the baked seafood platter. We got extra French fries. I sipped my drink. It was fabulous. My mother had been right. If the food was as good as the beverages, we were going to leave here full and happy.

"So how's your sister?" Lucas asked.

"She's doing okay," I said. "She's not really in the mood to talk, so I'm not sure what's going on in her head. But it can't be easy for her."

"I'm sure," Lucas said. "But she's got a great family supporting her."

"Yeah. She'll be fine. Anyway. Enough about that mess. Tell me about you."

"Oh. Okay. Well, what about me?" He shifted a bit in his seat. Was Lucas shy? How adorable.

"Well, you never told me a lot about your family or where you come from. Just bits and pieces. I want to hear everything." I propped my chin in my hands and smiled at him. It was true. For all our dates, our conversations seemed to always get sidetracked onto other topics and we still hadn't completed the getting-to-know-each-other phase.

"Yeah? It's not that interesting." He swirled his drink in the glass, watching the ice cubes clink together. "I grew up in Virginia and pretty much stayed there through college. Virginia Tech." He glanced at me.

I nodded. "You did tell me that. But you never told me your major." I glanced up as the hostess led a table full of jabbering women to the next table and sighed inwardly. A whole restaurant and they had to seat them next to us? Really? They looked like they were in their late thirties or early forties and kind of reminded me of Holly and Heather Hawthorne, just from the snippets I overheard as they filed into their seats.

Stop thinking about that! I forced my attention back to Lucas.

He smiled. "Business. What else?"

"What? Yes. Major. Of course. Makes perfect sense." I should've known we had that in common too—especially since we both ran businesses.

"So after school I was supposed to start working with my dad. He owned the plumbing business, remember? But the thought of it . . ." He shook his head. "I couldn't see myself doing that for the rest of my life."

"So you went to dog grooming school?"

"Not right away. First I thought I might want to make a lot of money." He smiled wryly. "I tried my hand at the corporate life. Not my thing."

I made a face. "I wouldn't think so. They would've made you cut your hair, right?" Lucas had really nice hair. Not too long, but not too short. Just right. Thick and dark and a perfect contrast to his gorgeous blue eyes.

"Yeah. And I needed it for the band." He grinned.

I pointed at him. "Because you were always in a band. That I knew."

The waitress came over and brought our oysters. When she'd left I turned back to Lucas.

"So when's the next gig?"

"Thursday night. Here on the island. And then in Boston next Saturday. Maybe . . . you want to go to one of them?"

"I'd love to," I said, just as I heard someone behind me say, "Now, if Felicia was here, you know she'd be picking apart this bread basket!" A titter of laughter followed.

Felicia? As in Goodwin? My ears perked up despite my very best intentions to stay laser-focused on Lucas. I leaned over just a bit, so I could hear them better. "So where are you playing?"

"Here on Daybreak, at Jade Moon. In Boston, a little club in the South End." Lucas started talking about the venue, which was pretty new but attracted all kinds of bands local and otherwise.

Meanwhile, behind me, one of the women was saying, "It's too bad all this had to happen. I do miss her, but what can we do?"

"Agreed," another one added. "We can't have someone who's cooking in other people's kitchens—and not well, from the sounds of it—in our circle."

A couple of cackles.

"Would you ever consider hiring her?" one of them asked after a moment's pause.

"Good Lord, no," the first one said. "I mean, it's not that I necessarily believe Heather's story about Gigi and the food, but it still wouldn't do to be associated with that. And I think it would be too embarrassing for her, the poor dear." Clucks of fake sympathy followed.

Heather. Heather Hawthorne? Heather and Gigi? What story about the food? Felicia's food? I leaned over further, silently encouraging them to keep talking.

"I heard she's having a hard time," the fourth one, who hadn't said anything yet, chimed in. "I feel dreadful for her. Plus all the problems she's had with Gigi otherwise. I mean, it can't be a very happy time."

By the silence that followed I guessed the others were giving their traitorous friend a look of disbelief. I wanted to turn around and ask her to elaborate, that I'd missed a whole piece of this story, but I managed to control myself. I kept one ear peeled for more on Felicia, but the Stepford Wives had moved on to the next poor person to decimate. Then I realized Lucas was staring at me.

"Maddie?"

"Yeah," I said, shooting him a brilliant smile.

He waited. Apparently he'd asked me a question, and now I had no idea what it was. I took a few frantic seconds to try and retrace the last steps of the conversation that I could remember.

I was coming up short.

"I said, do you think we're too old to be chasing gigs around Boston and surrounding areas?" There was a teasing tone to his voice, as if he already knew the answer and just wanted to see what I'd say.

I was grateful for his generosity. He could've made me squirm for a bit. "I'm sorry," I said. "I thought I heard a name I knew behind me. No, I don't think you're too old at all." Lucas had just turned thirty-three—he'd told me the last time we'd gone out. "Besides, age is silly. It's just a number."

"I'm glad you think that way," he said.

"Hey, if it's what you love to do, why would you not do it? Age doesn't matter." I waved my hand to dismiss it. "I mean, really. We're only as old as we act, right?"

He nodded admiringly. "I like the way you think. So tell me about your family? The rest of them, I mean. I know a bit about your grandpa and Val, but what about your parents?"

Before I could answer, I was distracted by a man moving swiftly between the tables, a cell phone pressed to his ear, his voice slightly louder than what was acceptable. And that voice sounded familiar.

My mouth dropped. It was Cole.

Chapter 39

My first reaction was rage. This jerk was out at a nice restaurant tonight, after ice cream last night, while my sister was in such a state of upheaval? I turned to see where he was heading, and saw him vanish through the doors in the back leading to the bathrooms. I frantically sorted through my options. I wanted to see who he was with. Then I had to confront him. This was the perfect moment. He wasn't expecting it. I had the element of surprise, and I couldn't let it go to waste. I sent a silent apology to Lucas and a quick prayer to the universe to hold the rest of the date together, then slid out of the booth.

"Hold that thought," I said to Lucas, fumbling to act normally. "I have to run to the ladies' room." I pointed at my whiskey glass apologetically. "Will you get me another one if she comes back?"

He looked at me curiously. "Of course."

I bolted from my seat and hurried toward the bathrooms. I skidded to a stop in the hallway. Obviously I had to wait for him to come out, so I used the time to try and rehearse a script. *You lying scum* probably wouldn't do as an opening, but where to start? Righteous indignation for my sister? Or a pointed question about what had happened to Holly and his role in her life—or death? Of course Daddy would've coached him to within an inch of his life about how to answer questions, but that was for the police and attorneys. He might just fumble under the wrath of his crazy sister-in-law who was willing to accost him in a bathroom hallway.

Man, he was taking a long time. I shifted from one foot to the other, moving out of the way as a woman passed me, headed for the restroom. She gave me a strange look. "Is there a line?"

I shook my head. "Sorry, just waiting for someone."

She disappeared inside. I leaned against the wall. Then noticed there was another door down the hall past the bathrooms, and it was ajar. I crept over.

A back exit. And I heard voices outside. Angry ones.

I inched closer to the door. One of the voices was Cole's. Higher-pitched than the other. Nervous, almost, but trying to maintain authority. "I'm telling you, I didn't see anything . . ."

The other voice, deeper, angry. I couldn't quite make out the words, but there was something slightly familiar about it. I tried to pin it down, but it hovered just out of my reach.

Shoot. I wanted to lean through the door and listen, but I wasn't sure where the two men were in relation to the door. And I wanted to hear what they were saying without alerting them to my presence.

Cole's voice again, almost pleading. "I swear to you. I was leaving. I had to go out the back way. I didn't see anything else."

"You're lying," the other man's voice hissed, a spring coiled tightly with rage. "You had to see something. And you've been talking to the police. Why would you do that if you had nothing to tell?"

"I had no choice! They've been on me since that night . . ."

Someone left the men's room next to me and let the door

slam shut behind him, causing me to jump, jamming my arm into the exit door handle. Which of course caused the door to creak as it moved. I winced. The voices outside paused. I held my breath. The man leaving the bathroom gave me an odd look.

I ignored him and refocused on what was happening outside, my heart pounding. This had to be about Holly's murder. Did this mean Cole really was involved? Or had he seen something he wasn't supposed to see and was trying to cover it up? Who was this other man? My skin broke out in a cold sweat despite the warmth of the night.

Outside, it was still silent. Then I heard a thud, like someone was being slammed up against a wall.

"You better tell me. You better tell me everything you saw," the other man said, his voice a dangerous thrum of warning.

Cole made a strangled sound. "I'm telling you. Nothing. Nothing."

The sound of a fist striking bone, loud enough that I could identify it through the door, and an accompanying cry of pain caused me to gasp out loud. Thank God I had my cell phone in my pocket. I pulled it out and dialed 911, babbling the restaurant's address to the dispatcher. "There's an assault in progress. It might be related to a murder case. They're out in a small alley behind the Saltwater restaurant in Turtle Cove," I whispered as loudly as I could, then disconnected and pressed back against the door.

Should I go out there? I didn't love my brother-in-law, but could I really stand by and watch—or rather listen—to him getting beaten up? Possibly worse, if this was Holly's killer?

Or had they been in it together, that little voice whispered in my ear. And this was just two bad guys, each trying to save himself?

I shoved the door open and stepped outside. I was in a small lot with room for a couple cars and a Dumpster. The alley that led to the street was barely wide enough for a truck to pass through. Cole was on the ground, looking dazed and bleeding from his nose. The other man was gone, but I heard footsteps pounding up the alley. I raced after them, skidding to a stop when I heard an engine fire to life. I pressed myself against the side of the building as a van shot past the alley entrance. A dark blue van. With the words QUINN BUILDERS on the door. I stared after it, stunned. Gabe? Adele's nephew? Is that why the voice sounded familiar? I'd only met Gabe once, but he did have a distinct voice.

But what on earth did he have to do with this? Unless he was the type who doled out vigilante justice and was going after anyone who had been at that house that night to try to protect his aunt.

I remembered Cole and ran back to where he was still sprawled on the ground. Cursing, I dropped down next to him. "Cole. Are you okay? Who was that who hit you?"

Cole's head rolled to the side and he tried to focus on me. He was going to have quite a shiner tomorrow. "Maddie?" he said, wincing with pain, his voice thick from the damage his nose had sustained. "God. Is this a bad dream?"

I sat back on my heels. Charming as usual. "No. Who were you talking to out here? Was it Gabe Quinn?"

He tried to roll away from me, but not before I saw the panic flash through his eyes. "Don't worry about it."

"Don't *worry* about it? You've got to be kidding me. I already called the police."

"The police?" That got him up. He sat, wincing, trying to stanch the blood flowing from his nose. "Why would you do that?"

"To save your sorry behind." I stood up. "What were you talking about? Holly? What did you do, Cole? And why won't you just be straight with Val about whatever's going on? She doesn't deserve this."

"Go away, Maddie." He looked miserable, pulling himself unsteadily to his feet. "And mind your own business for once."

I bristled. My family was my business, thank you very much. I stepped forward, all set to tell him that, but two cops rounded the corner of the alley, hands on their weapons. They took one look at Cole's bleeding face and me, poised to pounce on him, and I could see the wrong idea blossoming in their minds—that I had done this.

"Both of you, hands where we can see them," one of them, the older cop, said.

I immediately raised my hands, palms up. "You've got this wrong," I said. "The other guy took off. I'm the one who called it in. I'm former Police Chief Leo Maloney's granddaughter."

"Great." The younger cop stepped forward. "Turn around and face the wall."

"You've got this all wrong," I said, but did as I was told.

He motioned to Cole to do the same. Cole did. Once they'd checked us for weapons, I was hustled off to the side by the younger cop, while the older one grabbed Cole. People had started poking their heads out the back door of the restaurant, drawn by the flashing lights of the cruiser parked beside the restaurant. I thought of Lucas, of our unfinished conversation, and wanted to die. I'd sworn I wasn't letting anything wreck this date, and then I'd gone off and wrecked the date. He probably thought I took off on him. He'd probably left already. I'd probably never hear from him again. Hot tears stung my eyes, a combination of anger and loss. Why was I so stupid? Why did I always do the wrong things with the nice guy?

"What happened out here? You punch him?" The cop's eyes bored into me.

I stared at him, torn between being offended and flattered that he thought I could punch Cole's lights out like that. "No! I'm the one who heard the fight and called it in."

"What's the other guy look like, then?"

"I don't know. I didn't see him." It wasn't a total lie. I hadn't seen Gabe. Just his truck driving away. And maybe that was a coincidence. Maybe the guy who punched Cole had taken off on foot, and Gabe had just been driving by at the wrong time. Or maybe someone had stolen Gabe's truck.

Problem was, I didn't believe in coincidence.

He raised a skeptical eyebrow. "How did you hear the fight then? Weren't you inside?"

I hesitated. "I was. I . . . went to the bathroom and I heard shouting. It sounded like it was getting violent, so I called you guys."

"And you said it might be related to a murder case? What murder case?"

I glanced at Cole. He hadn't heard the question. He was busy answering his own cop.

"The Holly Hawthorne case. This . . . gentleman was there the night she died."

The cop stared at me. "And?"

"It sounded like they were talking about that night. Maybe you could ask him?" I motioned to Cole.

The cop didn't look impressed.

"Or not. Listen," I said. "Call my grandfather. He'll vouch for me. He's my brother-in-law," I said, jerking my head in Cole's direction. "As much as I want to punch him out, I didn't. The other guy got to him first."

The cop watched me for another few seconds as if weighing how much of a liar I looked like, then he sighed. "Fine. You can go."

"Thanks." I started toward the door, then glanced back at Cole. "What about him?"

He glanced at the other cop, still grilling Cole, and shrugged. "Probably a broken nose. And he'll have a nice black eye tomorrow. Hope he doesn't have any fancy parties coming up."

Chapter 40

I pushed past the crowd gathered in the back door, intent on finding Lucas, then stopped short when I realized he was at the back of the crowd, staring at me with an unreadable expression as I emerged in front of him.

"I'm so sorry," I burst out. "I went to the bathroom and Cole was outside and he got in a fight with someone . . ." I trailed off, looking around to make sure the crowd was dispersing, or at least not paying attention. "And I think it might've had to do with Holly's murder," I finished in a stage whisper.

Lucas looked unimpressed. "Really," he said. "Find out anything good?"

I shook my head.

"Let's go," he said. "I better get you home."

"Home? But we didn't eat yet," I said, feeling my heart sink.

Lucas shrugged. "The food came. I wasn't sure what happened to you, so I had it boxed up when I realized that you were involved in whatever the ruckus was outside. I'm glad you're okay, because I was worried for a bit."

But not anymore. Not when he realized I'd blown him off. I hadn't meant to, of course, but how would he know that? What normal girl runs out on a date with a guy she allegedly really likes, to stalk her brother-in-law whom she supposedly really dislikes, and get involved in a murder investigation about someone else she disliked?

I mean, he kind of knew I wasn't normal, but still. "Lucas." I tried again, not wanting to reduce myself to pleading with him, but I knew I was seriously close to messing this up permanently. "I'm really sorry. Let's just go eat, okay?"

"I already had them put it in a box." He strode back to our table.

I followed, swallowing back tears. What was wrong with me? Why did I keep doing this?

He grabbed two paper bags of food off the table without pausing to see if I was behind him, and continued to the front door. I snatched my wrap off the back of my chair and followed, not really wanting to be stranded in this restaurant. I caught up with Lucas at his car. He opened my door for me, polite as ever, and closed it after I tucked myself in.

I waited until he'd pulled out into traffic, heading in the direction of Daybreak Harbor, before I turned to him. "Lucas. I'm really, really sorry. I went to the bathroom and heard Cole outside arguing with someone. It sounded like it was about what happened at Holly's. Given all the questions about his involvement, I was trying to hear what he was saying. You understand that, don't you?"

He kept his gaze straight ahead. "And before that you were distracted by the people at the table behind us. Am I that boring, Maddie, that you can't keep your attention on our conversation?" He shook his head. "Look. Forget it. It's fine."

"It's not fine. And you're not at all boring, Lucas. I was looking forward to this date all day." I slumped back miserably in my seat. "I can't help it that there's always some stupid drama lately," I mumbled.

Now Lucas looked over at me. "No. You can't. But you

can help how much attention you give it." He turned his gaze back to the road. "It made more sense last time. When your grandfather was involved. But I'm not sure why you're so concerned this time."

I sat up, my hackles up suddenly. Even though the rational, calm Maddie was trying to be heard—*Shut up, shut up, just shut up*—the impulsive, gotta-be-right Maddie had to get the last word in. "I'm concerned because my sister is heartbroken that her husband was involved in all this. I'm also concerned because a woman who works with me is possibly taking the blame for it. I'm sorry if you don't think that's a good enough reason." I turned my head to face out the window.

He didn't reply anyway.

As we got closer to Daybreak Harbor, the traffic slowed. People were just getting started on their night out. Pedestrians and cars vied for right-of-way. Kids raced through the crowd with ice-cream cones, laughing and shouting. Normal people, having normal fun on vacation. I leaned my head against the window and shut my eyes against the pounding headache that was creeping through my skull. Lucas drove like a man on a mission. Clearly he wanted to drop me off sooner rather than later. Well, fine. Who needed him anyway? Relationships always turned out to be trouble, no matter how good they started out.

By the time he pulled up in Grandpa's driveway, I'd almost convinced myself he was the bad guy here.

Almost.

I grabbed the door handle as soon as he pulled to a stop. "Maddie," he started.

I paused but didn't look back at him.

He sighed. "Forget it."

I climbed out and slammed the door. It wasn't until he'd driven away that I realized I'd left my food in his car. Not that I was hungry anymore anyway.

Chapter 41

I spent the night tossing and turning, thoughts and pictures racing through my mind. Cole, bleeding on the ground. Holly, jabbing a finger at Adele. What she must have looked like facedown in the sand, dead. Her sister's face, twisted in hatred before she chucked a bunch of greens at me. Felicia in the kitchen, pushing cinnamon buns on me.

Thankfully, no one had been around when I'd gotten home, so I didn't have to answer any questions about my disastrous date. Or why I was home when I hoped I wouldn't be. Or even worse, see Val and have to figure out how to tell her what I'd seen and heard. Not that I knew what any of it meant.

In lieu of dinner, I'd dug through my kitchen cabinets until I found a protein bar and took it upstairs with a cup of tea.

JJ waited for me on my bed. Well, maybe he wasn't waiting for me. Maybe he was secretly upset I'd cheated him out of a night with the bed all to himself. As a result, I was scrunched onto less than half the bed while he sprawled out on the rest. I'd like to say it was the reason for my miserable night's sleep, but I know it wasn't. I'd screwed up with Lucas—possibly irreversibly—and I knew it. Not to mention, I was dying to know what that conversation between Cole and the mystery man meant. And what food Heather Hawthorne and Gigi had in common. And, maybe worst of all, I couldn't stop thinking about what those women had said about Felicia and her catering. Had I completely screwed up by hiring her for the gala? If her food was bad, or if she poisoned everyone, I'd have to leave town.

Needless to say, sleep didn't come easily with those thoughts. When my alarm went off at six, I was wide-eyed and staring at the ceiling.

At least I had the cats and my new business to focus on today, hopefully taking my mind off all the crappy things. Lord knew there was plenty to do. But when I went downstairs, the place was thrumming with activity despite the early hour. Grandpa and Gigi were actually cleaning cages together, and they seemed to be having fun doing it. Grandpa was telling Gigi a story about one of the island's old-timers, Sal Bonnadonna, owner of a local liquor store, and his crazy dog.

"And every time I went in that store, if he thought I was there on official police business, he'd set that darned dog patrolling me like a beat cop gone bad," Grandpa was saying.

Gigi stared at him, fascinated. "Did it try to bite you? Would you have shot it?" For once, she didn't look sad or nervous. She seemed to be really enjoying the conversation.

Grandpa turned and stared at her. I could tell he was exaggerating his facial expressions for maximum effect, but Gigi couldn't. I bit back a smile as I watched him.

"Lord, no," he said in a tone suggesting she'd be mad to even think such a thing. "But I would've shot Sal!"

Gigi dissolved into giggles.

I stepped into the room. She immediately sobered and went back to work, like she thought I was going to scold her or something. "Morning," I said. "I'm so grateful for you two doing this."

Grandpa Leo turned in mid-scoop of one of the litter boxes and beamed at me. I was afraid he was about to start waving the scoop around and flinging litter everywhere. He wore a pair of denim overalls and one of his crazy cat shirts. "Mornin,' doll. Got in late?" He winked at me.

"I guess. You don't have to do that, Grandpa."

"Nonsense." He turned back to his task. "You need some help. You can't do everything yourself. Gigi and I are having a great time. Plus, this is my place too. I need to be more on task with my jobs. I get a little distracted sometimes. Must be old age."

"Old? You? Never. Okay, well, as long as you're enjoying yourself." I headed to the kitchen in search of coffee and Ethan, peeking inside before entering. No sign of Val, thank goodness. I had no idea if I should say something to her or not about what happened last night, although she'd find out eventually and be mad at me for not telling her.

Ethan turned when I came in and raised an eyebrow. To his credit, he didn't ask me why I was there, or how my date went. He simply filled a mug with coffee and handed it to me.

"Rough night?" His tone was matter-of-fact.

"You could say that." I sank into a chair and sipped my coffee. "You could also say I brought it all on myself."

"Oh boy." Ethan sat too. "Do I want to know?"

"I'm sure you'd find the story delightful, but I don't have the energy right now. Listen, can you help Grandpa and Gigi man the café today? I want to work on some of the behind-the-scenes stuff. I need to figure out this registration system."

Ethan nodded. "'Course. The food is on its way, so I've got plenty of time. So you're in hideout mode?"

He knew me so well.

"I guess," I said, taking a big swig of coffee. "How could you tell?"

"It's not that hard. So what happened last night?"

I was horrified to feel my eyes welling up with tears. "I messed it all up."

"What?" He leaned forward. "How?"

It all came out in a rush—my good intentions for our date, the women behind us talking about Felicia, Heather, and Gigi, seeing Cole, trying to hear his conversation with the mystery man who punched his lights out. How Lucas had packed all our food up because he was tired of waiting for me, and how I didn't blame him one bit.

"I wish I knew what they meant about Felicia. Is her cooking bad? Is she going to ruin the gala? But more importantly, Lucas. I like him s-so much," I choked out. "But now I screwed it up for good." I buried my face in my hands, waiting for sympathy.

It never came.

Instead, Ethan refilled my coffee cup and sat back down. He looked preoccupied, actually, staring off into space. I peeked at him through my fingers. "You got nothing for me?"

He refocused on me. "Just that you need to be honest about why you're not moving this forward. This guy really likes you. I can tell. But you're not giving him much to work with."

Sheesh. First Becky, now Ethan. What happened to best friends who let you cry on their shoulder and made you feel better?

"That's not true," I defended myself. "But all this crazy stuff keeps happening. I mean, how was I supposed to know I'd pick the one restaurant where that loser showed up . . ." I trailed off as the door to the kitchen opened.

Shoot. Val.

She looked at us suspiciously. "Why did you stop talking?"

"No reason," I said immediately. "Nothing about you."

"Yeah. That's what they all say lately." She sailed past us, her nose in the air, and went to get a mug.

Ethan jumped up. "Let me get it for you." He busied himself making her a cup of coffee. The fact that he added a quarter teaspoon of sugar and measured out the milk told me it wasn't the first time he'd done so.

"Thanks," she said, her tone decidedly warmer as she accepted the mug. Then she glared at me.

"What?" I asked.

"I have a bone to pick with you."

"Great," I muttered. "Who doesn't?" But my heart was pounding. I was afraid she'd heard about Cole and wanted to know why I hadn't told her yet. "What did I do now?"

"Dad asked you to help with the gala."

"Yeah." I waited.

She continued to glare.

"Is there more?" I asked.

"That's enough, isn't it? Why did Dad ask *you*? I mean, do you have to be the favorite for everything?"

That's what this was about? The relief was so strong I felt almost giddy. "Val. For real? You can have the job. Seriously. Dad thought you were under enough stress."

"Yeah, well, he didn't bother to ask me. I don't want it now." She took a noisy sip of her coffee. "But I don't think it's fair that you get all the glory."

"Believe me, there's no glory here," I said. "And I'm happy to have the help if you want to jump in."

"I'll bet," she said, still snooty. "That's all I wanted to say. I'll let you get back to your conversation."

"Okay. I'll, um, see you later," Ethan said.

No wonder he wasn't listening to me or offering me

sympathy. He'd been preoccupied with the Cole part of my evening, because he'd been worried about how it would affect Val. My business partner had clearly become smitten with my married sister. The question was, did she realize it?

I waited until she left then reached over and grasped his arm. "What is going on?"

He frowned. "What do you mean?"

"I mean, with you and Val."

"Nothing."

"Nothing? Ethan. Please tell me you don't have a thing for her. Because her life is really complicated right now—"

"Maddie," he interrupted. "Please. Leave it alone."

I stared at him. "Leave it *alone*? You can't be serious."

"I'm dead serious," he said, and for once, he sounded it. "Besides. You should worry about your own relationship. Or whatever you want to call it at this point. Maybe figure out why you keep sabotaging it."

And he left the room, leaving me speechless.

Chapter 42

I was about to go upstairs and hide in my room for the day when Gigi came into the kitchen looking for me.

"Gabe's here to see you," she said. "I'm going to run a quick errand before we open, is that okay?"

Gabe. My heart started to pound thinking of his van tearing away from the scene behind the restaurant last night. What was he doing here?

"Sure, go," I said. "Just come back, okay?"

Gigi gave me a funny look but nodded, then took off. I downed the rest of my coffee before getting up and following her to the living room.

Gabe stood in the middle of the room, staring out the window. At what I couldn't tell. He snapped to attention when I came in.

"Gabe. Hi," I said, shoving my hands into the back pockets of my jean shorts and trying to appear casual. "What can I do for you?"

"Morning, Maddie. Sorry to show up unannounced." Gabe looked like he hadn't slept in days. His eyes were bloodshot and his curls stood off his head in crazy tangles. His clothes were wrinkled, as if he'd been in them all night.

I snuck a discreet—I hoped—look at his hands. Would

Purrder She Wrote 217

I be able to tell if he'd punched Cole out last night? Or would his hands be all chewed up anyway from the work he did? I was out of luck for the moment anyway. His hands were shoved into the pockets of his sweatshirt.

He took a deep breath and looked around, as if the words he needed were on my walls, or my floor. "I wondered if you'd decided if I got the contracting job."

"The job," I repeated. His aunt was sitting in jail and he may have been involved somehow—and he wanted to talk about my job?

"Yeah. See, this thing with my aunt, well, I need to hire a lawyer. And I don't have the cash flow right now. So I need to make sure I have enough jobs lined up before I set things in motion."

Ah. Now I understood. But what was I supposed to do? "Of course. I totally get it." I took a deep breath, stalling for time. On the one hand, we needed the work done and contractors weren't busting down my doors to do it. On the other hand, last night's scene had been disturbing on a lot of levels. On the third hand, he could've been trying to help his aunt by forcing Cole to tell the truth about whatever he saw, if he saw anything. On the fourth hand, maybe if he was around, I'd be able to get some info from him.

I was running out of hands, and he was waiting for me to say something. "Yes, you got the job, Gabe. Ethan and I are looking forward to working with you."

It took him a second, then a smile broke out. "Really? You mean it?"

I nodded. "Yeah. We need the work done. The sooner the better, you know?"

He grabbed my hand and pumped it up and down. I glanced down. Nothing. No blood, anyway. It was moving so fast I couldn't tell much more than that. "Thank you. Thank you so much. I'll start tomorrow, if that works. I'll go get the permits today."

Well, I'd said I wanted the job started sooner rather than later. "Um. I guess. We can at least talk about the schedule," I started, but a knock on the door interrupted.

So much for wanting to avoid people. "Hold on," I said to Gabe, then stopped and stared. Lucas was at my door. Maybe I hadn't screwed it up as badly as I thought. Maybe he thought he'd overreacted and had come to tell me. Maybe he was here to ask if we could try again tonight. Then I remembered that I was dressed in clothes I had picked up off my floor and barely brushed my hair, and cringed. I went over and unlocked the screen, holding it open.

He shuffled from foot to foot and nodded. "Morning."

"Hey." I motioned him in, trying to play it cool. Maybe if I didn't call attention to my rat's nest hair Lucas wouldn't notice. "How are you?"

"Fine. I'm here to groom the new cat."

"The new . . . oh. Myron," I said, suddenly feeling stupid. The cat that hated the car so much he tried to climb out the window after escaping from his carrier. "That's right, Katrina told me. I'll, um, go find him." I turned away, completely embarrassed. Of course he wasn't there to see me. Because I'd screwed everything up. Tears pricked my eyes and I blinked them away, trying to see past the blur to find our new resident and not make a fool of myself. Well, any worse than I'd already done. "Lucas, this is Gabe," I said, waving in Gabe's direction.

Then I realized they were staring at each other in kind of an odd way. Lucas nodded. "Hey," he said.

Gabe mumbled something.

I let them do their caveman routine and went to look for the feline in question. "Myron," I called, then immediately felt stupid. Myron had been a stray. Katrina had probably named him in the van on the way over. He wouldn't know it was his name. And even if he did, he wasn't a dog. Luckily, I caught sight of him curled up in the cubbyhole of one of the cat trees. "Ah, there you are." I peered in. He blinked lazily at me. I reached in to pet him. He came out and head-butted me. I scooped him up and handed him to Lucas. "You can use the downstairs bathroom," I said, pointing. "There are towels in the closet."

"Thanks."

Our eyes met.

Then Lucas turned away and headed to the bathroom.

I felt my heart break a little bit. I took a minute to blink away the fresh tears that filled my eyes, then turned back to Gabe. "So. Anything else for today?" I asked brightly.

"Can I take a quick look at the rooms again? I want to do some measurements," Gabe said. "Then I'll get out of your way."

"Sure. Help yourself. Oh, by the way?"

He looked at me, expectant.

"I was just curious. How is Adele?"

He shook his head. "She's okay. Home now, thank goodness. But I don't think she's out of the woods yet. And it's killing me." He looked really sad.

"I'm sorry," I said quietly. He seemed so broken up about this. Maybe my theory was right about him taking matters into his own hands.

But how would he have known Cole had been the one to call in the body, unless he'd been there too? Was it possible he'd heard me talking about it while he was here? I didn't think so. I tried not to mention that whole thing a lot around the house because of Val, and certainly not in front of strangers.

"Yeah, thanks," he said. "I'm sorry too."

I waited until he'd left the room, then weighed my options. I could pretend Lucas wasn't here and go hide upstairs. Or I could go try to talk to him.

My inner voice was screaming at me to go talk to him.

And usually when I ignored that voice, things didn't go so well for me.

I steeled myself, went down the hall and knocked on the bathroom door. The running water stopped and Lucas cracked the door.

"Yeah?"

"Can I come in?" I pushed the door open without waiting for an answer. Myron was in the sink huddled in a ball, looking miserable.

"Sure. It's your house." Lucas went back to bathing Myron.

So that's how it was going to be. "Lucas. I'm really sorry, again."

Silence.

Seriously, he was going to make me beg? Before I could decide what to say next, he finally spoke.

"He working for you? That guy Gabe?"

I nodded. "Yeah. He's Adele's nephew." Saying her name gave me a stab. "She heard me saying I couldn't find a contractor and set me up. I was going to give him the job anyway but he was in a real hurry to get started because he needs to hire a lawyer for Adele. Why? You know him or something?"

"Kind of. I groomed his dog," he said. "Did a drop-off for him because my schedule got backed up and I felt bad."

"Oh." I frowned. "Is he mean to his dog or something? Did he not pay you? Or was I imagining you were looking at him weird?"

"Nothing like that. I don't even know him. But the person he was with when I went to his house . . ." He shook his head. "I got the sense he was trying to hide her. But she answered the door, so it was kind of a moot point."

Her? What the heck was this about? "Okay," I said. "Who?"

He took a deep breath. "Holly Hawthorne," he said. "Wearing a T-shirt and nothing else."

Chapter 43

That was not what I was expecting. I stared at him. "Holly . . . are you sure?"

"I guess I can't be sure which sister it was. It wasn't like I was introduced," Lucas said dryly. "I didn't know she had a twin until . . . all this. But the one who died had a diamond in her nose. I could see it in the picture they ran in the paper. The one at Gabe's did too. Do they both?"

I thought back to my altercation with Heather. Before the veggies started flying, I'd been face-to-face with her and hadn't noticed any piercings. Which made sense, because Becky said she worked in some fancy banking job. Lord knew they probably frowned on nose rings.

So it had to be Holly. Which meant Holly and Gabe were an item. Gabe. Adele's nephew. Adele, who hated Holly's guts and threatened to slash her tires. Or worse. Had she known about this? If she had, it had to have fueled the fires of her already intense hatred for Holly. Or what if she hadn't known and recently found out . . . I could almost hear her reasoning: *if she treats cats the way she does, I'm sure she'll treat my nephew even worse.*

And what did this mean for Gabe? His aunt was accused of killing his lover? Did he know more than he was telling?

Had Gabe been there that night? Had *he* killed her? And now he was panicking because his aunt was taking the fall?

Holy cow, what a mess. "Wow," I said finally.

"Yeah," he said. "I didn't know anything about either of them at the time, so I didn't think anything of it. But when I saw her picture in the paper, I recognized her but couldn't place her. When I saw him it clicked." He turned off the water and rubbed a towel over Myron's fur.

"When was this?" I asked.

Lucas thought back. "Probably a month, month and a half ago?"

"That recent. Wow. Okay." So that changed things. I wondered what happened between them. Had they broken it off and that was why Holly was with Cole? Rebound, or revenge? Or had they not broken it off and Gabe caught Holly and Cole and killed her in a jealous rage? Of course, that assumed my original theory of Holly and Cole being an item at all was correct. And what about the cat toy?

Lucas lifted Myron out of the sink and toweled him off. Myron hissed. His ears were flat. Lucas didn't seem fazed by this, which I loved. So many groomers didn't want to deal with cats, but he was clearly gifted. And fearless.

I didn't want to have lost my chance. Desperate to keep the conversation going any possible way, I blurted out, "I think Gabe is the guy who punched Cole out last night."

That caught his attention. He looked at me sharply. "You saw him there?"

"I saw his van speeding away when I went down the alley after him. And the guy's voice sounded kind of familiar, so I'm guessing I'm right. So the question is, was Gabe there that night?" I thought back to what I'd overheard. The voice I thought was Gabe's wanted to know what Cole saw. Which could mean either Gabe was there and wanted to know if anyone saw him, or hadn't been there and wanted to know who had been.

Lucas, meanwhile, was now staring at me as if he'd never seen me before. "You went down the alley after someone who'd just committed an assault? Why would you do that, Maddie?"

I tried a small smile to ease the tension, even though I felt more like throwing up than laughing. "I didn't think you still cared."

He didn't smile. "I'm not laughing. That whole thing last night was . . . not good. For a lot of reasons. This being probably the biggest one. You could've gotten hurt. Or worse."

"I know. I'm sorry. But I'm even sorrier that I upset you. Lucas . . ." I went over to him with the idea of grabbing his hands and looking deep into his eyes, convincing him to fall completely in love with me and forgive all my transgressions. But I'd forgotten about Myron. The phrase *angrier than a wet cat* had always seemed like just a figure of speech, but I was sadly misguided. Before I could even reach for Lucas's hand, Myron sensed the distraction and seized his chance, leaping from Lucas's arms like a cougar, using Lucas's chest as a springboard. I could see the blood from the scratches blooming under his white T-shirt. Guess they hadn't reached the nail-clipping portion of the program yet.

"Oh my God. Shoot. I'm so sorry. Here, let me put something on that." I spun around and yanked open a drawer, hoping for some antibiotic cream or something. I couldn't even do that right. All I could find was an old tube of toothpaste and some of Grandma's unfinished prescriptions. Helpless, I slammed the drawer shut. "Hang on, let me just run upstairs and get something to clean that . . ."

Lucas, to his credit, barely reacted. With hardly a wince,

he reached down and scooped up an unhappy Myron, whose great escape had been thwarted by the closed door. "Don't worry about it, Maddie," he said, and whatever opening I'd had vanished. "I need to get back to work, okay? We'll talk later."

And he turned away. Apparently he was done with me.

Chapter 44

Once Gigi returned and she and Grandpa assured me they would hold down the fort, I grabbed JJ and slunk upstairs to my room, locking myself in under the guise of work I needed to catch up on. I think JJ was a bit disgruntled at not being able to hang with his pals downstairs, but I was being selfish. I needed his company.

I had to get updates for the Web site over to my Webmaster—the guy Ethan and I used out in California for the juice shop—and formulate my social media strategy, which at the moment was basically called winging it. I had to put a deposit together with our revenues from this weekend, and try to do some cash flow estimates. I needed to work on the budget, and factor in Felicia. I also needed to get the money in order for Gabe's contracting services, although at this point I was a little worried that I'd hired either a murderer or an accomplice. Then I needed to get to work on the gala. And figure out what to do about Lucas. If there was anything left to do at all.

It all seemed daunting enough that I just wanted to crawl under my covers and cry.

But I put my chin up and got to work. I tried to push the whole mess out of my mind and spent the next couple hours sorting out the auction part of the hospital gala with Dad's point person, Charlotte. She was lovely and just needed direction. We put together a game plan and some names to help her get the rest of the auction items collected and she seemed much less likely to have a nervous breakdown. I gave her my mother's number and told her she'd be happy to help oversee the remaining tasks. That gave me a little bit of pleasure.

I'd made enough progress that when my phone rang just after lunch I was annoyed by the distraction. But I reached over and grabbed it. My dad.

"Maddie. I got your message about the caterer. That's wonderful news."

"Yes. The caterer," I said, remembering I needed to probably show up at today's meeting too. So much for not having to face people. "Meeting at three today. We've got it."

"Great," Dad said. "So which company is it?"

"Felicia Goodwin's."

A pause. "Felicia Goodwin?" he asked finally.

Same reaction as my mother. "Yes. Why? Something wrong?"

"No, it's just . . . how did you come across her?"

"She's helping us out here at the café, she's eager for work, and you needed someone by three today. What's the problem, Dad?"

He sighed. "I don't know if she's the best person for this, Maddie."

I gritted my teeth so hard I worried I'd chipped a couple. "Why on earth not? I've tasted her food. It's great." Granted, my tastings were limited to cinnamon buns, but if she could cook salmon or beef with half the same success, the event was in good hands. I was seriously getting annoyed now. Bad enough this got dumped on me, and now my father was going to make matters worse by micromanaging? I took a breath and reminded myself that my type A personality hadn't just dropped out of the sky. Cass would tell me we have to embrace the aspects of ourselves we might not like that other people mirror back to us.

Crap. I hadn't meditated today.

"I've had her food too," my dad said. "But she may not feel comfortable given that she's not a guest."

"I think if she cared, she would've said no. I get the sense she'd rather get paid than sit there and pretend to want to socialize. What's really going on, Dad?"

I heard him get up and close his door, then come back to his desk.

"Look. How much do you know about the Goodwins?"

Clearly not enough, and I hadn't realized the answer had been sitting under my nose the whole time in the form of my parents. "Just that she runs a catering business and doesn't get along with her daughter, who also volunteers for me and acts like she's on something half the time."

"Well. I don't know anything about that. But the Goodwins were pretty big names on the island. Michael Goodwin was on the hospital board for a while. Felicia was . . . typical of that crowd."

I knew what he meant. But I couldn't picture Felicia sitting around lunching and gossiping.

"Then about three years ago Michael died unexpectedly. Had a heart attack at the gym. But when he died, Felicia found out they were broke. Michael had made some bad investments, among other things, and, well, long story short once they paid for the funeral there wasn't much left. The daughter had to leave college and everything. It was . . . shocking to the family."

"I bet." Now the dysfunction kind of made sense. What a sad story. It had to have been a terrible shock for Felicia. And an embarrassment, especially if she was used to holding a certain level of status around town. This place could be quite fickle. Which was obvious by those women at the restaurant last night. Probably Felicia's old friends. I felt sorry for her all over again. And Gigi, who'd had to leave school because she was suddenly broke. Still, I wondered why she and her mother seemed to have so much animosity toward each other. "Dad, that's sad, but I think it underscores even more why she'd want the job. It pays well, I'm guessing. She's going to be out back cooking and running the kitchen. It's not like she'll be out in the mix with all the snobs who used to be her friends. I still don't see the problem."

"There were some problems," my dad said bluntly. "With her business. Specifically, with the Hawthornes."

"You don't believe in burying the lede at all, do you," I muttered.

"Excuse me?"

"Nothing. Newspaper talk. You can ask Becky about it. What happened with the Hawthornes?"

"She was catering a party for them last summer. Her daughter was working for her. Something happened with her that night—of course the details change with every telling. But apparently Heather Hawthorne fired them. Because of the daughter. She's apparently a bit unpredictable. It was quite the talk of the town."

"Thanks for telling me sooner, Dad. She's only working here. Plus I didn't know you got involved in all this crazy gossip."

"Believe me, I try not to. But these people are all part of the hospital. And Anne Marie loved to regale me with the latest tale. I'm sorry I didn't warn you. Truly. I don't think it fully registered with me that Gigi was your other volunteer. I've been distracted."

"It's okay, Dad." I sat back and tried to think. What exactly did he mean by *unpredictable*? Unpredictable enough to kill someone? Sometimes talking to my dad when it was a subject he wasn't comfortable with was like pulling teeth. "Okay. Well. I don't know what to tell you. You wanted my help, we've got Felicia. Unless she poisoned an entire party of people, I'm going to say we go with her. Speak now or forever hold your peace."

I could hear my dad's brain humming as he frantically weighed his options. Finally he sighed. "Make sure she makes the meeting today."

"I'm heading there myself to meet her."

I hung up, my own brain humming with this news. My dad could give Becky's society-page reporter a run for her money. His tidbits were interesting. And disturbing. Heather Hawthorne had fired Felicia, and Gigi was at the crux of it. What had she done? I wondered if Holly had been part of it too. And if they'd embarrassed Gigi enough, had she saved up her revenge until she had the perfect opportunity?

I called Becky as I was getting dressed for the hotel meeting. "Did you know Gigi Goodwin got her mother's company fired from catering for the Hawthornes?" I asked when she answered.

"Huh. No, I didn't. Then again, I'm not up on all that gossip," she said dryly. "I just try to report the news."

"Well. Apparently it was the talk of the town. Don't you read your own society pages? Plus it seems the result was Felicia being blackballed from all the fancy parties. Which explains why she was so hot to work for me. And why she cried when I asked her to cater my dad's gala."

"When you did what now?" Becky asked. "Why are you hiring people for your dad's gala?"

I sighed. "Long story. I can't get into it now because I have a meeting at the hotel where the gala is taking place."

"I don't even think I want to know," Becky said.

"You probably don't. But can you ask Jodi about it? Maybe she knows the details."

"Why do you want to know that?" Becky asked.

"Well, because if Gigi—or her mother—had a reason to want revenge on the Hawthornes, maybe they're the ones the cops should be looking at." That realization had just hit me too. What if Gigi and her mother had cooked up some scheme to kill Holly? Or both of the twins, and they just didn't get to the other one yet? A chill slid up my spine. What was it they said about all murders—they were driven by love, money, or revenge? This tale had the money and revenge components for sure.

"Maybe," Becky said slowly. "But I think it's a moot point. I mean, since I heard they are really close to an arrest. And you didn't hear that from me. It's not confirmed yet."

My heart nearly stopped. "You're kidding. Who? Adele?"

"My source didn't offer a name, but he seemed pretty sure things are about to break. Guess they got the evidence they need."

Chapter 45

"So how did the meeting go with Felicia and the hotel?" Ethan asked the next morning. We didn't open until one today, so he was sitting on the porch swing with his cup of coffee, taking in the sight of the ocean glittering just beyond our backyard.

I took a moment to drink in the view and the scent of the salt air myself, then went and sat next to him, wrapping my hands around my own coffee. I'd briefed Ethan yesterday on the conversation with my dad, and my renewed concerns about Gigi. And now Felicia. Although I didn't want to let one gossipy conversation by some mean women change my mind about her when I hadn't even given her a chance yet. Still, it felt better to talk it through with Ethan.

Our conversation had been polite, but we never strayed from the topic at hand. I probably shouldn't have voiced my concerns about him and Val. After all, he was probably just being Ethan—helpful and caring. And now I'd made things weird between us. Apparently socially awkward had become my new norm.

I pushed those worries aside and tried to act like nothing odd had happened. "It went well, actually. Felicia sounded very competent. She's got people lined up to help serve, she already has a menu thought out, and it sounds like it's going to be fine." I hesitated. "She did tell me she's going to ask Gigi to help out. Said she wants to get her back working for her. I tried to get her to tell me why they stopped working together, but we kept getting interrupted. I feel like I have to know though. For the sake of my dad and the gala."

"People try to protect their kids as much as possible." Ethan touched his foot down and set the swing rocking gently back and forth. "And they give them lots of chances."

"I wonder how much she's going to need to protect her from," I said softly.

Ethan frowned. "What do you mean?"

I sighed. "Ethan. What if this thing with the Hawthornes was more than just a misunderstanding, or a spilled glass of wine? What if Gigi used her mother's business as a way to get in there and get some kind of cat-fueled revenge on Holly and it went really wrong?" We were both silent as we thought about that.

"Maddie. Are you seriously concerned about Gigi?"

"I'm concerned about a lot of things relating to this mess. But yes, Gigi is one of them."

"Do you think we should let her stay on here?" Ethan asked finally. "I mean, if you're worried about her . . . state of mind?"

"I thought about that too. But I feel like that could really have an adverse effect on her. She likes it here." And though I didn't say it out loud, I felt a little bit like I owed it to Adele to keep an eye on her. Adele had taken her under her wing, however misguided, and now she was indisposed.

It sure sounded like, from what Becky said, she was in big trouble. Even if they hadn't named her, who else could it be? Unless they'd been working a whole other angle to this case and had a surprise up their sleeves.

"You're not responsible for her," Ethan said, as if he'd read my mind.

"I know. But I feel bad for her."

We both turned as a van, followed by two cars, pulled into the driveway. Gabe and his crew. I'd almost forgot they were coming over today to start working. I was surprised, given the Adele situation, but then again I understood he needed to raise the money for her defense.

"Is that the contractor?" Ethan asked.

"Yeah. I may have forgotten to mention he wants to get started right away."

"That's good. Is he going to work around the café hours?" Ethan asked.

"With the really noisy stuff, yes. And once the season winds down it will be easier. I figure he'll start the brunt of the work once September rolls around. Right now they need to do prep work and all that."

Ethan nodded. "Makes sense."

I hoped it did. Part of me still wondered if Gabe was really the bad guy here. The problem was, there were potentially a lot of bad guys here. I mean, Gigi clearly had some issues—and some issues with the Hawthornes—but that scene with Gabe and Cole in the alley had been incredibly suspect. And given what Lucas had said about Gabe and Holly . . .

But that also strengthened the case against Adele. Because if her favorite nephew was dating a woman she despised, that could only bring problems to the family. Would she have taken measures that extreme to keep Holly away from him?

By the time Gabe got out of his van and reached the porch, I was on the verge of calling the whole construction project off until this got sorted out. I didn't need any more drama at my café.

"Morning," he said, trying to sounding chipper despite the fact that he looked, once again, exhausted.

"Morning," Ethan said, looking curiously at me when I just stared at Gabe.

"Hi. Yes, good morning," I said when I realized everyone was waiting for me to talk. "How are you, um, how are you doing?"

Gabe shrugged, eyes dropping to my porch floor. "Had better days. But work will take my mind off it, I hope."

"Yeah. About that." I took a deep breath. "Gabe, do you think we should postpone this for a bit? Until things are a bit more . . . squared away? Maybe until after Labor Day?"

Ethan was staring at me like I had five heads. And Gabe's face fell even lower than it already was. But the more I heard myself talking, the more I convinced myself it was the best thing for right now. There was too much going on, and what if Gabe *was* involved in this murder? Selfishly, I didn't want him ripping holes in Grandpa's house and then getting hauled off to jail. I also didn't need the police coming here to arrest him and turning this place into another circus.

"Postpone it?" he repeated. "Why? Maddie, if you're worried about disruption I'm well aware how to work this so your operations aren't disturbed."

"I'm sure you are," I assured him. "It's me. My planning was poor. I should've waited until we'd wrapped up the last few weeks of the summer season. And now I have another project that's going to take me away from things this week, so the timing is just bad. Is it possible to work your schedule so we start in early September?"

He was mad. I could tell by the tightening of his jaw, the vein that pulsed in the side of his neck. His fist, unconsciously closing and releasing at his side. I watched him curiously. Was he about to show me a different side of himself? A side that maybe killed his girlfriend in a jealous rage?

The three of us hung there in limbo for a long moment, while around us the island hummed to life. Gabe's workers stood in the driveway around the cars, drinking coffee and laughing. Two dogs barked at each other from opposite sides of the street. I heard the ferry's horn in the distance as it prepared to dock and deliver a crowd of people onto our island. Above me, the sun beat down, already hotter than Hades.

Finally, Gabe seemed to pull it together. He nodded, his hand at his side. "Fine," he said. "But I'll still need to do some prep work so we're ready to start right after Labor Day. Anything past that and my schedule is already set, and then I don't know when I'll be able to get to you."

"Understood. That's perfect. Thank you, Gabe," I said.

He nodded curtly. "I'm going to pick up some supplies and bring them back, then."

"That's fine."

He turned and went down to the driveway, conferred briefly with his people, then they went around the side of the house.

Ethan looked at me. "You sure about this?"

I exhaled. "I'm not sure of anything except there's enough insanity going on around here right now. I don't really want to add to it. I'm not sure of Gabe's involvement in this murder, Ethan. Honestly? I'm not sure of anyone's involvement. And it's starting to really freak me out."

I faltered as Gabe came back around and motioned to me. I hurried down the porch steps. But before he could ask me whatever he was going to ask me, his phone rang. He answered it, turning away from me. But I clearly heard him say, "What happened?" and "When?"

Then, he abruptly hung up and looked at me. "I have to go. I'll be in touch."

Then he jumped in his van and peeled out in a move oddly reminiscent of the night at the restaurant.

Chapter 46

Despite the murder, the gala, and Gabe's odd behavior, I still had litter boxes to clean. I left Ethan on the porch and went to fetch one of the forty-pound boxes of litter I kept stashed out on the back porch. I hefted the litter box and hustled through the door, almost knocking Gigi over on her way in.

"Oh. Hi," she said, wringing her hands together. "I was coming to get that."

"You were? Brilliant. I love you. Here, I'll bring it in." I lugged the box into the café. The girl didn't look like she could carry this. In fact, she looked like she might fall over if a strong enough wind came through the island. But I didn't have time to worry about her right now. I was curious about Gabe's phone call. Did it have to do with his aunt? Had they arrested her yet? I needed to talk to Grandpa.

I dropped the litter in the middle of the floor and turned to Gigi. "You take those boxes, I'll take these," I said, waving to the left side of the room. "You want something to drink?"

Gigi shook her head and got to work. We got into a good rhythm, and we actually finished in record time. Either that or the cats hadn't been too messy last night. Whatever the reason, I was grateful. "Are you going to hang around today to man the open hours?" I asked her.

She nodded. "I love doing that. And lots of people are filling out applications too."

"I saw the pile. It's great." I had to start answering them too. But then Grandpa walked in the door. He blew me a kiss, then headed for the basement.

I turned to Gigi. "Can you take over for a bit? I need to talk to Grandpa."

She nodded. I followed him downstairs.

"Grandpa," I called. "I need to talk to you for a minute."

He turned expectantly as he reached his desk. "Morning, doll. What's going on?"

I sank into a chair and propped my feet up on the other chair. "Everything. Did they arrest Adele?"

He hesitated. "What have you heard?"

"I haven't heard anything. But Gabe got a phone call and tore out of here, so I assumed it was something bad. And I heard . . . something might happen today."

"Ah." Grandpa nodded. "I forgot you have your own sources. Anyway, there's a bit more to it than that. Yes, she's been arrested. But Maddie—she confessed."

My feet dropped to the floor and I sat back, stunned. "She *what*?"

"Confessed. To the murder. That's why they arrested her. And she backed it up with a lot of knowledge about how Holly actually died, even though they didn't release that information publicly."

The hits just kept coming. "But, Grandpa. Why? She's been saying all along that she's innocent, that she's going to get blamed for something she didn't do. How could she confess?" I pushed myself to my feet and paced the room, trying to work this out in my mind. Adele had not seemed like she was putting me on that morning when I went to her house. She'd seemed genuinely distraught. And scared.

"Maddie, maybe it's time to face the fact that she did it," he said grimly. "People don't just confess to murders because they want to learn about our justice system."

I shook my head. "No way. I don't buy it. Grandpa, listen. I have a lot to tell you. I've been thinking, and there are so many scenarios." I filled him in on the Cole situation at the restaurant the other night, and how I thought the other guy might've been Gabe.

"Maybe Gabe had something to do with it and Adele found out. And she's trying to protect him? She would totally think Holly's life wasn't worth him losing the rest of his own over it. And then there's Cole. I'm sorry, but something about the Cole piece of this isn't sitting well with me. He could've been involved with either of them. They all had something to lose."

Grandpa frowned at me. "Why didn't you tell me about Cole earlier? This was Tuesday night, you said?"

I nodded. "I'm sorry. I had a lot on my mind. And I didn't want Val to know, and I figured if I told you I'd have to end up telling her."

"That's a bad reason, Maddie."

"I know. Apparently I can't make any good choices lately," I muttered. "But Grandpa, this doesn't add up. And then there's Gigi. And . . . her mother." I had to tell him all of it. Every crazy idea that had been floating through my head. If anyone could help make sense of it, it was Grandpa. And with four or five other viable suspects to Holly's murder, I couldn't just sit back and accept that Adele had killed her.

Even if something had caused her to confess.

"Gigi and her mother? What about them?"

I told him my theory about Gigi's altercation with the Hawthornes, after what I'd heard from those women, and my dad. "Either she or her mother could've been hell-bent on revenge. If the Hawthornes were messing with their business?"

"But you said Heather's name was mentioned as the one who did the firing?"

I hesitated. "Yes. That's what I heard."

"Then why kill Holly?"

"Aren't they interchangeable?" I threw up my hands. "I don't know, Grandpa. But with Adele adding fuel to the fire, especially if Gigi told her what happened, who knows. Gigi could've gone right off the rails. And maybe Adele feels bad because she kind of took her under her wing. And didn't Adele say she gave some of the mice to Gigi and Katrina before she brought them over for the opening?"

Grandpa listened intently to my theories. I loved that about him. Even if he thought they were ridiculous, he still listened. "So if you had to put money on someone today," he said slowly. "Who would it be?"

I took my time answering the question. As much as I wanted to say Cole, that wasn't the first answer that came to my mind. Heather, Cole, Gabe—they all seemed like reasonable choices given what I knew. But my gut was screaming at me that this had something to do with the Goodwins' catering business.

But what, I hadn't figured out yet. "We need more time," I said. "They can't just close the case, can they?"

Grandpa sighed. "Doll. You know as well as I do that once they have someone in custody, it's over. Now, I don't disagree that this new development with Adele seems very out of the blue. But I don't think it matters, unfortunately. The only thing they wanted was to hear someone say the magic words. And now she's said them. As far as they're concerned, it's over."

Chapter 47

The news broke a few hours later. The Daybreak Harbor Police Department announced that they'd officially made an arrest in the Holly Hawthorne murder case. Adele Barrows was in custody. Case closed. That's all, folks.

My mom always had a sixth sense about her family, and when things weren't going well. Whatever she knew about what was going on, in true mom fashion, she organized an impromptu family dinner and insisted we all go—me, Val, Grandpa, and Ethan. She wanted to make sure we were all okay, she said. While I didn't doubt that, I trusted in her ability to wrangle a few details about the Holly Hawthorne case. Also, I suspected Dad wanted to interrogate me about gala progress. I did have good news to report, but I also knew he was worried about the whole Felicia thing. Plus, Val was still mad at me about the whole stupid gala thing. Which I couldn't quite wrap my head around.

But when she wasn't downstairs half an hour before we were supposed to be there, I was elected by Grandpa to go up and get her. Grudgingly I trudged up to the third floor.

"Ready?" I asked from the doorway. "We have to leave."

"I don't want to go," Val declared from the bed, where she sat cross-legged flipping through a magazine. She wore a Fleetwood Mac T-shirt that had seen better days and a pair of jean shorts with holes in them.

"You have to."

"No I don't."

I felt around in my pocket to see if I'd grabbed my phone, then turned to my sister with a sigh. "Val. Mom won't let you off the hook. You know this. Why waste the time and energy arguing with me about it?"

Val tossed the magazine aside. "Cole's been calling me."

I sank down next to her, my heart sinking with me. "And?"

She shrugged. "He wants me to come home."

"So you're going."

"I didn't say that," Val said slowly. "I'm not sure yet."

I looked at her. "You're not?"

She shook her head slowly. "No. Because I still can't get a good answer out of him about what he was doing at that house that night." Val picked at her cuticle. "And I think he owes me an answer to that, don't you?"

I nodded slowly. "I would want one."

"Yeah. Well, he doesn't think he needs to provide one. So we're kind of at a stalemate."

"So you're not going back yet, then?"

She shook her head. "Not today, anyway."

"Oh. Well. That's good," I said.

She gave me a funny look. "Good?"

"You know what I mean," I said, hoping she wouldn't push the issue. "Anyway. We need to go. Mom's expecting us. Grandpa and Ethan are waiting." I got up and headed to the door.

"Ethan's coming?" Val asked, sitting up.

I turned around and looked at her. She sounded perkier at this bit of news. "Yeah. Is that okay?"

"Of course. I mean, if he wants to. But I guess I should go change. What time are we supposed to be there?" She was already up and heading for her closet before I could answer.

Fifteen minutes later we all piled into Grandma's car. Grandpa insisted on driving. I sat up front with him, JJ on my lap. Ethan and Val were in the back. "This will be fun," Grandpa said brightly, glancing at Val in the rearview mirror. "Right, Valerie?"

"Sure," she said.

I glanced behind me in time to catch Ethan watching my sister.

When we got to Mom and Dad's, it was already a full house. Dad was home early from work and already changed, attempting to help Mom in the kitchen. Which meant she was spending more time trying to get him out of the kitchen than getting dinner ready. Grandpa immediately went to intervene. My youngest sister, Sam, was in the living room. She had some guy with her who I'd never seen before. He wore some kind of flowy pants and had bare feet and a shaved head. He may or may not have been stoned. Val took one look at him and, in typical Val fashion, rolled her eyes in disapproval. Even with everything going on she was still kind of a snob.

I elbowed her. "Be nice. You know Sam always finds her fellow free spirits." I led Ethan into the living room and plopped on the couch, setting JJ on the floor next to me. "Hey Sam." I smiled at her friend and offered my hand. "Maddie. This is Ethan."

He nodded at us and shook our hands. "Jeremiah."

"We met at a sound healing retreat," Sam said. "Jeremiah does amazing things with singing bowls." She gazed at him adoringly.

"Maddie! Ethan! Good to see you." My dad came in, beaming at us. "Shall we sit? It's about time for dinner. So Maddie, how's the gala planning going?"

"Fine, Dad. Charlotte's got her marching orders for the

auction and Mom's helping her. They're moving along nicely. She sent me an e-mail today."

"Dinner," Mom announced as she and Val brought the food in and set it in the middle of the table. It wasn't lost on me that Val took the seat next to Ethan. That was when I noticed there was an extra place setting at the table.

"Who else is coming?" I had a moment's panic that they'd invited Craig or something in a pathetic attempt to get us together. Or Lucas. Would they have invited Lucas, not knowing that I'd managed to tank things?

But my parents exchanged glances. Nervous ones. "What's going on?" I asked.

"We may have some company for dinner. But it's not definite yet," my mother hastened to add, looking to my dad for help.

"What company?" I pressed. "What's the big secret?"

Val passed the plate of tofu around. My mother was still on a vegan kick. My father had grudgingly accepted it. Jeremiah spooned a heaping portion onto his plate, his expression radiant.

"Well." My father clasped his hands together. "Mira Tanner called today."

The plate of potatoes Val held crashed onto the table. Tiny roasted potatoes rolled around madly. Ethan jumped up and began spooning them back into their plate.

"Please don't tell me . . ." Her voice cracked and she swallowed, trying desperately to compose herself. "Mom. Dad. You didn't invite her over."

"We actually didn't," my mother said. "She asked for you and I told her you weren't here. She said she knew you weren't staying at your house. I didn't tell her where you were staying, but told her you'd be here tonight. She said she'd like to stop by."

"Mom." I shook my head. "Why?"

"I figured it was better if she came when we were all

here. Better than if she cornered Val somewhere alone," my mother said. "I'm willing to be polite. You are still married," she pointed out to Val. "But honey. Of course you know if she steps out of line in any way she'll be escorted out of the house."

"And unfortunately, she's on the hospital board," Dad added. "So I'm obligated to be somewhat polite in that capacity as well."

Val's face had gone so white I was afraid she'd pass out. Without a word, she fled out of the room. I heard a door slam upstairs.

The rest of the table had gone completely still. Grandpa's face had slid into cop mode, which I've realized is a defense mechanism for him when he's uncomfortable. Sam's gaze bored into her plate. Only Jeremiah seemed unfazed. He speared a rogue potato and popped it into his mouth.

"Delicious," he said, smiling at my mother.

And then the doorbell rang.

Chapter 48

I was torn between wanting to stay and see what would happen and wanting to go upstairs and check on Val. My mother hurried to the door. I barely registered Ethan slipping out of his chair at the same time, I was so distracted. I looked at my father. "Bad idea, Dad," I said.

He nodded. "I'm afraid she was very persistent."

"Mom doesn't usually let people push her around like that," I said. "How'd this lady manage it?"

Before he could answer, my mother returned with Cole's mother in tow. What a big wuss that guy was. Seriously. Sending his mommy to fight his battles? He made me sick.

His mother reminded me of Emily Gilmore of *Gilmore Girls,* one of my favorite shows of all time. The difference was I loved to hate Emily on the show because the actress was so great. Mira Tanner actually thought this was an appropriate way to act in real life.

Her eyes scanned the room when she entered, landing on my mother. "I thought you said she'd be here," she said, without bothering to say hello to any of us.

My father rose. "Mira. We've set a place for you. We've just begun dinner. Please, sit."

She looked like she'd rather jump in the ocean fully

clothed, but she did. She sat in Ethan's chair, which is how I noticed he hadn't returned in all the commotion.

"We're having marinated tofu with stir-fry veggies," my mother said brightly. "And roasted potatoes. What can I get you to drink?"

I had to nearly chew my tongue off to keep my mouth shut. Why was my mother pandering to this insane woman? Deep down I knew they were trying not to cause more problems for Val than she already had, but it still seemed crazy. Sophie James didn't let herself be cowed by anyone, never mind someone like Mira Tanner. And there was the small matter of her being on my dad's board, which definitely complicated things. But I let it play out, fascinated to see what would happen next.

"I really don't need anything," Mira said, clearly horrified at the thought of eating tofu. "I'd just like to speak to my daughter-in-law for a few moments. My son is distraught, and this unpleasantness needs to stop."

This, I was thankful to see, gave my mother pause. Her smile dropped, her eyes narrowed, and she leaned forward in her chair. "*Your son* is distraught?" she repeated. Her tone was still pleasant, but I knew what was coming. Sam did too. I could see her holding her breath.

Mira looked at my mother like she might at someone who had clearly escaped from an asylum. "Well, of course he is. His wife has vanished and shown him no support whatsoever. Not to mention, she's been out with other men during his time of need. It's quite distasteful." She glanced at my father now. "I would've thought, at least with *your* standing, Brian, that she would've been counseled to behave a bit better."

The implication being that my father had a respectable job and position in the community, and made enough money that he deserved some respect. Whereas it was clearly a slight to my mother, with her gypsy skirts and scarf tied around her unruly curls, who made no secret around the island that she still loved to live a bit of a bohemian lifestyle, doing what she wanted, designing scarves and clothing for her Etsy site one day and writing a mystery novel the next. If Val hadn't married her son, Mira Tanner wouldn't have given my mother a second look if she'd been on the ground in the middle of the street during rush hour.

"Now, you wait a minute," Grandpa Leo said indignantly, at the same time my father said, "Mira, that was uncalled for."

But my mother had clearly exhausted her efforts to remain pleasant and open-minded. All pretenses of happy hostess had fled. She rose slowly from her chair so she stood over Mira Tanner. Even Jeremiah, intent on the tofu and potatoes up to this point, could sense the atmospheric change in the room and watched with wide eyes.

"You really do have some nerve," my mother said quietly. "You're in *my* house, speaking about *my* daughter. Who had the unfortunate urge to marry *your* son, who lied to her, was out at another woman's house, and was in or near the vicinity when this woman was murdered. And you're telling me *he's* distraught? My daughter should've filed for divorce that night, if you want my opinion on the matter. And I don't recall Cole being keen on explaining himself. So you can spin this all you want, Mira, but the reality is, your son is not worthy of my daughter, and if anything good has come out of this mess, it's that now she's maybe realized that. Now. If you don't want anything to eat, you should go. I don't think Valerie is in the mood to discuss this with you."

Mira's perfect red lips thinned until they about disappeared. Clearly she wasn't used to being spoken to that way. I could barely hide my smile. My mom hadn't let us down after all.

Mira rose slowly from her chair and straightened her dress.

"I'm very sorry you feel that way," she said, her tone haughty. "Clearly your family has never appreciated the partnership with our family. Surprising, especially since Erik had to . . . assist with Leo's troubles so recently." She glanced at Grandpa, a triumphant look on her face.

That was too much for me. I jumped up. "Hey. You leave my grandpa out of this. Your son is more in need of his daddy's services than Grandpa ever was."

The entire room was silent. Even Mira. I was silent too. I'd surprised myself with that last bit, but I had to admit it felt pretty darn good to tell her off.

She, however, didn't appear to feel good about it. But for once had nothing to say. If this was a sci-fi flick, I would've been vaporized by the lasers of death coming out of her eyes.

"I'll see myself out," she said coldly. And she strode out of the dining room before anyone else could even react. We heard the front door slam a minute later.

We all looked at each other. Then my mother reached across the table and high-fived me. "You saved me from having to punch her out," she said.

"And me from having to arrest her," Grandpa grumbled.

"You're not a cop anymore," Sam pointed out.

He turned his level gaze on her. "So? I still have handcuffs."

"I appreciate the celebration," my father said dryly, "but unfortunately I need the Tanners—and the Hawthornes—to not boycott my hospital gala. Or have me fired. In case you'd forgotten, Sophie."

My mother made a face. "They won't boycott it. It would look bad." She enunciated the last words with air quotes. "And they wouldn't fire you. Everyone loves you.

And the rest of the board would laugh them out of the room. Besides, what would you have me do? Let her insult our daughter and my father?" My mother's voice had turned dangerously cold. "This gala is really important to you, I guess."

"Sophie. Of course I wouldn't let her insult our family. But we could have perhaps handled that differently."

"Differently?" my mother said, almost hissing the word.

I hadn't witnessed a lot of fights between my parents over the years. Not because they hid it from us, but because they very rarely fought. But when they did, it wasn't pretty. It seemed this might be one of those times.

And I didn't really want to see it. Plus, I had a feeling I might be dragged into this, since I'd delivered the parting shot.

"I'm going to check on Val," I said, and fled upstairs. No one noticed I was leaving, except Sam, who shot me a helpless look. I ignored her.

Upstairs, I went to Val's old room. The door was closed so I figured she was in there. Without bothering to knock, I opened the door and poked my head in.

And had to blink to make sure I wasn't seeing things. But no, the vision was still the same when I opened them again.

Val and Ethan. Kissing.

Chapter 49

Saturday morning, and my first Pet Pantry on Wheels run. Katrina had left me a message last night, during the disastrous dinner at my parents' house, to make sure I was still on board. Well, I hardly had a choice. Her exact message had been, "I'm sending someone over with the food. We'll load it into whatever car is in the driveway."

Which had been Grandpa's truck, because we'd all gone to Mom's in Grandma's car. At least she'd made it easy for me. I was actually kind of glad for the distraction today. Good thing she'd called, too, because I probably would've forgotten all about it.

I hopped into the truck and placed JJ next to me. He'd love this. Visiting people and being adored was high on his list of favorite adventures.

I'd managed to get out of the house without seeing anyone. Which was a blessing, because I had no idea how to address what I'd seen last night. My married sister and my business partner. Kissing. Oy. As if this crazy situation couldn't get any worse. I had no idea what to even think about it. At one point I'd wondered if I really had seen it, or if my brain had been so overloaded it was playing tricks on me. I wasn't even sure Val and Ethan realized I'd seen

them either. I'd managed to pull the door shut pretty quietly. The only noise I made, in fact, was when I tripped
and fell halfway down the stairs. But I recovered quickly
and went to hide in the bathroom for a few minutes. The
drive home had been silent, with Grandpa making a few
attempts at jokes that fell flat. When we'd arrived, everyone had retreated to their corners and the house had gone
completely silent.

Thank God I could get out for a while this morning.

I pulled into the first coffee shop drive-through I found
and ordered a large black coffee. It wasn't the day for anything fancy. I just needed a clear head for once. As I waited
for my order, I studied the note Katrina had left, which de-
tailed the stops and what I was dropping off at each. I figured I'd start at the westernmost point of the island, in
Fisherman's Point, to beat the traffic, and do the Daybreak
Harbor stops last, since I had to be back at the café by
eleven to open. I plugged the address into my Google maps
app, turned up the radio, and hit the road.

I pulled up to the first stop about forty minutes later. It
was in one of the island's only trailer parks on the far west
side of town. The little old couple were waiting anxiously
on the run-down porch with their dog, a beautiful golden
retriever. They thanked me profusely for the month's worth
of food I gave them, and hugged me a few times before I
went back to the truck. I told myself it was allergies when
my eyes blurred as I drove away, watching the golden's tail
wagging in my rearview mirror.

By the time I got to the third stop in Turtle Point, my
heart was full and I hadn't thought about any of the mad-
ness in the last two hours. The house I pulled up to was
small, with a tidy yard and flowers blooming in pots on
the porch. A smattering of pansies circled the mailbox. I
got the delivery—two boxes of wet cat food and a bag of
dry food—out of the truck and went to the door.

A woman about my age answered. She was dressed in gym shorts and a T-shirt. I could hear music playing behind her.

I smiled. "Hi. I'm Maddie with the Pet Pantry on Wheels. I have your food."

"Oh! Thank you. Come on in." She swung the door open. "I'm Crystal. You can just drop it in the hall."

I placed the boxes down. A black cat appeared seemingly from out of nowhere, twining his long, slinky body around my legs.

"Jack! Manners," she scolded.

"It's fine. I love cats. My guy is in the truck." I motioned outside, where JJ lounged against the open window, sniffing away. "I run the new cat café in Daybreak Harbor."

Crystal lit up. "You're Maddie James! I've been dying to go." Her smile faltered. "Although my funds are pretty limited these days. Hence the charity." She waved at the food, clearly embarrassed about whatever situation had brought her to ask for the help. "I lost my job on the mainland. So I'm trying to figure out my next move and picking up work around the island to pay the mortgage for now. Stinks."

"I'm sorry," I said. "But I'm not here to judge you. Katrina set up this program to help people who need it. We're not here to decide who's worthy or not."

Crystal blinked furiously, trying to hide the tears. "Thank you. I'm so appreciative. And once I'm back on my feet I want to help."

"No problem," I said uncomfortably. "Listen, feel free to come by the café whenever you want. On the house. Good for a cup of coffee and a muffin too."

"Really? That's so sweet of you. But you don't have to—"

"I know I don't. But the café is supposed to make people happy, aside from taking care of cats. It's not really there to rake in tons of cash." I grinned and handed her a card from my pocket. "Just e-mail me here and tell me when you want to come. I'll save you a spot."

She clutched the card. "Thank you. Really."

"No worries. What kind of work do you do?" I wondered if I could hook her up with some kind of job.

"I worked in marketing up in Boston. But everyone's cutting back. So now I'm waitressing. I picked up a gig at Saltwater, though, so that's been helping. The tips there are way better than the other places I've worked, even though it doesn't come close to a corporate salary."

Saltwater. The place I'd been with Lucas Tuesday night.

"Really," I said, trying to sound casual. "How long have you been there?"

"I guess about six weeks."

"Were you there Tuesday night by any chance?"

"Tuesday." Crystal thought for a minute, then lit up. "Yes! That was the crazy night where there was a big fight outside." She looked at me curiously. "You heard about that?"

"I was there," I said.

"Oh wow. Yeah, that was crazy. I felt kind of bad for Cole."

My heart skipped. "You know Cole?"

She nodded. "Just through the restaurant. He comes in on the weekends with his girlfriend. Seems like a nice guy."

His girlfriend? Could she mean Holly? "Who's his girlfriend?" I asked casually.

"I don't know her name. She's older than him though. You can kinda tell." She looked immediately apologetic for saying that. "Sorry, do you know Cole?"

"Um, yeah. Kind of," I said. "We went to high school together." It wasn't a total lie. "So, older, huh?"

"Yeah. Probably ten years, maybe more. I mean, I don't care. I don't even know why I mentioned it."

"So it wasn't . . . the woman who died last weekend?"

Now Crystal looked at me like she was worried about my mental health. Which she potentially should be.

"Died?" she repeated. "I have no idea. I didn't know anyone died."

Apparently her newspaper subscription had been one of the first things to go with her new budget. Either that or she really didn't get out much.

"Never mind," I muttered. "Good luck with your job search." I fled out to the truck.

Chapter 50

I headed toward Daybreak, grabbing my phone out of the console with one hand and scrolling for Becky's number with one eye on the road. When she answered, I blurted out, "I just talked to someone who said Cole's girlfriend is older than him."

A pause. "Sorry?"

"Holly didn't look older than him. Holly looked like she'd had enough plastic surgery that she looked like a . . . really weird twenty-year-old. Who is Cole's girlfriend?"

"Maddie. I have no idea what you're talking about and I'm kind of busy—"

"I know. Adele confessed. You're going to be busy for a while with that," I muttered. "But listen. I was just doing the Pet Pantry on Wheels run and I delivered food to a waitress who works at the place where Cole got punched out the other night." I filled her in on the rest of the conversation.

"Hmm. That's interesting," Becky said. "So he wasn't seeing Holly, but he did have a girlfriend."

"It sounds like it. What do I do with that?"

Becky thought for a second. "I could go back to Jodi and see what comes up on the guest list from the party that night that Holly was killed. If Cole was there, he probably brought his girlfriend, unless he was cheating on her, too, with Holly."

"Not funny, but entirely plausible," I said. "Yeah, if you could look that would be great. Thanks, Becky." I hung up and refocused on my GPS. I needed to plow through the rest of these deliveries and get back to the café.

I finished my rounds and made it back in time to do a quick check of everything before I opened. Ethan and Gigi had covered the morning shift while I completed the duties of my third job. Ethan had set up a nice spread of Felicia's food, which included some chocolate puff pastry that nearly made me swoon when I bit into it. Otherwise, the house was quiet.

I wanted to ask Ethan where Val was, but I didn't think it wise to open that can of worms. So I slunk into a corner and wondered what was going to blow up next.

When my phone rang a few minutes later, Becky's number flashed on the screen. I glanced around to make sure the guests were occupied, then slipped into one of the rooms earmarked for construction.

"Hey," I said.

"So an interesting thing," Becky said without prelude. "Jodi got the guest list for the party and one of the names on it sounded familiar. I remember reading a blurb from the cop logs the other night with this name. So I checked with my cops reporter, and apparently there was an incident at Holly and Heather Hawthorne's house. A couple hours before Holly's body was called in. They called the police on some guy with the same last name as a woman on the guest list."

"Okay. What does that mean?"

"Well. A woman named Diane LaPlante was a guest. A man named Sean LaPlante apparently showed up unannounced at the house and 'created a disturbance,' according to the report. Holly called the police on him. Or Heather. One of them."

"So . . . who is Diane LaPlante?" I was thoroughly confused.

"I have no idea. A friend of the Hawthornes, I guess. Jodi wasn't sure. Thought I would pass it along in case it means something. And, Jodi remembered the story about Gigi and the Hawthornes. The big firing. Something about Gigi taking food out of the kitchen for the cats during some fancy party. Heather caught her and lost it. She made a huge deal, claiming unclean food practices, and called the board of health on them. Guess it got pretty ugly."

"Wow. So Felicia and Gigi had a really big bone to pick with her," I said slowly.

"Sounds like it. Look, I gotta go back to work."

I hung up and thought about all this. Then I called Grandpa's cell phone. Ten minutes later we had a plan. I sat back and watched the clock move more slowly than it ever had.

Chapter 51

After the café closed around three, I drove to meet Grandpa at our designated meeting spot—the beach. Ever since I was a kid, Grandpa's place had been the beach. He went there for everything—to relax, to think, sometimes to brood. He always went there when he needed to work out something particularly troubling. And now that he was retired, I guess he came here to do his work.

When I pulled in with Grandma's car, I had to laugh. Grandpa waited for me in his truck, dressed all in black, complete with Jack Bauer-style sunglasses. "I think you missed your calling," I said, sliding in next to him. "You should've been an FBI agent. Or some kind of fancy undercover cop."

"Nah. I liked being in charge too much." He flipped open a small notebook. "Diane LaPlante. She works with Heather Hawthorne. She's Heather's boss, to be exact. And it appears Ms. LaPlante has been coming down to the island most weekends this summer. Staying at the Hawthornes' house."

I frowned. "So she's a dead end."

Grandpa shook his head. "Not exactly. She's not coming down here for the sea air and some quality time with her star employee."

"Wait! She's Cole's girlfriend," I said as it dawned on me. "The older woman."

"'Fraid so."

"And her husband is Sean, I'm presuming?"

"Right again. He must've finally decided enough was enough and came down to confront her."

"The same night Holly ends up dead." I blew out a breath and slumped in my seat. "Do you think Holly was the one who outed them in the first place? That would give him cause to kill her."

"That I don't know, but she sure saved him by calling the cops. I heard things were on their way to getting violent."

"So what about Heather? Maybe she was mad that her sister called the cops and her boss's husband got hauled away to jail? Maybe she thought it would reflect badly on her at work?"

"I'm sure she thought all of those things. But once the cops took him away, she whisked her boss away somewhere. Didn't come back to the house at all that night. And Holly was still standing when they left. And after getting threatened to within an inch of his life, I heard Cole went upstairs to hide."

"But he stuck around," I said.

Grandpa nodded. "Probably his knees were shaking too hard to walk."

I digested this. "You've been busy, Grandpa. Should I ask about the detective work that led to this wealth of information?" I tried to keep my tone light, but I was still concerned about all of this.

Grandpa shook his head. "Nope. Private investigators are like journalists. We don't reveal our sources."

"I see."

"Cole didn't kill anyone, Maddie. He's too stupid. And passive. Now I'm just concerned for your sister. I want her to see this guy for who he is so we can get her out of the situation. The sooner the better."

I agreed with that, but I still wasn't convinced Adele was the killer. There was still Gabe, Gigi, and Felicia to consider. But Grandpa must be really worried about Val to support going after Cole like this. "Fine. Have you talked to Val since last night?"

He shook his head. "No. But I feel like Cole is about to turn all the charm on to get her back. And I worry that she's susceptible to his BS."

I wasn't so sure of that, given how cozy she and Ethan had looked last night, but I kept that to myself too.

"He has been trying to call her. But she told me she hasn't taken his calls. So where's Cole now?"

"At his and Val's house. I followed him there earlier."

I hid a smile. I could just picture Grandpa tailing Cole all over the island, documenting his every move. And Cole was not smart enough to catch on. "Perfect. I'm going to talk to him."

"What are you going to say?"

"I'm not totally sure yet. But I'll think of something." I wasn't being entirely truthful. I did know what I was going to say to Cole, but Grandpa would probably try to steer me to a different tactic. I could picture him wanting to run this like one of his SWAT team takedowns, with a rehearsed script and a backup plan in place.

He didn't look convinced. I needed to distract him. "You didn't just find all this out since I called you. How long have you know about this woman?"

Grandpa shrugged. "I have my ways, Mads. I haven't lost my touch." He winked. "Also, a couple of Patriots season tickets in the hands of the right people can help."

Chapter 52

I drove to my sister's house, my anger mounting with each mile marker. Who did this guy think he was, cheating on my sister? I wondered if that was the example his father set. Get married, have the nice house, the outward picture of happiness, but then do whatever you want to do while things collapsed from the inside out. No wonder Mira Tanner seemed so . . . sour.

I pulled up and parked on the street, not wanting to alert him by driving into the driveway. I wanted him to be surprised when I rang the bell.

But it took me three rings and some pounding before he opened the door. I had to admit that the more I thought about it, the more I knew Grandpa was right. Cole was a lot of things, but he was too weak to be a killer.

He opened the door, peering out behind me. His black eyes had turned into greenish-blue bruises, giving him the look of a Halloween character too early for his holiday. "What do you want, Maddie? Is Val with you?"

"No. But I need to talk to you."

"About what? I'm not feeling well—"

"I don't care," I said. "My sister hasn't been feeling well for a week. Probably longer."

Cole half smiled at that. "It sounds like she's doing fine. Already got a new guy, from what I heard. Did you set her up?"

I stared at him with full-on daggers until his false bravado faltered and he stepped back, silently letting me in. I followed him inside. He remained standing. So did I.

"You need to tell me the truth about what happened at Holly's," I said. "I know you're protecting Gabe Quinn."

He gaped at me. I tried to assume an air of assurance, as if I knew this for a fact and would go to bat for it in a court of law. Of course, I'd made it up on the way over. I had no idea if Adele was protecting her nephew or her protégée, but I had to find out what Cole knew. He'd been at that house, in a unique position to see who was there and, possibly, what had happened.

"Protecting him from what? I have no idea what you're talking about. I guess all that time on the West Coast with those wackos really got to you, huh?" He folded his arms across his chest and tried to assume an authoritative stance.

"I heard the whole thing between you two the other night," I said, not even acknowledging his lame attempt at an insult.

He said nothing, but his right eye twitched. Finally, confirmation. It was Gabe who'd punched him out. "What was Gabe doing there? Was he still seeing Holly? What's he hiding?"

Cole turned away. "You need to leave."

I moved around him so I was once again in front of him. "I'm not going anywhere, Cole. If you don't tell me what you know, I'm going to make sure Becky prints everything about your sordid affair with Diane LaPlante all over her society pages. You can kiss whatever assets you hoped to retain in your divorce from my sister good-bye. I will make sure you're the laughingstock of the island and your precious father wants to crawl under a rock because you're such an embarrassment. And I have your girlfriend's husband on board as the main source of the story."

I was pretty pleased with myself for thinking that bit up on the fly. But given the look on his face, it must've hit some nerve. Public ridicule, especially for a family like his, could be a powerful persuader.

Cole closed his eyes for a moment. When he opened them, he moved to the cabinet and pulled out a bottle of vodka. He splashed some into a glass, added an oversized ice cube from a tray in the freezer. He didn't offer me a drink.

After taking a swig, he dropped into a chair. He didn't invite me to sit. I didn't mind. I liked standing over him.

"Well?" I demanded, after a few moments of silence. "I don't have all day, Cole. Becky's got the piece ready to go, so if it gets too late she's sending it as the front page of the living section."

"I'm not protecting him!" he blurted out. "I have no idea what he did. There were so many people fighting at that house that night that I'm surprised only one person walked away dead!" He frowned. "That didn't make sense, did it. She didn't walk away."

I rolled my eyes. He really wasn't that smart. "Was Gabe there?"

Cole nodded. "He was with Holly. They'd been on and off for years. But he broke it off with her for good earlier in the summer. She was torturing him. God, she was out of control. She had so many boyfriends I wasn't sure how she ever kept them straight. She and I have been friends since high school," he said in response to the question on my face. "She told me all of her drama. Between her boyfriends and the battle to the death she had with her sister, I'm surprised she made it as long as she did." He sounded sad about this. "She wasn't a bad person. Just messed up."

I didn't think he was in any position to judge, but I held my tongue. At least I had him talking now. "So she and Gabe were split up? Or together?"

"Split, technically, but since he was the one to break it off with her this time, she felt like she needed to get him back just so she could break up with him herself. She had a thing for being in control."

"She sounds delightful," I said dryly.

Cole shrugged. "She didn't have the best role models. Anyway, she got Gabe back for a while, then she dumped him. But he showed up that night to talk to her. He wasn't angry. Or drunk. He was really sad, she said."

"So you talked to her after she saw Gabe?"

He nodded. "It was before all the drama with Diane. He told her he really loved her, that he didn't love the girl he was with, that he wished they could just start over. She told him there was no future for them, that he'd been a lot of fun but she needed to move on."

"That could've changed things from sad to angry," I pointed out. "Are you sure he left after that? He could've pretended to leave then circled back and killed her, Cole."

Cole shook his head slowly. "He left. I saw him drive away." He drained his glass then glanced up at me. "He's not that good of an actor. He wouldn't have been able to hide it. And honestly? He wouldn't have been able to do it. Holly always talked about what a pushover he was under all that brawn."

"Well, someone killed her," I said bluntly.

"Yeah. And that someone confessed to it." Cole slammed his empty glass down on the table. "I have no idea what you're trying to prove here. Gabe didn't do anything. His crazy aunt confessed. Which means she did it, unless she's really crazy."

"Was she there? Did you see her?"

"No, I didn't see her," Cole snapped. "But that's the whole point if she's the killer, right? No one should've seen her. Look. I'm sure she had a way in, since her crazy little friend-in-training was serving that night—"

"Wait. What?" I interrupted. "What crazy little friend? Serving what?"

"That girl. The one who looks anorexic who's always following Adele around. She was part of the staff serving that night for the party."

The staff. Serving. Caterers. I hadn't even thought of that. Had Felicia's company catered this party? They couldn't have. From what the group of vipers had said at the restaurant the other night, that whole crowd was boycotting Felicia.

So if Heather and Gigi had been involved in an altercation, how had she landed the gig?

"Do you know what catering company it was?" I asked Cole.

"I don't know. Food was pretty much the last thing on my mind," he said. "But I did see their vans in the driveway. They were purple."

Purple vans. That was something. There couldn't be a lot of those on the island. "Thanks," I said, and turned to go.

He called me back. "Are you going to run a story?"

Disgust flooded my body and turned my cheeks bright red. "A better question would be, *What's my wife going to think about all this?*" I said.

He dropped his gaze.

"So what is the deal? Are you still seeing your girlfriend?"

"You don't understand," he said softly. "I didn't want to hurt Val. It just . . . happened."

"Well. Far be it from me to stand between you and true

love. If you had any morals at all you'd cut Val loose and stop messing with her. But honestly, Cole, I hope she files for divorce as soon as she can find the best lawyer in the state. Then you can do whatever you want. Unless your girlfriend's husband kills you first."

I walked out, slamming the door behind me.

Chapter 53

Grandpa would be waiting for me to check in. I drove downtown and parked at the nearest coffee shop, then called him.

"Meet me at Grounded," I told him, then hurried inside.

By the time he arrived I was seated, drinking an almond-milk mocha with an extra shot of espresso and Googling catering companies on Daybreak Island. Along with Felicia's, there were three others. I went to each of their Web sites, but only found pictures of food and smiling people eating. No pictures of vans, purple or otherwise. I made a sound of frustration as Grandpa slid into the seat across from me.

"So how did it go?"

"Do you know any caterers with purple vans?" I asked.

He frowned at me. "That's a weird question given the topic of conversation."

"It's not though. Do you?"

He thought. "I'm not familiar with a lot of caterers," he admitted.

"Nothing you can remember seeing on the street? Purple vans aren't that common."

"Why are you asking?"

I filled him in on what I'd learned from Cole. "I'm still suspicious about Gabe being there that night. I feel like Adele may have thought that he did something and confessed to cover for him," I said. "But if Gigi was there, that's an even bigger red flag. I mean, if her mother's being black-balled because of something she did, and she somehow got a gig with another caterer . . . wait a minute." I stared at Grandpa. "I bet the caterers weren't from the island."

"You're right. Otherwise they would've heard about whatever altercation happened and would never have hired Gigi. It's too small an island for her to disguise herself that well. Smart girl," he said with a touch of admiration.

"Thanks," I said, grabbing my phone again.

"I meant Gigi," he said with a chuckle. "I mean, you're not so shabby yourself. But really. If she wanted revenge for something, that would've taken some careful planning. And research. It doesn't fit with the persona she projects, but that's all the more reason to look at it carefully."

I held up my phone triumphantly. "Nantucket." Another island off the coast. The caterers were called Purple People Pleasers, known for their catering of high-society events and fleet of purple vans.

What I couldn't figure out was how Gigi got herself hired. Unless she was a better actress than any of us thought.

After Grandpa left for some undisclosed errand—I swore he was working a top secret government job, the way he came and went since I'd been home—I ordered another coffee and sketched out my plan for when I called the caterers. Then for the heck of it, I called Becky first. "Do you know anything about a catering company called the Purple People Pleasers?"

"Never heard of them," she said. "Why, do you need a caterer?"

"I don't. They're based off of Nantucket. But they catered the Hawthornes' party last weekend."

"Really."

"Yup. And I heard they had an interesting server working that night."

"Who?"

"Gigi Goodwin."

"Gigi. Your volunteer? The one whose mother runs a catering company?"

"The very same. Also the one who had some kind of issue with the Hawthornes."

"So how . . . ?"

"No clue. I wonder if your society person has any insight?"

"I'll call her."

"Aren't you at work?"

"Of course I'm at work. I'm always at work. But she's off today. Must be nice to have a nine-to-five reporting job."

I smiled. Becky could complain all she wanted, but she wouldn't have it any other way. Her life was in that newsroom, especially during a time like this.

She called me back a few minutes later. "Jodi's going to call you directly. She wants to know if you want to be her pinch-hit reporter when she needs a day off."

"Depends on how much it pays, and if I can quit my other two side jobs," I said. My other line beeped. "That's her. Call you later."

"So you wanted to hire a caterer?" Jodi asked when I answered.

"No. I just want to know their deal," I said. "Why would they be catering a Hawthorne shindig?"

"Well. Word on the street is they have this rivalry thing going with Island Catering. They're the top dog around here for the fancy people. And they've done some jobs on Nantucket, so the purple ones are feeling like they're encroaching on their territory. Since they're top dog on Nantucket." She sounded amused. "Sometimes this beat is better than the reality shows. Maybe I should try writing a TV series. I bet it pays better."

"Probably," I said. "So how would they make contact over here?"

Jodi thought about that. "Maybe someone's used them off island, or maybe they have a contact. You know, an in."

"Did the Hawthornes use Island Catering?"

"I really don't know. I only know about the purple people because they were at an event I covered last year. Hope this helps."

I thanked Jodi and ended the call. Then I dialed the number on the Purple People Pleasers' Web site. Voice mail. I'd expected that, since it was a Saturday, but had still hoped for a person. But I was ready.

"Hi," I said. "This is Maddie James, and I'm helping my father, the CEO of Daybreak Island General Hospital, with the annual hospital gala next week. Our caterer just quit, and everyone on the island is so booked. I'd heard about your company and wanted to see if you might be available. Please call me." I left my number and hung up.

If they were really serious about getting business on Daybreak, they wouldn't let this go for very long.

Chapter 54

By the time I got home, it was nearly eight. Which meant that the party was just getting started downtown. A ferry had just arrived as I drove by, so I waited for the throng of people to cross the street before I could continue down to our house. It was a beautiful night on the island, clear and warm, the smell of salt air hanging over us. The sky was just beginning to go dusky, and the stars were extra bright against the backdrop. There was a frantic energy as people tried to pack in everything they could before they had to head home to their real lives.

Grandpa's truck was still gone. I had no idea if Ethan or Val were home or not. I checked in on the cats in the café. JJ was snuggled up on the top of the tallest tree, overseeing the kingdom. I left him to it and went upstairs to my room.

And almost jumped a foot when I realized Val was curled up on my bed. I couldn't see her face to tell if she was sleeping or not. But as I moved quietly through the room she spoke.

"I'm not asleep," she said.

"What are you doing?" I asked. "Were you waiting for me?" Although I had a feeling I knew why she was here.

"I was." She sat up and hugged her knees into her chest. "Cole called me. Again."

"Oh yeah?" I pulled out my desk chair and sat, stalling for time and trying to look innocent. "What did he say?"

She looked me in the eye. "That you went to see him."

"Val. Don't be mad. I hate him for treating you like this and I wanted to know what he'd been up to that night—"

"I'm not mad," she interrupted. "I just wish you'd told me about the thing at the restaurant." She half smiled. "I'd have liked to imagine him getting punched in the face." The smile faltered. "What did you tell him?"

I hesitated. "I told him he should do the right thing by you."

"The right thing. That's funny. I don't think Cole would know the right thing if it jumped up and bit him." She didn't sound mad, simply resigned. "I know he's been seeing someone else. I'm glad it's not the dead girl, but it's still . . . a lot."

"I'm sure." I took a breath. "So what do you think you're going to do?" I asked casually. I didn't want her to think I was prying, or pressuring her.

"I don't know yet," she said. "I'm really dreading dealing with his parents. I'm expecting a summons from them any minute now."

"So what?" I asked, outraged. "You ignore them. You don't owe those jerks anything. They owe *you*."

She waved me off. "They've got that whole *boys aren't responsible for their actions, she must've seduced him* mind-set. They'd do anything to defend him. They'll expect me to march home and forgive him."

I couldn't imagine our parents ever giving us that much leeway. They were our staunchest supporters and would do anything for us, but if we did something wrong we were always held accountable. "They can expect all they want. Doesn't mean you're doing any of it. No way." I got up and walked around the room in a circle. "You didn't sign a pre-nup or anything, did you? You'll at least get the house in the divorce. Then you can sell it and move wherever you want. We can find you a place. I'll help."

"Maddie." Val cut me off. "Stop. I can't think about that right now. I have to figure out how I actually feel first."

"You're not saying . . . Val. You aren't considering staying with that dirtbag, are you?"

She looked away. "It's complicated."

"Complicated?" I shook my head, trying desperately hard to retain control of this conversation. Val would shut me right down if I got too judgy or adamant about what she needed to do. *It's her life,* I heard Cass say in my mind. "Val. It's really not. Are you happy?"

She cocked her head at me. "What do you mean?"

"Happy. You know. With Cole. With your life."

Val was silent for so long I thought she'd fallen asleep. When she finally spoke she didn't look at me. "Happy," she said slowly, as if she was testing the word on her tongue and found it strange, exotic. "What does that even mean, Maddie?"

I didn't know how to respond to that. I'm not often speechless, but my twenty-six-year-old sister sounded like a middle-aged woman who'd come to terms with the fact that her life was pretty much the same mundane thing day after day, like a life prison sentence with no chance of parole.

"Happy," I said finally. "It shouldn't be something you have to look up in the dictionary. It means you wake up every day looking forward to what's going to happen. You love spending time with your husband. You do fun things together. You have friends. You enjoy your house. I didn't think it was that foreign of a concept."

She shrugged. "We're fine. I mean, we don't do a lot of things together, but we have different interests, you know?"

Fine? Clearly he didn't think they were fine if he was seeing someone else. "There are different interests and then there are incompatible people," I said.

"We're compatible enough."

I resisted the urge to press that specific issue and instead tried another tack. "Val. You haven't even hit thirty yet. If you can't be happy in your twenties . . ."

"Are you happy, Maddie?" she asked, leaning forward. I could hear the edge in her voice. "Do you wake up every day looking forward to what it will bring?"

I felt my cheeks heat up. I'd always thought of myself as happy. But was I? I spent so much time running around fixing things and people and running businesses and helping everyone, but at the cost of other things that meant a lot to me. Like Lucas. And a chance at a real relationship. Not that relationships were the only way to be happy, but they were a big piece of happiness. A big piece that I'd been missing out on for a long time.

Val was still waiting for an answer. "I'm happy enough," I said. "And yeah, I think every day brings a new set of possibilities. That shouldn't change just because you've been married to someone for a couple years." I knew that lately I hadn't exactly been living this mantra, but deep down it's what I believed. And she was right. I needed to do a better job of practicing what I preached.

She watched me, an unreadable look on her face. Then she took a breath. "I've sort of started something with Ethan."

I didn't have to feign surprise—I was shocked that she'd actually told me. "What kind of something?"

"I don't know what it is. I don't know if it's just because he was nice to me after everything that happened. Lord knows he's not my type. But I like him. He makes me feel good. He's kind. He can talk me off a ledge. Do you know how many people can talk me off a ledge? Pretty much none."

"I know," I muttered.

She shot me a look. "My point is, I just met the guy. It's kind of crazy to think I'm falling for him. But what could I do about it anyway?"

I sat down next to her on the bed. "Val. Forget Ethan for a minute. Don't get me wrong, I think he would be great for you." I wasn't so sure how she would be for him, but that was for him to figure out. "But the real question here is, do you love Cole? Are you willing to forgive the way he's treated you? How he's dishonored you? Because you're the only person you should leave Cole for. Now. If you're looking at Ethan and seeing what you might be missing out on and that's prompting you to make a decision, that's something entirely different. And something I would applaud."

She looked at me, amused. "Maddie. I'm sure you'd be the last person in the world to be sad if I left Cole. You don't have to pretend otherwise."

"Val, that's not true. I just want you to be happy."

Her smile faltered. "There's that word again."

"Well, I stand by it."

"Yeah. You always were kind of a romantic." Her eyes took on a wistful look I hadn't seen in years. "I just wish I believed it was possible."

Chapter 55

I woke up the next morning to my phone vibrating incessantly under my pillow. I'd shut the ringer off in an attempt to have some peace and sleep in a bit, but clearly that wasn't happening. JJ, who'd come up sometime during the night and curled up on top of said pillow, was not impressed with this wake-up call either.

I fumbled around under my pillow and finally fished the phone out. The first thing I registered was my parents' number. The second was the time. Seven ten. Why were my parents calling so early on a Sunday?

"Hello," I muttered.

"Maddie." My dad.

I sat up. "Yeah? What's wrong?"

"I thought I told you to stay away from the Tanners and the Hawthornes."

I frowned. My dad, usually way laid-back and calm, sounded agitated. I guessed Cole had gone running to mommy and daddy about our . . . conversation.

"I have stayed away from the Hawthornes," I said indignantly.

"And the Tanners?"

I shrugged, even though he couldn't see me. "Mostly."

"Mostly? Madalyn. What possessed you—"

"Dad. Hold on a minute," I said. "I went to see Cole. Cole doesn't count. I didn't go see Erik or Mira."

"But they heard about it. And as I suspected, Mira is trying to cause problems for me with the gala. And, quite possibly, with the rest of the board."

"If I recall correctly, Mira was already mad because of the episode the other night," I pointed out. "So I think she already had a bone to pick, Dad, no offense. I was trying to stick up for my sister." I couldn't believe I had to explain this to him. I got that he was under a lot of pressure, but this was crazy.

"Well, it certainly added fuel to the fire," he said. "My reservations person told me the Coopers canceled. Followed closely by the Berkinhowsers."

I had to bite my tongue to keep from saying something I'd regret. "Dad. Maybe something came up. You immediately assumed it's my fault?"

"I'm asking you again, Maddie. Stay out of this. Stay out of your sister's marriage, stay out of this murder. It's been solved anyway, granted with a sad outcome, but solved all the same. I need to try to repair this relationship so I still have a job next week." And he hung up.

My own dad. Hung up on me. After calling me at seven in the morning on a Sunday.

I spent the morning stewing about the whole sorry situation. I went to Val's room to see if she'd gotten a similar phone call, perhaps asking her to avoid filing for divorce until after the gala, but she wasn't there. Ethan was nowhere in sight either, which led me to believe they'd taken off somewhere. And there wasn't even any coffee. I made some and then wandered into the café. We weren't opening until noon, but I figured I'd get the chores done.

But I was pleasantly surprised to see that the room had

been cleaned and freshened, and the cats fed. So all I had to do was sit and play with them and get snuggles. JJ eventually came down and wanted in on the action too, so we all had a little lovefest. Until my phone rang again.

Wary, I picked it up and checked the screen, fully prepared to ignore it if it was another lecture. I didn't recognize the number. At least it wouldn't be someone yelling at me. Hopefully.

I answered and heard a chipper voice on the other end asking for me.

"This is Maddie."

"Hi, Maddie! This is Julie from Purple People Pleasers! I understand you're interested in a caterer?"

The caterers Gigi had worked for. I'd almost forgotten. "Yes, thank you for calling me back!" I stood, disrupting Moonshine's cuddling in my lap. As a parting gift, he dug his nails into my leg. I gritted my teeth against the pain. "I heard you catered an event last weekend for the Hawthornes."

Julie must have been prepared for this, because she didn't miss a beat. Despite the fact that someone was murdered at that party, she was focused on their food. "We did. It was a lovely, low-key gathering for a group of friends. What kind of event were you looking to have catered?"

I nearly laughed out loud. Lovely and low-key, huh? "It's actually a bit fancier," I said. "But I'm just curious, how did you come to work with the Hawthornes?" I hoped my question sounded casual enough.

"Of course, I should've said that up front. So sorry," Julie said. "We were lucky enough to make a connection with someone who lives on Daybreak who's had some experience as a server. She mentioned that some folks in town were in the market for something new cateringwise, so we just made the calls and wooed them. Apparently it worked!"

"I guess so," I said. "That's great. Who's your connection? I actually know a few people in the area through my dad's work. Just curious, of course."

"Oh, of course. Her name is Gigi. I can't remember her last name—I'm not in charge of staffing—but she's a dear. So, now, tell me about your event."

Chapter 56

I hung up after giving Julie my e-mail so she could send me a proposal for catering services for the gala, which of course I didn't need. All kinds of warning bells were going through my brain about Gigi. So when she showed up at the door five minutes later, I nearly jumped out of my skin.

"Hey," I said, heading over to unlock the screen door. "I didn't know you were coming today."

She looked at me like I was crazy. "I'm working the café hours today. I thought I'd come by a little early and visit with the kitties."

"Oh. Cool. Okay," I said. "I'm going to get some coffee. Want anything?"

She shook her head no. I went into the kitchen and leaned against the counter. There was a strong possibility that Gigi had been responsible for Holly's death, and Adele had felt responsible for her part in dragging Gigi through her drama with Holly. But Gigi had her own bone to pick with Holly and Heather, as the ones responsible for Felicia's declining status as a caterer on the island.

So had she orchestrated this whole scenario as a way to get close to the Hawthornes and get revenge?

The kitchen door opened and Ethan came in. He looked surprised to find me standing there. "Hey. You waiting for coffee? I can make some," he offered.

I shook my head. "No. Just taking a breather. What are you up to?"

He shrugged. "I took Val to breakfast," he said, looking me in the eye. She must've told him she'd talked to me. But I had bigger fish to fry today.

"Good," I said. "I hope you went somewhere yummy." I glanced at the clock. Eleven. I went back out to the living room and found Gigi on one of the floor pillows. Moonshine had convinced her to take up where I'd left off and was curled in her lap, kneading contentedly.

Something told me he was about to get mad at me again.

"Gigi. Can I talk to you for a second?" I asked.

She looked up. That panic was in her eyes again. At this point I figured it was an act. Clearly she was a good actress. "Sure," she said, her voice unsteady.

I shut the front door. I didn't need any early visitors as an audience. "I know you worked with the caterers at Holly Hawthorne's house the other night," I said. No reason to pussyfoot around. Cut to the chase and catch her off guard.

She went whiter than the walls in Dad's emergency room. "How . . . how do you know that?" she asked.

"Doesn't matter. But now I'm wondering why you were really there. Especially since I know you and the Hawthornes had some major issues."

Gigi said nothing. Moonshine, sensing the tension, meowed softly.

"Gigi?"

"I needed some money," she said.

"Money? Come on. Then why didn't you work for your mother?"

"Because she doesn't have that many jobs," Gigi blurted

out. "And it's my fault. It's all my fault that Heather Hawthorne and her nasty family were trashing my mother all
over the island."

"Why? What happened with the two of you?"

Gigi resumed petting Moonshine, almost with a vengeance. "It's stupid," she muttered.

"Enlighten me."

Gigi looked up at me, and for a split second I saw pure,
raw anger glittering in her eyes before they transformed
back to wounded puppy. "Why do you care?"

"Why? Because you're working in my café, for one.
And two, because I don't believe Adele killed Holly. I
think she's taking the rap for someone else."

It took her a minute, but then she got it. She leaped to
her feet, sending Moonshine racing to the nearest cubby
for cover. "You think I killed her and she took the blame?
You're crazy!"

"Then what were you doing there?" I challenged. "Even
if you did need money, why didn't you go work for another
caterer on the island at a different job? How did you even
get back in their house if they have such a problem with
you?"

Gigi laughed, a harsh sound. "They're too stupid and
snotty to even look at the servers. Lord Voldemort could've
gone in there with a white apron and pants on and they'd
never have noticed. They don't pay mind to the hired help.
And I couldn't go work for anyone else. She badmouthed
me to enough people that none of the other caterers would
hire me, and I don't have experience with anything else!"
She stalked around the room, her hands moving in useless
circles as she tried to work out whatever was in her head.

"You still didn't tell me what caused the problem," I
said. I could tell she was thinking, *Do I have to?* She was
definitely more calculating than she usually let on. Which
made me even more suspicious of her.

In the end, she must've decided she had to tell me something, even if it was not the whole truth. She stopped pacing and stood near the far wall. "I took some of the extra food from one of the parties and gave it to the cats," she said, crossing her arms defensively over her chest.

"Okay," I said.

"Okay what? That's what Heather got mad about!"

I frowned. "Was it food that should've been served, or was it about to get tossed?"

"Tossed."

"Then why would she care?"

"Because she hated cats. Especially outdoor, *dirty* cats." She made a face. "Loser. Especially when it was her sister who caused some of them to live outdoors!"

Heather hated cats. So what would've happened if Holly had brought Georgia home? The whole thing made my head hurt.

"Gigi. Did you take that job so you could get in there and have access to Holly? To . . . do something to her? Because it's not right to let Adele take the blame for this. Listen. You have to tell me." I closed the gap between us, imploring. "Let me help you—"

The doorbell rang, startling me enough that I jumped. Muttering a curse, I stalked over to open it.

Craig was on the porch. In uniform.

If I didn't know better I'd assume he'd had the place wiretapped and was coming for Gigi. Except she hadn't said anything incriminating yet. And certainly wouldn't now. I turned around to see if she'd seen him.

She was gone.

Chapter 57

I swore out loud this time, then flipped the lock on the screen to let Craig in.

"What's wrong?" he asked.

"Gigi. She must've slipped out the side door."

"She trying to get away from you?" he asked, only half kidding.

"Yes! And we were just . . . having an important conversation," I finished lamely. "Hang on a minute."

I left him standing in the living room and hurried through the house to the other side, exiting near the garage. Just in time to see her bike disappear down the street.

When I went back in, Craig was playing with one of the new kittens. He glanced up from the laser toy. "Everything okay?"

"Not really." I squared my shoulders and faced him. "Craig. I'm worried about Gigi's mental health."

He stood up slowly. "Explain."

I told him everything I'd found out about the party and Gigi's elaborate scheme to get on the catering staff. "Don't you think that's suspicious?" I asked. "That she went to so much trouble to work in that house on the night Holly died?"

"Of course it's suspicious," he said. "But since we have the killer, I'd say maybe she was planning something else. Maybe she wanted to poison the Hawthornes, but Holly dying put a wrench in her plans."

I couldn't tell if he was kidding. "So you don't believe me."

"I believe you that it's suspicious. But I also believe Adele when she says she did it."

"But—"

"Maddie. I didn't come here to argue with you about this again. I actually came to ask if I could take you to dinner. We've been crossing paths a lot lately with . . . all this stuff but we haven't had a chance to talk. I'd like for us to be able to talk."

"Craig." I tried to soften my words. "I appreciate the gesture. Really I do. But I don't think it would be smart for us to try and date. Look. Going backward has never worked for me. No matter how tempting it is."

"And yet," Craig said, "you came back here. That's the ultimate going backward, no?"

I looked out the window at the ocean beyond while I tried to figure out how I felt about that. The ocean—this little piece of it, anyway—knew my secrets, knew me better than I knew myself. Was Craig right? Had I made a mistake coming back here? My entire family had fallen back into their old ways of coming to me to solve everything, beginning with Grandpa's house issues that had sucked me in in the first place. My sister Val's life was falling apart. My mother wanted me to save the day. My dad wanted me to help him run his professional life. Craig wanted to get back together with me. And in less than three months, I'd been dragged into the unraveling of two murders.

On the other hand, I'd opened a brand-new business, reconnected with old friends, and had met an amazing new guy. Who I promptly drove away, but still. I'd given my business partner a chance to embrace a whole new life, with a new venture in a new setting. Ethan was adaptable enough that he'd slipped right into this brand-new world with nary the blink of an eye. He seemed to be doing better than me, actually, but perhaps that was because his entry into this world didn't come with five or six people who still hadn't resolved their key dependency issues.

This was all too much to think about this early in the morning, in the face of a terrible murder. With my ex-boyfriend as witness, no less.

"It wasn't going backward. There was a chance to start something new here. A new business, a new life for Grandpa." But now that I was back here, I wasn't sure how to quite fit in.

"Did you ever think it was something else that brought you here?" Craig asked.

"Something else?" I arched an eyebrow at him. "I think I would know if there was anything else that brought me here."

"Would you?" Craig asked. "Maybe it was some, I don't know, some pull you couldn't explain."

"Since when did you become all romantic and woo-woo? That's not really a cop trait," I said, trying to inject a teasing tone into my voice. I didn't know what else to do. Yes, I loved Craig. I really did. But I loved him in the way old friends loved each other, not the way he seemed to want.

He blew out an impatient breath. "I meant, did you come back because maybe you thought you had something unfinished here? Like us?"

"Craig," I said gently. "Look. I know you think we can pick up where we left off, but it's not that easy. We're different people."

"Which makes it better," he said. "I don't want to go back to high school. Believe me, Maddie."

"That's not the point." I took a deep breath. "Listen. I really like Lucas. I have to see where that goes." I hated breaking it to him like that, but he seemed to need me to be direct. "I'm sorry. I want us to be friends. Craig." I grabbed his hand, forced him to look at me. "I really want us to be friends."

He smiled, but there was no humor in it. "Yeah. But we can't always have what we want, can we?" He gave my hand a little squeeze, then released it and walked out the door.

Chapter 58

Monday morning. The café was closed and I was happy about it. Aside from my newly adopted antisocial behavior, I also had work to do on the gala. My father had been sending me messages through Charlotte—apparently he was still mad at me about the whole Cole thing—and I had to get the menu from Felicia so it could be approved, and help them sort out a few last-minute auction details, and a thousand other stupid details that I'd never have thought of myself because I wasn't a party planner.

I could start a business from scratch and make it work any day of the week, but clearly this was not my forte. Finally I got up, grabbed Dad's stupid binder, and marched up to Val's room. She was still here, and I was glad about it. She didn't seem to be going anywhere soon, either, although I hadn't asked.

"Please. Take it away," I said, handing her the binder.

She looked at me suspiciously. "What's this?"

"The binder for the gala. I need help. I have no idea why Dad asked me, and I don't want the job. Please, Val. Help."

"What's the catch?"

"Catch? There's no catch. I was only doing this to stay in the will," I said, only half kidding.

"I thought you wanted to do this so Dad thought you were the shining star again!"

"Oh, Val." I shook my head. "I don't want to be a star. Please. Help?"

She smiled. "Yes. Absolutely."

"Okay. Let's go downstairs and have coffee and I'll tell you where I'm at."

She followed me down, JJ leading the way, flipping the binder as she walked. "Wow. This is a lot of stuff. I would so love to put this party together from scratch," she said.

I paused on the stairs and looked at her, almost causing her to run into me. "You would?" I asked.

"Totally. I've wanted to do stuff like this forever."

Another thing I didn't know about my sister. "Well, you're in luck," I said as we hit the first floor. Ethan wasn't in the kitchen but his spirit was there, along with a lovely fresh pot of coffee. I glanced at Val, curious. "How is everything with Ethan?"

"Fine," she said, trying to sound casual, but I saw red creeping up her neck. "So what's got to get done?"

I poured two mugs of coffee and perched on a chair, one leg under me, to walk her through what I'd managed to cobble together as a to-do list. But I'd barely gotten to the second task when the doorbell rang. She stood. "I'll get it."

I took the opportunity to refill the coffee mugs, feeling a sense of relief I hadn't had in more than a week. Val would save the day. She seemed to like this stuff. And maybe it would give us a chance to work together on something.

My happy-family thoughts were chased away when the kitchen door opened and Val came in, Craig right behind her. Val looked disturbed.

"What are you doing here?" I asked Craig. I hadn't expected to see him again, at least not here, after the way our conversation played out yesterday. Unless something bad had happened. "What's wrong?"

He looked at me with an almost pitying look on his face. "It's Gigi."

"Gigi? What about her? Oh God. Did you find . . . was I right?"

He shook his head. "No. You weren't right. We found her on the beach. She tried to commit suicide, Maddie."

I felt my knees go weak and grabbed onto my chair. Val came over and squeezed my hand. "What do you mean? Is she okay? What happened?"

"We're not exactly sure. Someone found her facedown on the beach, barely breathing. They rushed her in to the hospital. She's stable now. I didn't get the details on what she took or her prognosis, but I wanted to tell you." He paused. "I'm sorry, Maddie."

"This is my fault," I said, sitting down hard and looking him in the eye. "Isn't it?"

"God, no. That's nuts," Val said, looking to Craig for confirmation. "Isn't that nuts?"

"Of course," he said, but he didn't sound convinced. "You shouldn't blame yourself."

"But I basically accused her of killing Holly."

Now Val turned to gape at me. "You did what?"

I nodded miserably. "It makes sense if you know the whole story. But we never got to finish talking and she took off. She must've been . . . really messed up about it."

"But that other lady confessed." Val looked from me to Craig. "Clearly I'm missing something."

"It doesn't matter." I turned to Craig. "So now what? Will she be okay?"

"All I know is what I told you," he said.

"Should I go see her?"

"Um. Probably not the best idea," Val said, looking to Craig for confirmation.

To his credit, Craig didn't respond. He just kept looking at me with those sympathetic eyes.

"Stop looking at me like that," I said. "I feel bad enough as it is. What should I do?"

He shook his head. "There's nothing you can do. Listen, I'll check back in on how she's doing and let you know. Will that help?"

I nodded. "Yes. Please. That would be great."

"Okay, then." He hesitated, and for a minute I thought he was going to hug me. But he didn't. He turned and left.

Chapter 59

The rest of the week passed surprisingly uneventfully, if not crazy busy. I was back to no volunteers. Ethan, Grandpa, and I made a schedule that worked for all of us for cleaning, and we got into a comfortable rhythm. Val made no move to go back to her house, and instead jumped full-on into helping get Dad's gala up and running. She had totally come through and helped me with all the outstanding items, including decorations for the room and finding some fab last-minute auction items, letting my mother off the hook too.

I didn't ask about her and Ethan. It was their business, not mine, and I'd already mucked up enough things by sticking my nose in other people's business. I still hadn't heard from Lucas. My dad was still basically only speaking to me through a third party, and only to make sure I hadn't screwed up anything else about the gala. A couple of other high rollers had canceled and he was majorly stressed.

As for Gigi, she was recovering from her suicide attempt. She'd gone on a drinking-and-pill binge, and given her tiny size it hadn't taken much to send her system into shock. I heard from Felicia—who didn't know about my conversation with Gigi, at least that she'd let on—that Gigi had been released from the hospital on Thursday and was home with her mother. It sounded like they were bonding, or maybe that was just Felicia's interpretation of it. In any event, Gigi wasn't living in a tent at the beach anymore, which was positive.

I was still conflicted about her presence at the Hawthornes' house that night, but as far as everyone else was concerned, the case was closed and I felt guilty enough to let it go. Grandpa had tried to comfort me by praising my investigative and deduction skills, and saying he would've pursued the same avenue if he'd been on the force and had gotten the same intel. I appreciated his words, but I still felt like crap.

The café had been steadily busy all week, with food sales skyrocketing with the combination of Felicia's food and Ethan's coffee. People had even taken to dropping by for a snack, even if there were no cuddling spots open, which made Ethan really happy. It reinforced Ethan's desire to turn the garage into the café. Which I hoped was really going to happen once I got Gabe back here in a couple of weeks.

If he really did come back, but I couldn't worry about that now.

In a nutshell, everything was going along swimmingly. Unless you counted the Lucas thing. Which I didn't feel like I had a right to, given how I'd mucked it all up. I still hadn't heard from him. I was debating calling him, but I didn't want to come off as pathetic. Then again, it was my drama that had caused this, and it really was on me to make the first move. I was still figuring it out.

So I moved through the week going through the motions, feeling numb and off center most of the time, despite my attempts to do Cass's rituals.

And soon enough it was Saturday night, the night of the

gala. Showtime. It had been two weeks since Holly's death. I felt like tomorrow was a day of reckoning, that I'd have to take stock of everything that had happened and everything I'd done—like nearly driving a young woman to kill herself—but for tonight, I had to put my brave face on and get through it.

"Ready?" Val asked, squeezing my hand as we stood inside the decorated room. I had to admit it looked gorgeous. So did she, for that matter. Poised and confident, she was not the same girl I'd picked up at her big empty house nearly two weeks ago. Despite the toll this whole debacle had taken on her, tonight she looked . . . peaceful. And she'd outdone herself for the party. She really had a knack for this stuff. She'd decorated everything with a Reach for the Stars theme, and had transformed the room so it felt like we were sitting under a gorgeous night sky. Black velvet curtains, dim lighting, and funky colors and stars projected onto the ceiling gave it a sense of an outdoor camping trip on a beautiful clear night, without the bugs. Everything glittered with confetti stars, including the table holding the plethora of auction items. I could see the guests fighting over the centerpieces, a mixture of stars and flowers. It was all elegant too. Nothing cheesy or cheap here.

Dad would be pleased. And he would wonder why he hadn't asked her in the first place.

"As ready as I'm gonna get," I said. "The food's almost ready, and that's more important." Felicia and her team had been here since noon, prepping and chopping and all the other things chefs did to make a huge meal. She'd brought a team of five people, and the hotel had provided three of their own servers to assist. While I'd known her food would be a hit, I hadn't known what to expect about her logistical operation and the people she'd bring with her. But everyone looked and sounded professional, and no one seemed overly klutzy. One of the servers, a young Hispanic man, seemed to notice how uptight I was and made it a point to try and put me at ease every time our paths crossed, which was sweet.

And not totally working.

I rubbed my hands together nervously. "I just wish it was over."

"Don't worry so much," Val said. "It will be great. I can just feel it." She winked. "Trust me."

Chapter 60

By the time guests began arriving, I'd relaxed a bit. Or it could've been the one drink I had to calm my nerves. So I was able to appreciate how many people were streaming through the door. My parents were in the first wave, of course, and I could see my father looking around anxiously, taking it all in, hoping for a smooth, stress-free night. My mother saw me and Val and waved.

Looks great, she mouthed, flashing us a thumbs-up.

I waved back, wishing for another drink. Then I blinked. And poked Val. "Aren't those the Berkinhowsers?" I couldn't believe I actually recognized them. If it even was them. Because according to my dad, they'd canceled and it was my fault because I'd yelled at Cole.

Val's eyes followed my finger. "Why yes, it is them," she said, smiling.

"They canceled. Unless Dad was somehow mistaken."

"Or maybe they reconsidered," she said, and I swore I saw a twinkle in her eye.

"Val. How did you—"

But she'd already sailed away to greet some people. I shook my head, watching her. She certainly looked in her element. Maybe she had a future in entrepreneurship herself.

My happy thoughts were suddenly derailed when I saw Sergeant Ellory come in, a pretty brunette on his arm. He wasn't wearing a uniform, but he never did anyway so I was immediately on guard. I made my way over to him just as one of our registration people finished handing him the program and a bid card for the evening.

"Sergeant."

He smiled. I didn't think I'd ever seen him smile before. He actually wasn't bad-looking when he did. "Maddie. This is my wife, Caroline."

"Nice to meet you," I said, then turned back to him. "Here to support the hospital?"

He nodded. "Absolutely." His calm, cop eyes stared right back into mine.

"Well," I said. "Enjoy. It should be a low-key night."

"I certainly hope so," he said.

I turned to go back to my post near the door, when out of the corner of my eye I saw Heather Hawthorne strutting into the room. I nearly cringed. I had to be sure to steer clear of her at all times, lest my father get the wrong idea.

It was going to be a long night.

I was hiding out by the bar, keeping an eye on the servers as they passed out main courses, when my mother joined me. She slipped her arm around my waist and kissed my hair.

"It looks amazing in here. And everyone is having a wonderful time."

I squeezed her back. "Thanks, Mom. But Val ended up doing a lot of this."

"I know she helped out. But Maddie. Don't downplay what you did. You really jumped in and took charge. Dad is very grateful."

"I don't know about that. Dad thinks I messed everything up."

"Honey." My mother took my face in her hands. "Dad is grateful. We are both so proud of you. I wish you'd give yourself more credit. Besides. Those silly people who canceled just needed to have some sense talked back into them. Nothing your sister and I couldn't handle." She winked at me.

I stared at her. "You got those people back on board?"

My mom nodded. "I wasn't about to let them ruin this for Dad *or* you." She hugged me. "You know I'd do anything for you, Maddie."

I watched her slip back to her seat, my heart swelling with gratitude. My mother was amazing. I was one of the lucky ones, for sure. And I had no doubt that she would do anything at all for me.

Most mothers would, I reckoned. Even if their kid screwed up. It was part of the job.

And maybe some mothers took that job way more seriously.

I'd been looking at this all wrong after all.

Chapter 61

Val grabbed me as I was heading for the kitchen. "Bathroom break?"

I glanced at the door and decided five minutes wouldn't hurt. We detoured out into the hall together and headed to the ladies' room.

"Okay, spill it," I said to Val after I'd checked under the seats to verify we were alone.

"Spill what?"

"The canceled people. How'd you and Mom do it?"

She shrugged modestly. "We just told Mira that you weren't kidding about the newspaper story. And we namedropped a fancy lawyer who I told her I was contemplating hiring to represent me in the divorce, and that I'd up the ante if she messed with Dad's job."

I squealed and hugged her. "And she caved? Just like that?"

"Of course. There's nothing people like her hate more than their precious names being dragged through the mud. She got her people back on board."

"That's amazing." I hesitated. "So you're . . ."

She nodded. "I'm going to file for divorce. I should've

done it a long time ago. Actually, I shouldn't have gotten married in the first place, but what can you do?"

I studied her. "You seem so calm about this."

"Yeah, well. Ethan's been teaching me some coping strategies."

The door banged open and two tipsy women entered, laughing a little too loudly. Conversation over. For now. I gave her a hug.

"Thank you," she whispered in my ear. "For everything."

Once we were back in the room, I slipped out back to check on the desserts. Felicia had outdone herself with that too. She was serving minicakes, a choice of chocolate or vanilla, coated with blue frosting and silver stars traveling up the sides. A tiny silver planet floated from a gold toothpick over the creation.

The servers were bringing the desserts any minute. The food part was basically over. I took a deep breath and pushed open the doors into the kitchen. While I was here, I figured I'd get a picture of the cakes as the servers arranged them on platters. I'd managed to remember to take plenty of pictures during the night for Dad.

Felicia glanced up and smiled. "You like?"

"They're gorgeous. Everything's been gorgeous. Thank you so much for jumping in and doing this."

"Thank you for the job," she said. "I'm blessed for the opportunity."

"You deserved it. Your food is awesome." I slipped my phone into the pocket of the little jacket I'd thrown on over my dress to combat the air-conditioning and moved closer to watch her put the finishing touches on the last few cakes. "How's Gigi?" I asked finally. We'd barely spoken about her, and I wasn't sure if Felicia wanted to or not. But I felt like I had to tell her about my conversation with her daughter. Get it off my chest. It was eating away at me.

"She's doing much better," Felicia said. "It will take a while. But she's seeing a therapist now, and I'm hopeful it will help."

"That's good." I nervously linked and unlinked my fingers. "Felicia." I lowered my voice so the staff still in the room couldn't hear me. "I have a confession to make."

Her fingers stilled briefly over her work, then resumed. "Okay," she said without looking up.

"Gigi and I were having a conversation. Last week, before . . ." I cleared my throat. "Anyway, I said some things that may have put her in a bad place. I was struggling with Adele's confession. I couldn't accept that she'd actually done it, and I found out some things about Gigi that put her at the Hawthornes' that night. I asked her about it, and about the things that happened in the past between her and the twins. I'm afraid I caused this." I stopped talking, waited for a reaction.

Felicia was silent for so long I wondered if she was maybe counting to one hundred, or one million, in order to not lose it and stab me with something during the event and risk not getting paid. When she finally spoke I realized I'd been holding my breath.

"I know about your talk," she said. "Gigi left a note. I don't think she meant it for me, necessarily, but the police gave it to me." She lifted her arm and swiped at her eye with her wrist. "She said she wanted everyone to know that she really didn't do it. That she was sorry about the problems she thought she caused me, and was trying to find a way to right it." Finally she looked up. I didn't think I'd ever seen anyone look more sad. "She was going to try and sabotage the new caterers. That's why she took the job. She was convinced she could put things right for me, convince the Hawthornes to stop badmouthing my company. Misguided, sure. Like most things Gigi did, it wasn't well thought out. In the end she couldn't do it. But she was terribly sad that anyone would think she would let her friend be blamed for something she did."

Hearing the confirmation and feeling the guilt fresh nearly brought me to my knees. "I'm so, so sorry," I said. "And I know now that I was wrong. Gigi didn't kill Holly." I looked her square in the eyes. "You did."

Chapter 62

Felicia put down her spatula and pushed her sleeves up. I noticed that for the first time since I'd met her, she looked calm. Her hands weren't shaky, and she seemed sure of herself.

"I wondered when someone would figure it out," she said. "But I guess that girl had so much else going on that it wasn't immediately clear, was it?"

I was a little surprised that she'd admitted it so easily. Or what if this calmness was just an act? What if she tried to do something and get away? I started to sweat. I glanced casually—I hoped—around the room. The staff were far enough away and making enough noise with their dishes and pans that no one was hearing us. I just hoped they'd notice if she made any quick moves. Like, if she tried to shove a catnip mouse down my throat.

Felicia must've sensed how jittery I'd become. "Don't worry. I didn't expect to get away with it, Maddie. Honestly, I'm surprised no one's figured it out yet. But when Adele confessed, I admit I had a few moments of thinking maybe I could get away with it. But that wouldn't have been right. I made a choice in the heat of the moment, and

I'm willing to accept the consequences. As long as Gigi is all right, I can accept whatever they want to do to me."

She shoved a piece of hair out of her face, leaving a smear of frosting over her eyebrow. "I wanted to do this job. I wanted to prove to all those people out there that I am good at what I do. That no matter what those nasty women said about me and my daughter, it didn't change that fact. And I wanted to make some money for Gigi. So please, make sure the money from this goes to her. I added her name to my business account so she can access it. Will you promise me that?"

"Felicia—" I had no idea what to say. Was she going to turn herself in? Kill herself? Then I had another thought. What if she decided to do something crazy and dire as the grand finale to the evening? That would certainly top the announcement about how much money was raised.

"Please, Maddie. I did a terrible thing, thinking I was doing it for my daughter, and my family, and all the pain they caused. But I couldn't live with myself very long. These last two weeks have been . . . stressful, to say the least. And I certainly can't live with the pain my daughter is in over this, never mind the poor woman who for some reason I will never understand confessed to something she didn't do."

I could hear the live auction through the doors, in between the kitchen noises. *I hear a thousand! Can I get eleven hundred?* The dessert trays were disappearing one by one as the servers rushed in and out with them. And yet here we stood, frozen in this terrible moment, like one of those videos where life is rushing on around the tragic figures in a blur as they tried to figure out what to do next. For the first time ever, I was glad that Sergeant Ellory was nearby. I wanted to run out and get him, but I was afraid of what would happen if I left her here.

"I think Adele thought either Gigi or her nephew had

actually done it," I said quietly. "And she thought it would be better for her to take the rap."

Felicia shook her head sadly. "She should've just let it be. They never would've figured it out, probably."

I doubted that, but I didn't want to say so and make her mad. But it still wasn't obvious to me how she'd come to shove a mouse down Holly's throat. "But how?" I blurted out. "How did you get in their house? Did you go there just to . . . to do that?"

She shook her head. "Adele called me. Told me about what Gigi was doing there. She'd gone over for her own reasons. I think she was trying to see if Holly had gone elsewhere and gotten a cat or something. But she saw Gigi and called me, afraid that the whole thing would backfire and they would have her arrested or something. So I went over and entered through the beach." She shrugged. "I still had a key to the gate from when I catered for them. I thought the coast was clear, but Holly and her boyfriend were outside arguing. I waited until he left and I thought she went inside, but she hadn't. She spotted me trying to slip into the kitchen. We had words. I tried to take the high road but she was just . . ." Felicia blinked back tears. "She was just being so nasty. I just wanted her to stop. I asked her. I asked her to just stop, could we please talk this over, but she was yelling and screaming about how she was going to call the police. The music was so loud inside no one heard, but I needed her to stop. So I . . ." She swallowed. "I had a bunch of those mice in my pocket. Gigi had given them to me. For my cat, Samuel." She looked at me, hopeful again. "Will you take care of Samuel for me? Or find someone who can?"

Wordless, I nodded. She was losing it. Or maybe she wasn't. Maybe she'd lost it that night with Holly, and now she was just calm and focused on putting things back in order.

"Thank you." Visibly relaxing, she leaned against the counter.

"So then what?" I prompted. From the corner of my eye, I saw my friend the server and prayed that he'd stay far enough away so she'd finish the story.

"I just stuck it in her mouth. Really, I was trying to shut her up. I didn't mean to kill her. But I guess . . . I shoved a little too hard. It went halfway down her throat. Her eyes got all big and she tried to hack it up, but she couldn't. She got more and more panicked. And I just ran." Felicia's gaze dropped to the ground. "It was a very, very bad decision."

You think?

"Felicia," I said softly, putting a hand on her arm. "I'm not sure what you're planning on doing, but I'm sure we can get you some help. My dad knows a lot of people—"

"I don't need any help, Maddie," she interrupted. "Thank you, though."

We both turned as my server friend approached. "Excuse me," he said, nodding at me before turning to Felicia. "The party's starting to wind down. Desserts and coffee are done. Is there anything else we need to bring out before we clean up?"

She shook her head, the movement tired. "No, Jackson. Thank you, though. I think we're done here."

He nodded and walked out of the kitchen.

"So what are you going to do? Please tell me you're not going to try something like Gigi did. It's not worth it, Felicia. I bet they can make a deal or something. You'll still have a life when it's over. Please don't think about killing yourself."

She stared at me. "Oh, my dear. I'm not going to kill myself."

I wanted to scream as Jackson returned to the kitchen. But this time, he had Ellory with him. They walked directly over to where we were standing.

Ellory ignored me. "Ms. Goodwin. You need to come with us," he said. "We won't handcuff you and we'll take you out the back."

My mouth fell open as Jackson, who apparently wasn't merely a server, took her arm.

Felicia looked just as shocked as I felt, but she recovered nicely. "Well, you saved me the trouble," she said. "Maddie, I was going to turn myself in. I just wanted to get through tonight, as I told you." She looked at the cops again. "I'm ready."

Jackson looked at me apologetically before he began leading her away. "I'm sorry, Ms. Goodwin," I heard him say. "Your food really was excellent."

Chapter 63

Monday

"It's great to be back." Adele looked around the café as if she hadn't seen it in years, when really it had been a week. "And the renovations have started, I see." She motioned to the official blueprints Gabe had dropped off just that morning. The job was back on track.

I nodded. "Gabe has been great."

"I told you," she said. "Aside from his poor choices in women, he's a wonderful guy."

"I was afraid you were taking the blame for him," I said. "Once I found out he'd been seeing Holly and she'd treated him so poorly."

"Well," Adele said. "I have a confession to make."

Oh God. I didn't think I could take more intrigue. I held my breath.

"I thought I was taking the blame for him," she said. "Once I heard what happened. After I called Felicia about Gigi, I got the heck out of there. And I saw my nephew. I knew he'd gone there to try and repair things with her. So I immediately thought the worst when I heard. And then of course they thought it was me." She shrugged. "Which was crap, but at least it took the heat off him. But then all kinds of things started happening." She looked pointedly at me.

I flushed. "I never thought you did it. I didn't want you to take the blame."

"Yeah, well." Adele shrugged. "I feel awful for Gigi."

So did I. She hadn't taken the news about her mother well at all. Word had it she'd been checked into a psychiatric facility where people could keep an eye on her given her fragile state of mind.

Grandpa came in and beamed when he saw Adele. "She's back!" He went over and hugged her. To my surprise, Adele hugged him back.

"Now," she said briskly, wiping at her eyes when he released her. "Let's get these cats ready for showtime. We need to have some adoptions today!"

"I'm with you," Grandpa declared.

They started working, Grandpa chattering away, catching Adele up on everything that had happened at the café this week. I watched them with a smile. At least one person had a happy ending out of all this. A rap at the screen pulled my attention away. I glanced over. Lucas.

I must've forgotten that someone had a grooming appointment, but I couldn't think of who it could be. I went over and unlocked the door. "Hey."

"Hey," he said. "Can I talk to you for a second?"

"Sure." I waited expectantly.

"Like, outside?" he asked.

"Oh. Sure." I followed him on to the porch. We sat on the swing. He was silent for a minute while I wondered what this was about.

Finally he spoke. "Maddie. Listen. I'm sorry about the other night."

I looked at him, stunned. "You are? No, I should be sorry. I *am* sorry. Really sorry," I added, in case it wasn't clear. "I messed up. And I've regretted it ever since."

Lucas shook his head. "I overreacted. I was feeling really insecure because of Craig and all that. I was being childish. Of course this affected you. It was selfish of me to think it didn't."

"Lucas. Honestly, there's no need to apologize. Can we just . . . start over?" I held my breath, hoping he wouldn't say that he didn't want to do that, he just wanted to clear the air because we had to work together, or some other excuse.

But he reached over and took my hand. "I'm in," he said. "How about tonight?"

I hadn't felt this happy in weeks. "Tonight is perfect," I said.

"Good. Now. Can you avoid any dead bodies at least until then?"

I smiled. "I'll do my best."

Look for the next Cat About Town mystery,
available in the summer of 2019
from Cate Conte and
St. Martin's Paperbacks!